RUNS DEEP

R.D. BRADY

Scottish Seoul Publishing, LLC

BOOKS BY R.D. BRADY

Be sure to sign up for R.D.'s mailing list to be the first to hear when she has a new release!

PROLOGUE

Ten Years Ago

Upstate New York

SIXTEEN-YEAR-OLD STEVE KANE'S breath came out in quick pants. His palms were sweaty and the white dress shirt his grandmother had bought him was sticking to his back underneath his brother's navy blazer. He snuck a glance at the jurors from the corner of his eye. He'd heard that if jurors looked at the defendant when the verdict came in it meant they had voted not guilty.

Not a single juror looked at him.

Steve's heart pounded, and he gripped his damp hands together. His attorney, Mr. Hadley, reached over with a liver-spotted hand and clasped his. Steve held on to it for dear life as if somehow Mr. Hadley could save him from what was coming.

Mr. Herbert, the jury foreman, stood. Steve had known Mr. Herbert since he was a kid. He remembered him coming to his third-grade class and telling them all about being a high school football coach. The talk had been dry, but the cookies he'd brought had been awesome. And Mr. Herbert had been on the sidelines of every football game Steve had ever attended. But he'd never seen him in a suit. And he'd never seen him nervous. Right now, the slip of paper in Mr. Herbert's trembling hands shook.

The judge peered over her glasses at the jury. "Has the jury reached a verdict?"

"We have, Your Honor." There was a wobble in Mr. Herbert's voice, and he cleared his throat. "Not guilty of murder in the first degree."

An angry shout went up from the gallery, followed by a rumble of voices. Steve stared straight ahead, and spots began to appear around the edges of his vision. *This can't be happening. It's not real.*

The judge banged her gavel, glaring at the crowd over her glasses. "There will be quiet or I will clear the courtroom." She turned back to the jury. "On the charge of murder in the second degree, how say you?"

The paper in Mr. Herbert's hand shook even more now. He cleared his throat again. "Guilty, Your Honor."

All the air left Steve's lungs. He felt as if the strings that had been holding him up had been snipped. He stumbled. Mr. Hadley's surprisingly strong arm wrapped around him, keeping him upright.

Stars appeared in front of Steve's eyes. He sat, stunned, unable to process any of it. Behind him, the courtroom gallery exploded with gasps and shouts. People Steve had known his whole life screamed at him. Everyone seemed to have leapt to their feet. Some reporters scribbled furiously while others rushed from the room to be the first to get the news out; the judge had declared all phones off limits in the courtroom.

The jury had gone for the lesser count of second-degree murder, not premeditated murder, which could have carried the death penalty. Steve supposed he should be grateful for that small break, but somehow he couldn't work past the shock to get to grateful.

His lawyer whispered into his ear. "Steve, they're going to take you now."

Steve stared up into Mr. Hadley's face. He didn't know if his lawyer had believed him, but Mr. Hadley had certainly fought for him, and he couldn't mistake the concern in the older man's eyes now.

"Steve, how do you feel?" "Steve—are you worried about prison?" Reporters yelled their questions at him from the front row, trying to get one last quote before he was whisked away from the courtroom and out of their reach.

Flashbulbs exploded in front of him and he blinked. Apparently, once the trial was concluded, the reporters weren't worried about the wrath of the judge—not when weighed against getting one final shot of the baby-faced killer. Steve stood at only five foot six, with deep brown eyes and light brown hair. He was so skinny he'd been called "scarecrow" by some kids at school. He was not the typical murder defendant.

Bailiffs surged toward the front row, trying to block the reporters. More uniforms streamed in the doors as people rushed toward the courtroom gate. Steve flinched, stumbling back, covering his eyes. But then he forced himself to step forward, straining to see past the chaos in front of him.

His eyes latched on to his grandmother in the second row. Her yellow church suit stood out in the sea of dark colors. She collapsed against Steve's brother, sobs wracking her frame. Steve choked back his own tears, willing her to look at him. He needed to see her face one last time. But she was too overcome.

His brother, though, caught his gaze. Jack gave Steve a nod as he held their grandmother—a promise to take care of her.

Two officers pulled Steve away from the table. Their faces

were blank masks: no compassion, no uncertainty. They turned him around, pulling his arms behind his back.

Fear tore through Steve. *I didn't do this. This can't be happening.* He started to shake. He looked around wildly. His eyes locked on the dark-haired twenty-nine-year-old man pushing through the crowds to get to the front of the courtroom.

"Let me through. Let me through, damn it," Declan Reed yelled at the reporters as he shoved past them.

Declan flashed his state badge and pushed through the swinging doors. "Give me a minute," he said to the corrections officers.

"Sir, we have to—"

"*Give* me a minute," Declan ordered through gritted teeth.

"You've got one minute. That's it." The officers stepped back.

Declan dropped to his knees in front of Steve. "Steve, you have to remember what I told you. You stay tough inside. You don't let them see that you're scared."

Tears choked Steve's throat. "I didn't do it, Declan. I didn't do it."

"I know. But that doesn't matter now. Now you have to protect yourself. You shut all that away. You hear me?"

Steve looked out into the gallery where Mr. Granger, the man who had taken him and his best friend Julie for ice cream cones once a month since he was five, glared back at him.

Declan grabbed Steve's arms. "Steve."

Declan's eyes were bright with unshed tears. Steve could feel Declan's fear for him. But there was nothing Declan could do. There was nothing anyone could do. It was up to Steve now.

Steve nodded jerkily, pulling back his emotions. "I know."

Declan pulled him into a hug. "Rely on yourself. Stay strong. And remember, there are people out here who care about you— who love you."

One of the officers stepped forward. "We have to take him now."

Declan gave a nod and stepped away. "I'll see you tomorrow. I'll be there, okay?"

Steve just stared at him and swallowed hard, swallowing it all down.

The officers placed the cuffs on Steve and led him through the back door of the court. They made their way down a short hall, and then one of the officers pushed open the door to the outside.

Immediately, noise assaulted Steve's ears. Even here, the crowds had gathered. They lined the sides of the makeshift pathway blocked off by wooden sawhorses and police officers.

As they passed through the pressing crowd toward the waiting police van, one spectator tried to break through. Officers pushed the man back, but it was like a starting pistol had gone off. The crowd surged.

"Get him out of here!" one of the officers yelled. Steve was shoved forward. His knee slammed into the frame of the open van door as he was all but thrown into the white corrections van.

An officer followed him in. Steve sat on the one chair that sat in the middle of the cavernous space. Chains were connected to its legs and along its arms. It looked like something you would put a serial killer in.

Steve sat down, his legs weak. *Or just a regular killer.*

As Steve's hands and feet were attached to the chains, panic rolled through him. He couldn't move. He took short breaths, trying to calm his pounding heart. He watched the officer strapping him in. The officer gave the chains a tug. He was young, maybe a little younger than Declan. He didn't meet Steve's eyes. He offered no reassuring words or even sympathetic gazes. *Not for the killer of Simone Ganger.*

Flashes went off outside the van as reporters clamored to get the money shot of Steve in chains.

One last tug on the chains and the officer stepped out, closing the van doors behind him before climbing into the passenger seat.

Steve told himself to look straight ahead. But he couldn't help turning to look out the window as the driver took them past the front of the courthouse. The crowds that had gathered for the trial had only grown more agitated with the verdict. They yelled angrily at the cops that held them back. Some waved placards above their heads.

Death to the Murderer.

Justice for Simone.

God will Punish His Sins.

Declan's words floated through Steve's mind. *And remember, there are people out here who care about you. Who love you.*

Steve looked out the window, recognizing at least half of the people angrily yelling. *Yeah, but there are a lot more who hate me.*

DAY 1

"It's Monday, folks! This is Billy the Kid on KLNQ serving upstate New York. Today is going to be the last good day for a while, so get out there and enjoy it. For those of you who haven't heard, and that can only be those literally living under a rock, we have one heck of a storm heading our way. It's going to hit in the next two days, and flooding is not just predicted, it's a given. So if you haven't stocked up yet, now is the time!"

CHAPTER ONE

Present Day

Auburn, New York

STEVE KANE WALKED down the hall, his gray Converse sneakers making no noise on the institutional tile. He watched the pale yellow concrete walls as he passed, knowing it would be the last time he would see them. He was never coming back.

"You got a ride?" Heath, the guard walking next to him, asked.

Steve shook his head. "Nah. Figured I'd take the bus. Didn't want anyone going to any trouble."

Heath nodded his big round head. Some of the inmates called him pumpkin head, although never to his face. None of them were that stupid.

The barred door at the end of the hall buzzed as they reached it. A tightness started in Steve's chest.

Heath pulled the door open. "Just keep your nose clean. You've done real good here. Don't come back."

Steve stepped through, the tightening in his chest increasing, along with a little panic. "Don't plan to." He took a step, then turned to look back at Heath.

When he'd arrived at Auburn Penitentiary, Heath had scared the hell out of him. Standing at six foot four, Heath had been six inches taller than Steve but had easily outweighed him by a good seventy-five pounds of muscle. Steve had been all bone. But now, the height gap was only two inches, and the muscle gap only about ten.

Heath held out his hand. "Take care, kid."

Steve almost smiled at the nickname. After being transferred from a secure juvenile detention facility in Albany due to over-crowding seven years ago, he'd been a kid in every way when he'd arrived. Heath had looked out for him, helped show him the ropes. Even warned him not to let other inmates see him speaking with him too often. Being friends with a guard could have nega-tive consequences.

Steve shook his hand. "You too, Heath. And thanks. For everything."

Steve turned and walked quickly down the hall, surprised at the emotion he felt. It was foreign. He thought he'd shut all that down ten years ago.

But by the time he pushed his way through the heavy doors outside, he was back in control. He walked along the path beside the chain-link fence, focused on the gate at the end. When he pushed through, he stood still, hands shoved in his jeans, breathing deep, his eyes closed, his heart pounding.

Free.

He opened his eyes and looked both ways. Most prisons were located on the outskirts of town, but Auburn Penitentiary was situated right in the middle of the city. He was pretty sure there was a bus stop down the street to the left. And even if there wasn't a bus, he had no problem just walking for a while until he found one.

He flipped a mental coin and was about to head to the left when a whistle drew his attention to the right.

Stepping out of a blue Toyota Prius was a man with wavy dark hair and the build of a cycling enthusiast. Nothing about the man, from his appearance to his car, suggested he was law enforcement, but that's exactly what he was—Investigator Declan Reed, New York State Police.

Declan waved, a smile on his face.

Steve shook his head. He should have known. He walked over. "Hey, Declan."

Declan smiled, his blue eyes crinkling at the corners. "Thought you'd just sneak out, huh?"

"Was hoping."

"Hop in, I'll give you a lift."

Steve took a step back. "Thanks, but I don't think arriving with a cop is how I want to go. Bad enough I left with one."

Declan gave a little laugh. "All right, but I'm buying you breakfast. Then I'll drop you at the bus station."

Steve's stomach gave a growl. For the last week, he'd been planning his first meal. And the idea of it had kept him awake at nights. He didn't care that it was still morning. New York couldn't have changed that much. There must a diner around here somewhere serving burgers. "Cheeseburger? Fries?"

"You got it."

Steve smiled. "Well, all right then." He walked around and climbed into the passenger seat, pushing aside some of Declan's papers and wrappers. He raised an eyebrow. "Junk food? You?"

Declan shrugged. "Been a little crazy at work lately. Hasn't been much time to eat right."

Steve knew from Declan's weekly visits and emails that his

promotion to state police liaison with the local police, along with his regular investigator duties, was running him ragged. But the promotion had also allowed Declan to move back to Millners Kill. Steve pulled on his seatbelt and stared at the dashboard. It looked like something out of a spaceship. I mean, he'd seen cars on TV, but the last car he'd been in, besides the corrections vans, had been an old Lincoln with dials and knobs.

Steve felt the panic rise in his chest again. Everything was different out here. The world had moved on while Steve was still stuck in yesterday.

"You all right?" Declan asked.

Steve nodded. "Yup. Just a—just a little culture shock, I guess."

"It'll take a little time to adjust. But you will." Declan put the car in gear and pulled out.

Steve didn't comment. He just glanced behind him. The sun glinted off the barbed wire at the top of the fifteen-foot fence ringing the prison. The place looked ominous.

Built in 1816, Auburn Correctional Facility was one of the oldest in the United States. A maximum-security prison, Auburn was rimmed by multiple barbed wire barriers and armed guard posts. It was a cement monster that towered over the landscape, alone and desolate. *And my home for the last seven years.*

Steve turned around and faced forward. *But not anymore.*

Declan pulled into traffic. A Hyundai cut in front of them, its oblivious driver chatting on a cell phone. Steve gripped the side of the car.

Declan glanced over at him. "Welcome back to the real world."

Steve settled back into the passenger seat, prying his fingers from the car door. After a few minutes, some tension that had filled him had drained out, and he found himself enjoying the ride. He recognized a couple of chain restaurants and store names. Cars drove by them and no one glanced over or gave them a second look.

It's all so ordinary, Steve thought with surprise. It had been so horrible when they'd locked him up. Screaming protesters at the court, then yet more crowds when he'd arrived at the juvenile detention center.

Yet now, when he got out, no one was here to protest his release. He'd been sent away for a decade, and it looked like the world had forgotten about him.

He didn't know what he had expected. *Maybe everyone on the street to stop and stare at the ex-con as he left the prison?*

Feeling eyes on him, he turned. Two teenage girls were driving a bright red sports car next to him. The blonde behind the wheel nudged her friend, who glanced over at him. The friend leaned over and blew him a kiss before turning at the next corner.

Steve smiled. Maybe this was going to work out after all.

CHAPTER TWO

AN HOUR AND A HALF LATER, Declan pulled the car into the bus depot. Steve could see the bus for Millners Kill already heading down the road toward them.

Declan got out of the car and pulled a navy blue backpack from the back seat. "You sure you don't want me to drive you? I'm heading there, anyway."

"Nah. I'm kind of in the mood to take the bus." Steve looked away, not meeting Declan's eyes. He didn't want Declan to see his fear.

When he'd left Millners Kill, he'd been its most notorious resident. He wasn't sure what kind of welcome he was going to get now, but he wouldn't be surprised if it involved pitchforks. He didn't want Declan in the middle of that.

Declan handed him the pack. "Here, take this."

Steve took the bag, jiggling it. "What's in here?"

Declan shrugged. "Some changes of clothes, a few books, a cell phone. My cell number, your brother's, and your grandmother's are already programmed in, and I downloaded a couple good songs onto it. Just your basic get-started bag."

Steve looked at the bag, touched by Declan's thoughtfulness. He still couldn't believe Declan had stayed in touch with him the entire time he'd been locked up. And he knew that part of the reason Heath had looked out for him was because of Declan.

Declan had been on his side ever since this whole madness had begun. He'd visited every week, helped look out for his grandmother when he was back in town, and basically made sure Steve stayed connected to the world.

A few weeks after going in, Steve had begun to resent Declan. He'd thought there must have been something Declan could have done to keep him from being convicted. After all, Declan was state police, and both of them knew Steve hadn't committed the crime. They just hadn't been able to prove it.

He shook his head. He'd been a stupid, sixteen-year-old kid.

Over time though, Steve had come to realize that Declan had actually gone out on a limb for him. As a state policeman, he'd muscled his way into the case and tried to get more lines of investigation opened. Declan had put it all on the line to try to help him. Steve appreciated how much Declan had risked to try to prove his innocence. And now that Steve was older, he knew that just because you were right didn't mean the world was going to treat you fairly.

"Thanks, Declan." Steve held up the pack. "I appreciate this. And everything else."

Declan extended his hand. "I'm really glad you're going home." His voice softened. "You have a chance here, Steve. Take advantage of it."

Some of Steve's old anger boiled up. "Is that what I have—a chance? Because if I recall correctly, the whole town was pretty happy to see me go. Not sure they're going to be so happy to see me back."

Declan looked like he was about to disagree with him but then changed his mind. "You're right. It's not going to be easy.

But it is a chance, nonetheless. You've got your brother, your grandmother, me. We're all in your corner. We'll help you get through."

Steve saw people lining up for the bus. He studied each face. He didn't recognize any of them.

And he realized, with a start, that perhaps no one would even recognize him. Until he went away, he'd spent his whole life in Millners Kill. But now he'd changed so much.

The thought was both freeing and incredibly sad. What did it say about a person that the only people who really knew what he looked like these days were the involuntary guests of the state of New York?

Steve met Declan's eyes and saw the faith he had in him—as well as the fear. And he swallowed his sadness, hiding it the way Declan was hiding his concerns. "I know," he said. "And I'll make it work. Somehow."

Some of the tension left Declan's face. He blew out a breath. "That's good. I'll be in town later. I'll stop by."

"Um, I'm supposed to start my job tomorrow."

"At Mel's?"

Steve swallowed. "Yeah."

He'd worked at Mel's Diner before he'd been incarcerated. Every parolee needed to have a job as one of the conditions of their parole. Steve had been surprised when his brother told him Mel had offered him a position. Surprised and grateful.

"What are you coming to town for?" Steve asked.

Declan pointed at the gray sky above. "There's a storm moving in. It's supposed to be pretty ferocious. And as state liaison, it's my job to help with some of the prep." Declan looked over at him. "You know, there might be some things you could do to help."

"Yeah, well, we'll see." The bus pulled up to the curb. As

Steve started to head toward it, Declan's words resonated. He turned back. "How bad a storm is it supposed to be?"

"Pretty bad. They're worried about the bridge. It's not holding up well. And it got really battered last summer with all that flooding. If there's another bad flood, the whole thing could go."

Steve knew that would be disastrous. The bridge was the only thing connecting the town to the mainland. With the bridge, they could pretend Millners Kill was a peninsula, surrounded by water. But the truth was, Millners Kill was a small island in Lake Ontario between Rochester and Oswego, connected to the mainland only by that manmade structure of steel girders. If the bridge went, they'd be in serious trouble.

"Any chance they might evacuate?" Steve asked.

"I wouldn't be surprised."

Steve pictured all the citizens of Millners Creek crammed into some school gym on the mainland—and Steve standing in the middle of them.

His stomach plummeted. Just what he needed. He wanted to slip back into town quietly and get himself set up before anyone really knew he was back.

Better yet, he wanted no one to even know he had been there until after he had already left. Because that was his real plan: to get a job somewhere away from Millners Kill. Somewhere he could *really* start over.

But if the storm was as bad as Declan was suggesting, he might be crammed into a small space with the whole town staring daggers at him—if he was lucky. If he wasn't, they'd be *throwing* the daggers. *Great.*

He didn't share any of his concerns with Declan though. There was nothing he could do about it anyway. "See you."

And for the first time, Steve was glad he was going back to

Millners Kill. He didn't want his grandmother facing the storm of the century alone.

Of course, she wouldn't be completely alone. His brother Jack would be there to help her out. Just like he had been ever since Steve had been incarcerated. But now it was Steve's turn to shoulder some of the responsibilities.

He hiked the backpack onto his shoulder. He had no doubt Declan had also tucked some money into it somewhere. He promised himself that he would pay back every dime.

Steve got in line for the bus behind an older couple. The sign in the window read Millners Kill.

And even though fears and doubts crowded his mind, a little kernel of joy was also building. *I'm going home. I'm really going home.*

CHAPTER THREE

STEVE STEPPED off the bus in front of Millners Kill City Hall. Millners Kill—population five thousand, although that ballooned to close to twenty thousand during summer. A sleepy little town in upstate New York where nothing ever happened.

Except for me, Steve thought as he stepped past as a couple who embraced as soon as the woman got off the bus. Steve averted his eyes, but he recognized the woman—Mildred Pierce, the town librarian. Before prison, Steve had visited the library every week since he was eleven. In the summers, he and Julie had gone there two or three times a week. Mrs. Pierce had been a constant in his childhood. Not overly friendly, not mean, just someone who was always around. Steve turned his head and walked away quickly. He wasn't sure how Mrs. Pierce would react to him now.

He pulled up the hood of his gray sweatshirt, not knowing if it made him more conspicuous or less. With his height, he tended to stand out in a crowd. In prison, he'd used that height to his advantage, but now he found himself hunching his shoulders to make himself shorter, trying to blend in, or, better yet, not be noticed at all.

He kept his eyes low, not making eye contact, but watching everyone out of the corner of his eye. But no one seemed interested in him.

Hefting his backpack higher onto his shoulder, he skirted around the crowd that was waiting to get on the bus. It had turned a little colder. The fall air cut through his jeans and sweatshirt.

A woman dropped her pocketbook right in front of him. Its contents spilled across the sidewalk. Steve didn't stop. He didn't even pause.

As he passed, though, he realized that he should have helped. He shook his head. *Crap.* Life on the outside was different. Helping didn't make you look weak—didn't make you a target. He sighed. Apparently it would take a little longer than a few hours for him to shake off ten years of institutional life.

Steve crossed the street. He noticed the large puddle too late, his attention focused on the people around him. His gray Converses and the legs of his pants were soaked. *Damn it,* he cursed, but he kept his expression unchanged.

As he passed McCann's Drugstore, he stared at the ground, praying no one he knew walked by. He wasn't ready for that. Not yet.

The wind tugged at his hood, trying to shove it down. Steve tucked in his chin. The wind had picked up a lot since he'd left Declan.

He made his way down four blocks, noting that the town had changed little. There were still only about two dozen shops strung along Main Street. True, the old card store had been replaced by a trendy little coffee shop, and the Blockbuster was now a Payless, but other than that all the old stores remained.

The hardware store was up on the right, the supermarket on the left.

The bus had passed Mel's Diner on the way in. The thought of Mel made Steve smile. Steve had bussed tables for him for three summers, and Mel had taught him how to play poker, how to box, how to drive—all activities he had been banned from mentioning to his grandmother.

The smile faded as he realized that Mel would not be happy to see him now. He wasn't sure why Mel had agreed to hire him.

Feeling colder, he picked up his pace as he turned onto his grandmother's street. He could see her picket fence ten houses down, and his heart tripped a little.

A handful of kids were playing soccer in the street. A soccer ball came soaring toward Steve, and he quickly trapped it with his feet.

A kid, no more than six, bundled in a red fleece jacket and hat, ran down the sidewalk. The kid came to a halt when he caught sight of Steve with the ball. "Pass it back."

Steve shifted the ball from his left foot to his right, then kicked it back using the inside of his foot. The kid stopped it with both feet although Steve could tell it was pure luck and not talent that had allowed him to do so.

"Thanks!" The kid smiled and waved. Grabbing the ball, he turned and rejoined the other kids, all older and bigger.

Steve continued past them, but he watched them out of the corner of his eye. One kid, who looked too much like the red fleece boy not to be his brother, yelled, "Hurry up, slowpoke."

The other kids laughed. The red fleece kid passed the ball back. Then he went and sat on the stoop. Steve shook his head—the dynamics of brotherhood, consistent throughout time.

The red fleece boy waved at him again, but the others paid Steve no notice, too interested in their game. Without thinking, Steve gave a little wave back. The boy beamed at him.

Steve turned away, but the boy's smile stayed with him. There was a lot of joy in that little face.

Four houses down from the boys' soccer game, Steve stopped. He stood at the white picket fence and looked at the yellow two-story house with the big white porch. It looked like it had gotten a recent paint job, but otherwise it hadn't changed.

He'd lived the first decade of his life one block over. When Steve was only ten, though, his father had gone missing, and Steve had moved into his grandmother's house—this house—along with his brother and mom. Only a few years after that, his mom had been diagnosed with breast cancer. She'd fought it, but she eventually lost the battle. That was only a year before Steve's arrest.

Steve knew his brother had made sure their grandmother had whatever help she needed to maintain the house. Guilt nagged at Steve. He should have been here to help her as well, instead of locked away.

Jack was now a county district attorney. His job took him all over the county, but he kept an apartment in town to be close to their grandmother. And if Steve was considered the town demon, Jack was the town angel. He was always donating his time to help out, and donating his money, too, when needed.

Steve should probably have felt jealousy toward his brother, but Jack had been just as good to him, too. He'd written him every week, visited at least once every two weeks. He'd kept Steve going. Honestly, compared to a lot of other inmates, Steve had had a full-fledged support team behind him. And he was grateful.

Steve breathed in deep. He called up a few of the words dispensed in his required therapy sessions—some of the only words that had actually resonated with him: *You can't do anything about yesterday, but today is all up to you.*

He pushed open the gate and walked up the porch steps. He hesitated at the door. Should he just walk in, or ring the doorbell?

He couldn't in all his life ever remember ringing the doorbell. But like a lot of things, times had changed.

He rang the bell.

He heard the shuffling steps of his grandmother, and his heart picked up its pace. "Coming," a voice called.

The locks turned, and the door pulled wide. A woman stood framed by the doorway. She had light brown hair that had only started to gray, and brown eyes just like Steve's. Those eyes registered confusion for just a moment before a smile burst across her face.

"You're early!" Bess Davidson threw open her arms and dragged him into a hug. Steve's arms wrapped around her. She smelled like cinnamon.

Memories, good ones, from his childhood assaulted him. The tightness in his chest eased, and his grip on his grandmother increased.

I'm home. I'm really home.

CHAPTER FOUR

HE WALKED DOWN THE STREET, watching the preparations for the storm. Most of the stores had plastic or wood covering their windows. The coffee bar owner pulled in the placard that displayed the daily quote. Today's read: "Never put off for tomorrow what you can do today."

He smiled. *Excellent advice.*

People hurried past, a sense of excitement in the air. Everyone was getting ready for the latest storm of the century.

He turned in to the park, nodding as he passed a family he knew from church, and walked over to where Lake Ontario rushed by. Normally the lake was calm, but the storm had worked it up.

He'd always loved the water, but never more so than when it stormed. The wind tugged at his coat, trying to wrestle it off of him.

He breathed in the power in the air. It felt like the whole world was on the edge of violence.

He smiled. *And how true that is.*

Whitecaps crashed angrily against the rocks along the shore, sending a spray into the air. Even the water had a palpable anger and power to it right now.

Anticipation built inside him, and he clenched his fists, trying to hold in the laugh.

Steve was out.

And a storm was coming.

He couldn't have planned it better. He smiled even wider, rubbing his hands.

Time to play.

CHAPTER FIVE

DECLAN PULLED into the parking lot of the Millners Kill Police Department. The squat, brown brick building stood at the end of Main Street; a flight of cement stairs and a winding handicap ramp dominated the front, along with a flagpole. The town employed four full-time officers and five part-time, along with another half a dozen volunteers.

Declan had debated stopping by Bess's house just to see if Steve had arrived all right, but he knew Steve wouldn't have appreciated it. It was hard though. Even though Steve was a man now, Declan still thought of him as the little boy who'd lived a few houses down from him. Or the terrified boy who had been led away from the courtroom.

But Steve was grown up now. And Declan had seen the hardness in him that prison had created. But he'd also seen signs of that young boy he'd known. Prison hadn't been able to stamp that boy out completely.

With a sigh, Declan pulled the key from the ignition and watched the flag ripple in the wind. He took a minute to try and figure out what he was going to say. He was the liaison with the state police, so he could probably make it seem like he was here about storm business. But the chief would see through that flimsy reason in a second.

Of course, he thought, watching a deputy walk up the steps and disappear through the double doors, the chief wasn't exactly a Mensa candidate. Chief Keith Hodgkins was the same guy he'd been in high school—a bruiser. He'd made all state for football in his junior year. Declan and his friends had joked that he'd taken one too many hits to the head.

Declan clenched his fist, remembering Keith shoving him into a locker after holding him down while his friends wrote "fag" on his forehead—in permanent marker. Now that same Neanderthal was the chief—for four terms already, and a lock for a fifth.

Declan shook his head. After high school, Keith had washed out of Florida State's football program. Yet he'd come back to Millners Kill with his ego unharmed. Two years at the local community college, and he'd signed on as a deputy. Eight years later, he ran and won for Chief. And he'd remained chief for sixteen years now. Even with the complete clusterfuck that was the Granger case.

Grabbing the square box from the passenger seat, Declan opened the car door and steeled himself to face the jackass. *No, the chief*, he warned himself, trying to tamp down his old resentment. But those high school wounds felt awfully close to the surface whenever he ran into Keith.

Declan walked up the steps and held the door open for an older woman who was heading out. "Ma'am."

She gave him a small smile. "Nice to see manners haven't died."

"Yes ma'am," Declan said before stepping through the door.

Dee Pearson, who'd manned the reception desk almost since the station's inception, was under siege. The phone was ringing, and Declan could see all the hold buttons were lit up. Three people were standing in front of the desk arguing. Dee was ignoring all of it.

She caught sight of Declan and gave him a sour look. Declan didn't take it personally. On her best day, Dee wore the same look.

Declan walked around the crowd. He leaned on the desk and gave Dee a smile. "Hello, Dee."

She nodded at him. "Declan. What can we do for you?"

Declan slid the box of muffins he'd been hiding behind his back across to her. "You're looking lovely today."

A smile lurked around her lips, but Dee refused to let it through. "I'm on to your charms, Declan Reed. They won't work on me."

Declan held his hand to his chest and sighed. "Now you're breaking my heart."

She pulled the box of muffins closer and peered inside. "Blueberry?"

"Absolutely. I had to wrestle three men, large men, to get them. That's the last box from Tops." Actually that story was only part of an exaggeration. He did, however, have to snag the box before Carl from the fire department could nab them. Luckily no fists had been thrown.

"Stores are about run dry with the storm coming in," Dee said.

"Yeah. I'll be in town for it. I'm staying at my sister's. Keith in?"

Dee tilted her head toward the back while picking up the phone. "He's in his office. I'll tell him you're coming."

"Thank you, Miss Dee."

Declan headed through the swinging doors to the back. Four desks for deputies stood in a square behind Dee's desk. All were currently empty.

Deputy Russell Nash, Millners Kill's youngest deputy, came barreling out of the storage room, his arms full. Declan quickly sidestepped to avoid getting run over.

Russ looked down at Declan through a heavy set of dirty blonde bangs, a blush covering his cheeks. "Oh, hey Declan. Sorry about that."

Six foot four, skinny as a beanpole, Russ bore an uncanny resemblance to Shaggy from *Scooby Doo*. And the department's uniform of brown on brown didn't help dispel that image one bit. Not for the first time, Declan wondered why they had gotten uniforms that matched the building.

"That's all right. What's all this?" Declan eyed the tarps and ropes threatening to tumble from Russ's arms.

Russ shifted his load. "Storm prep. You here to see the chief?"

Declan nodded.

Russ stepped closer, leaning down. "Careful, he's in a mood."

"I'll keep it in mind. You need help with that?"

"Nah. I'm good. You going to be in town during the storm?"

"Yeah. My dad and I are bunking in with my sister."

Declan's dad still lived in town, as did his sister, Sylvia. But Sylvia's husband was in Afghanistan, and neither Declan nor his dad felt right about letting her and her kids ride out the storm alone. Besides, with Steve back, Declan wanted to stay in town anyway, in case there was anything he could do to make Steve's transition a little easier.

"That's good." Russ shifted his load.

Declan eyed the precariously balanced pile, but it held.

"It's getting crazy out there," Russ said. "I've written up three traffic accidents this morning and broken up two fights. I even had to put a guy in the drunk tank an hour ago."

"Storm's working everyone up."

"Yeah." Russ's face clouded a little. "It's good you'll be in town. We might need a little extra help."

Declan eyed Russ. "Something going on?"

Russ opened his mouth but then shut it quickly as another officer came out of the hallway leading from the cells. "Nah. It's good. See you later." Russ headed toward the front doors, his load wobbling the whole way.

Declan watched to see if Russ made it through the heavy front doors without dropping anything. The tall officer disappeared through them without incident. *Pure luck*, Declan thought.

He turned and headed back to Keith's office. He had the nagging feeling there was something Russ had wanted to tell him. Well, it would have to wait. There was enough going on without whatever was on Russ's mind.

Declan was still ten feet away from Keith's office when he heard Keith on the phone.

"Damn it, Marlene, I can't get to your mother's party this weekend. We have a storm coming in."

Keith's wife, Marlene, was rarely in town, preferring to spend her time down in Florida. She came from money, and Declan was pretty sure that was the only thing keeping Keith hanging on. Declan had absolutely no idea what was keeping Marlene in the marriage.

A silence was followed by, "Fine. You take that any way you want."

Declan hesitated a minute, making sure Keith was off the phone. After hearing nothing more, he stepped into the doorway and knocked on the frame.

Keith looked up, and Declan was once again shocked by the man's appearance. In high school, Keith had been all muscle, but now all that muscle had turned to soft fat. Large jowls hung around his neck, and his eyes seemed to have shrunk into his head.

Apparently the doctors were right: heavy drinking and an

unhealthy diet were not good for you.

"Declan." Keith leaned back in his chair. It creaked under his weight. He placed his hands over his stomach, which seemed to be straining to free itself from his shirt. "What can I do for the state police today?"

Declan leaned against the doorway. He didn't even consider taking a seat. Keith seemed to have found the most uncomfortable chairs in the history of mankind for his "visitors."

"Nothing. The state police are wondering what *you* need. Anything we can do to help with the storm prep?"

Keith shook his head. "We've got everything well in hand. But I'll let you know if you state boys are needed."

Declan glanced around the office. Marlene had decorated it: wood paneling, antlers hanging behind Keith's desk, old cowboy pictures hung at random spots, and a lamp with a cowboy boot for a base. And there was a new addition since Declan's last visit: a framed lasso over by the window, a small plaque underneath it that Declan couldn't make out.

Apparently Keith had never grown out of wanting to be a cowboy when he grew up.

Declan turned his attention back to Keith. "There's a possibility the governor might order an evacuation. He's supposed to make the decision within the next twenty-four hours."

"I'm aware." Keith narrowed his eyes, making Declan wonder if he could even see through them. "But we take care of our own here. We don't need to go running for cover because of a little rain."

Shit. Declan had been worried about just this reaction. He tried to figure out a way to handle Keith, but the truth was, the man was as stubborn as a goat.

"Keith, they're talking about an inch of rain or more per hour. And winds almost at hurricane strength. If that's the case, evacuation would probably be a really good option. Especially considering the condition of the bridge."

Keith waved away Declan's concerns. "You've always been a worrier, Declan. Millners Kill has been through worse."

Declan opened his mouth to argue, then shut it. There was no point. Besides, Keith wasn't the one making the call. It was the mayor. And hopefully, when the time came, the mayor would ignore Keith's advice.

Declan blew out a breath, trying to keep his voice even, professional. "All right. Well, I'm staying in town for the storm. So I'll be around if you need me."

Keith watched him for a moment before speaking. "Is that because of the storm or because your little pet project is back in town?"

Declan didn't bother to pretend he didn't understand the barb. "Steve's not a pet project. But I don't mind being around if he needs some help adjusting."

Keith scoffed. "Adjusting. Yeah, let's make sure the murderer doesn't get his feelings hurt now that he's out and free to kill again."

Declan considered for only a second explaining all the very good reasons why Steve was not the murderer of Simone Granger. All the data on the many innocent people who were wrongly convicted every year ran through his mind. Already, over three hundred convicted prisoners had been exonerated around the country thanks to DNA testing—and that was only where the funds could be arranged to test DNA, and where there was DNA available to test. There were also numerous studies that spoke about the inherent flaws in eyewitness testing, improper testing, inadequate counsel, and the list went on.

And then, of course, there were cases like Steve's: where everything rested on circumstantial evidence. Information that, taken individually, could never have convicted him—but which collectively looked damning.

He thought for just a minute about arguing with Keith one more time about Steve's innocence. But he discarded the thought almost immediately. Keith had always had a blind spot when it came to Steve.

"He's not a bad kid, Keith. He did his time. Even got his college degree while he was inside. He deserves a chance."

"He killed the Granger girl." Keith paused. "Of course, you never really believed that, did you?"

Declan didn't respond. At the time of Simone's murder, Declan had been Steve's strongest supporter, next to Steve's grandmother and brother—not that it had made any difference.

Keith fixed his eyes on Declan. "Nobody's going to forget what he did. Nobody should."

Declan knew that at least the first part of Keith's statement was true. The murder of Simone Granger had shaken up the little town of Millners Kill. Simone had been seventeen years old and a straight-A student with a full ride to Stanford.

She'd also been painfully shy. The prosecutor had argued that Steve, who had been in and out of the Granger house since he was a kid, was one of the few people who Simone would have let into her home on that fateful night.

"You never could come up with another suspect, could you?" Keith pressed. "And you know why? Because Kane was guilty."

"Even if that's true, he's done his time. He—"

"Lions don't change their stripes. Once a killer, always a killer."

Declan sighed. This had been a stupid idea. He knew who Keith was. And Keith was right even if his metaphor was wrong: *zebras* don't change their stripes. And that was especially true for Keith.

Keith had made the Granger case the centerpiece of every

one of his campaigns for office. He'd been the one who'd uncovered the bloody clothes in Steve's room. Of course, he'd also been the one who'd stomped all over the crime scene, contaminating any potential DNA evidence. *And* he was the one who'd lost the clothes from lockup. Unsurprisingly, those facts had been absent from Keith's campaign ads.

To be honest, the whole police department had been woefully out of their depth when the Granger case came along. Before Simone Granger, there hadn't been a murder in Miller's Kill in ten years, and that one had been the result of a bar fight with plenty of witnesses.

But once Keith focused on Steve, there was no changing course. He seized on everything that might be related to Steve's guilt and disregarded anything that might have helped to exonerate him. To say that Steve was railroaded would be a complete understatement.

Declan had been stationed on the other side of the state at the time, but he'd gotten himself reassigned to the Millners Kill area after hearing about Steve's arrest. Fact was, Steve held a special place in Declan's heart. After college, Declan had enlisted in the Army and had become a Ranger. And Steve, who'd been ten at the time, had sent him a Flat Stanley to keep with him. Declan wrote Steve regularly about Stanley's "adventures." That stupid cutout and the weekly letters from Steve kept Declan going when hell was literally exploding around him.

So when Steve was locked up, Declan had tried to repay the favor—writing Steve every week and visiting when he could. And the truth was, he still couldn't make himself believe that the kid he'd watched grow up had committed that gruesome crime.

"We've already gotten calls this morning about Steve being released," Keith said. "People are scared. They want to know what we're going to do to protect this town from him."

Declan stared, his mouth a little dry. *Shit*. He'd hoped Steve would have a little time to settle in before people knew he was back. "And what did you tell them?"

Keith met Declan's gaze, his eyes hard. "That it's the Millners Kills Police Department's job to protect this town. And that we will do exactly that."

Declan knew this was bad. Keith wasn't going to give Steve a chance at a normal life. He'd all but declared Steve as enemy number one. But he also knew there was no way to convince Keith that he was going about this the wrong way.

"Look, I'm not here about Steve," Declan said. "I'm here to help. So if you need anything, you let me know."

Keith smirked. "Sure, Declan, we need any help from the state I'll be sure to give you a call."

"Okay then. I'll see you later." Declan turned around without waiting for a reply. *Well, this was a stupid idea.*

Declan waved to Dee as he headed out. Pushing open the outside doors, he wondered if he should run by Steve's and warn him that the chief had it out for him. He shook his head. Steve was a smart kid. *Well, I guess "man" now.* He knew better than anyone how people in this town thought of him.

Declan sighed. *Just keep your head down, Steve.*

CHAPTER SIX

STEVE WALKED through the living room. It was weird. Nothing had changed. The same red plaid couch was over against the wall across from the kitchen. His grandfather's leather recliner was parked in front of the fireplace. The old tan carpet still ran through the whole house, and the same floral wallpaper dominated the walls in the kitchen and front hall.

And yet somehow it was all different, too. The carpet and furniture were a little more faded with a few more stains and scratches. And the house felt smaller, like it had shrunk since he'd last been here. He glanced at the stairs. He could have sworn they were a little more centered as well. The paint on the walls seemed a little duller too, and he noticed some cracks in the corners of the walls. *I'll need to fix those.*

He walked over to the mantel and glanced at the pictures lined up there. There were the same ones he always remembered —his grandparents' wedding picture, his parents, pictures of him and Jack as kids—but now there were new pictures as well, of Jack, graduating college and law school.

But there were none of Steve after the age of fifteen—because everything in Steve's life had slammed to a halt at that age.

He picked up the picture on the end of the mantel. It was of him, age fifteen, and he had his arm around his best friend—a girl with dark brown hair and braces.

"Steve, you hungry?"

Steve fumbled the picture before righting it and setting it back on the mantel. He turned around and smiled at his grandmother. "You just fed me. I don't think I could fit in another bite."

"Well, Jack will be by in a little bit. He's helping with the sandbags. He thought maybe you could help as well."

Steve felt a momentary panic at the idea of getting involved in a public event. The last thing he wanted was to dive right back into town life—but his grandmother was looking at him with such concern.

He nodded. "Yeah, well, we'll see."

He followed his grandmother into the kitchen. The old TV set on the counter was turned on to the local news.

"Steve, can you go turn up the TV?"

Steve crossed the kitchen and turned the knob.

"The counties of Oswego, Cayuga, and Wayne will be the hardest hit, with potentially over two inches of rain per hour. If you haven't gotten your supplies in, folks, you need to get them in a hurry. This storm is picking up speed, and it's going to hit our area by tomorrow afternoon."

Steve turned it back down as the newscast gave way to a commercial break. He turned to look at his grandmother. Her face was pinched.

"Grandma? You all right?"

Her features smoothed. "It'll be fine. They've been working everyone up into a frenzy about this storm. But I'm sure it won't be as bad as they say."

Steve took a seat at the kitchen table. "I'll make sure the house is secure, maybe tape up the windows."

"That would be wonderful, thank you. But I think we might need to buy the tape, and some other supplies. The stores are probably going to be completely out soon." She gave Steve the look.

He swallowed. *Oh, good. Shopping in town.* "Yeah, well, why don't you give me a list?"

Thirty minutes later, Steve was pushing a cart down the aisle of Tops, searching for beef jerky. His grandmother had been obsessed with the stuff for as long as he could remember. Steve had never understood it. Even though prison food hadn't offered much, it still hadn't made him appreciate the uniqueness of jerky. Finally spying the familiar red packaging, he snagged three bags.

He looked around. This actually hadn't been too bad. So far, no one had recognized him. And it was actually kind of nice, just buying stuff. But he was still having trouble with the newness of everything.

It was the small things that kept tripping him up. The cars on the walk over here, for instance. They all looked so high-tech. And there were no pay phones any more; everyone had cell phones. In fact, it seemed like every kid he saw was staring at a phone or some game thing. When did that happen? When did electronics take over? And it struck him as surreal to think that those kids had internet access everywhere they went. At Auburn, they'd still had dial-up.

It all made Steve feel like a time traveler who'd just been dropped in the future. Declan told him he'd catch up, but he didn't think so. He felt like he was already so far behind, he'd never catch up.

He turned at the end of the aisle.

"We need to get milk. I told you—" A blonde woman banged into Steve's cart.

"Oh, I'm sorry." She glanced up. Then, gasping, she took a quick step back. It was Cheryl Summers, two years ahead of him in school and the popular girl. "It's you."

Steve went still—not sure what to say. He gave her an abrupt nod and moved his cart around her. As he passed, her husband stared daggers at him.

Steve recognized him too. He'd been a friend of Jack's.

"I can't believe they let him out," Cheryl whispered to her husband.

Steve tried to ignore their muttering, but his chest felt tight.

He managed to get the supplies they needed. Everything except for the batteries—the store was completely out. He hoped his grandma had a cache somewhere in her house because one store was as much as he was willing to do today.

He made a beeline for the register. *Time to go.* He made a point of keeping his eyes down, only looking up enough to avoid running into anybody else. He got in the first line he saw open. A couple was ahead of him. Luckily, they didn't seem to know him and he was pretty sure he didn't know them.

After loading his goods onto the conveyor behind the couple, he pretended to read the magazine headlines, but his heart pounded and he was overly aware of the people around him. He moved up to the cashier as the couple ahead of him finished.

"Paper or plastic?" the blonde teenage girl at the register asked. Her nametag read Elise.

Steve tried to calm his breathing. "Um, plastic."

Elise leaned far enough over that her blouse fell away from her chest. "You ready for the storm?"

Steve averted his eyes. "Uh, yeah, sure."

"I haven't seen you around before."

"Yeah. I just got in town."

"Well, some people are going down to the shore tonight.

Bringing some beer before the storm hits. You should think about coming if you're going to be in town."

Steve stared at her for a minute before her words clicked. *Holy crap. She's flirting with me.* Steve took a look at her. She couldn't be any older than sixteen.

"You work out over at Gold's? I go there sometimes," she said.

He struggled not to laugh. Work out—for fun. Right. In prison, muscle was protection. Working out wasn't a hobby. It was a religion that kept you safe. "Yeah. How much will that be?"

The girl's smile wobbled as she glanced back at the register. "$38.78."

Steve handed her two twenties. She took her time making change, but Steve didn't make eye contact. He busied himself with looking around the store.

Finally, she handed it over. "Well, take care." She smiled, her eyes lingering on his face.

"Yeah, you too."

Steve ducked outside with his bags. Shaking his head, he gave a little laugh. Someone had actually flirted with him.

But his smile disappeared when he remembered Cheryl and her husband. He hunched his shoulders, staring at the sidewalk. Every time someone walked past, he tensed, expecting them to recognize him and say something. He'd almost made it to the end of Main Street when a dark Acura pulled up next to him.

"There he is."

Steve glanced over, his muscles tight. Then a smile crossed his face. "Jack!"

Steve's brother got out of the car and came around it, wrapping Steve in a hug. Steve felt the stares of passersby, and it made him feel self-conscious. But Jack didn't seem to care.

When Jack stepped away, he held Steve at arm's length and looked him over. Steve did the same. There was no denying they were brothers, but Steve was a good three inches taller than Jack, and while Jack was slim, Steve was more muscular.

"You look good," Jack said. "I need your workout regimen."

Steve laughed. "It's easy. Get convicted of a crime you didn't commit, then workout every day in the yard for a decade."

Jack's smile dimmed. "Hey, that's all behind you now. Sorry I couldn't be there to meet you when you got out. I had this law conference in Albany."

"No problem." Steve shifted the bags in his hands.

Jack glanced at them. "You shopping for Grandma?"

Steve nodded.

"Did you see Elise Ingram? She's grown up pretty well."

Steve paused, not making the connection until he realized Jack was talking about the cashier. "That was Elise Ingram? Holy cow."

Steve remembered Elise as this little girl with pigtails and braces. He shook his head. Time really was marching on. Jack looked so professional: dark business suit, crisp white shirt, purple tie. Steve was pretty sure there was a matching briefcase in his car somewhere. He looked like a lawyer or a politician. *Speaking of which...* "Grandma mentioned you might be running for mayor."

Jack gave him a slow smile. "I'm tossing around the idea. But we can talk about that some other time. Right now I'm headed over to help fill sandbags along the levee. They could use you too."

Right. Hanging out with all the good townsfolk. Fun, fun, fun. Steve held up his bags. "I need to get these supplies back to Grandma."

"I told her I'd find you and bring you back after. She's okay with it. And I already picked up some wood at the hardware store to board up her windows. We can do that together after we help out."

Steve looked away, watching people heading into the super-market or packing their cars with their supplies. But what he really saw were the angry screaming faces that had protested outside his trial. The same Millners Kill residents that Steve had known his whole life.

He looked back at Jack. "Look, I know you mean well, but the rest of the town didn't exactly rally to my side. They all still think I killed Simone."

"Not all of them. Some think Keith botched that investigation so bad, we'll never know for certain. But the fact is, you're back. People are going to see you at some point or another. It might as well be doing something that helps out the town."

Steve sighed, knowing Jack was right—like he always was. He also knew that fighting Jack was a useless endeavor. Once Jack was focused on something, he never let it go. And apparently, Steve's successful reintegration into Millners Kill was his latest project.

Steve sighed, resigned to his fate. "Fine. Let's go."

CHAPTER SEVEN

JACK DROVE SLOWLY through Millners Kill, pointing out to Steve what had changed while he'd been away. Steve knew Jack was doing it to be nice, but the whole exercise just made it more apparent to Steve how much of an outsider he really was.

He remembered riding his skateboard down Main Street, which was good. But then he thought about how he'd never gotten to be part of another Fourth of July parade. And now he couldn't imagine standing in a crowd cheering as the floats went by. When Jack drove him by the high school, all Steve could think about was the fact that he'd never gotten to graduate from there. Never went to prom.

In fact, the more places Jack pointed out, the more apparent it became to Steve how hard it was going to be to live here. If he showed up at any of those places that, as a kid, had embraced him, he'd be a pariah.

By the time Jack pulled into a parking space behind the bait and tackle shop, the good mood Steve had developed from seeing Jack had evaporated. He was back to feeling like Steve the ex-con.

Jack put the car in park and looked over at him. "You okay?"

Steve nodded, looking through the windshield at the water. The wind had picked up and whitecaps had begun to form. "I'm going down by the water for a bit."

Jack opened his door. "Okay. I'll find out what they need us to do."

They both stepped out of the car, and Jack headed around the building. Taking a breath, Steve headed in the same direction. Jack was speaking with a big man with a clipboard. After taking a breath, Steve made his way over to the beach.

There were about three dozen people scattered across the beach. Some were filling bags. Some moved overburdened wheelbarrows. Some loaded trucks. Steve turned away from them and walked to an empty area. He stared at the dark water as it tossed and raged. God, he'd missed this. There was something incredibly freeing about being next to a large body of water. It was primal and untamed. And everyone was equal before it.

While he was on the inside, he'd tried to picture the water, but it had never resulted in the same feeling. Now he closed his eyes, breathing deep, smelling the lake in the air and feeling the spray lick at his face. A peace settled in his chest. *Yeah. This is home.*

He opened his eyes as his brother walked over. "Got our assignments." Jack held up a shovel.

Steve took it, raising an eyebrow. "You seem to be missing *your* shovel."

Jack smiled and ignored the barb. He pointed at a group of men and women farther down the bank. "You'll be helping them fill sandbags."

Steve looked at Jack in his pristine suit. "And what are *you* going to be doing?"

Jack grinned. "They need some administrative tasks done."

Steve shook his head. "Shocking. I'm doing the hard labor and you're pushing paper."

Jack whacked him on the shoulder. "Go on. It'll be good for you. Make some new friends. And play nice with the other kids."

"Shut up, Jack."

Jack might be joking, but Steve did feel like a little kid starting at a new school. A little kernel of nervousness began to build in the pit of his stomach. It was different from the fear he'd known in prison. Then, he'd been fearful of physically getting hurt. Now, he was fearful of what other people would say. He'd been reduced to an insecure twelve-year-old.

Steve glanced over at the group of people he was supposed to work with. They looked normal enough, and he didn't recognize any of them—but from this distance, that didn't really mean much.

"Hey, you good?" Jack said.

Steve straightened his back. "Yeah, sure."

"This is a new beginning. Show them who you are not who they think you are."

Steve nodded, his face feeling tight. "Yeah. I know. See you later."

Hunching his shoulders, Steve walked over to the group. A small guy with a dark complexion shoveling sand into a bag caught sight of him. "Hey. I'm Carlos. Grab a bag and start filling."

Steve nodded. "Okay." He reached down and grabbed a few bags and headed to an empty spot next to the pile of sand.

He paused for just a minute, but no one paid him any attention—and not in a "don't look at the criminal" kind of way, either. They were all simply focused on their own tasks. So Steve bent to his. *Well okay.*

CHAPTER EIGHT

THE MAN WATCHED Elise Ingram as she stepped out of Tops. Her blonde hair blew around her in the wind, and she impatiently tried to push it down.

He smiled. *What a pretty, pretty girl.*

Elise pulled a knit hat out of her bag and tugged it on before turning to the right and heading down Main Street.

He fell into step along with her, but on the opposite side of the street. She didn't even glance over at him. He struggled to keep the smile off his face. *Oblivious.*

Elise reached the corner and stopped, waiting for a minivan to drive by. Then she quickly crossed. He turned away, then turned again down an alley that ran parallel to Main Street. Elise would turn up again at the next corner.

He skipped a little, his joy too overwhelming to contain.

The game was on. He picked up his pace, and sure enough, Elise was just rounding the corner, turning away from him. He stepped out of the alley and hurried after her as she walked down one more block and crossed the street. He pulled down the edge of his cap and tugged up his raincoat collar.

Ahead of him, he could see Elise pulling out her phone and typing something, slowing her pace. He put on a little speed and moved ahead of her, juggling his two grocery bags.

The next alley was just up ahead. When he reached the opening of the alley, he pulled at the small hole in the brown bags he had created earlier. With a tearing sound, both bags ripped, and their contents spilled across the sidewalk. A few cans rolled into the alley.

"Oh, no." He stood and stared at the mess of groceries.

A can of peaches rolled toward Elise, and she stooped to pick it up. She gathered a few more dropped items and made her way over to him. "Hey. Looks like you could use some help."

He stood, his hands full of groceries. "Oh, thanks. Bags just gave out."

"Oh, hey, it's you. I didn't recognize you."

He smiled. "Thanks. Just pile it on top."

Elise eyed the groceries already in his arms. "Um, are you going far? Maybe I could help carry them?"

"That would be great. Thanks." He smiled, and together they gathered up the rest of the stray groceries.

He headed into the alley. "My car's just on the other side. How's school?"

"Good. It'll be nice to have the next few days off, though. College is tougher than I expected. I have a history project due right when I get back, so I really need the time."

Oh, you'll have more than just a few days off. Out loud, he said. "You're at the community college, right? First year? Do you have plans for after that?"

Elise shifted the load in her arms. "Yeah. I'll stay for the two years and then transfer out, see if I can get into a state school."

"Good plan. It'll be a lot less money that way. Hold on a second." He stopped next to an old table someone had discarded in the alley and put his armful of groceries down. With his back to Elise, he pulled the knife from the sheath on his belt, under-neath his raincoat.

"You need me to take some of those?" Elise asked, leaning forward.

He smiled as he turned. With one quick slash, he opened Elise's neck. Her eyes went wide, and she grabbed on to him. Groceries crashed to the ground and rolled along the alley floor.

He took her in his arms and pushed back her hair. "You're such a pretty girl, Elise."

Elise grabbed at her throat, blood pouring over her hands.

He smiled. "Well, at least you don't have to worry about that history project."

CHAPTER NINE

STEVE SPENT over an hour filling bags before Carlos tapped him on the shoulder. "Hey. You want to help me move these over to the levee?"

"Yeah. Sure." Dropping his shovel, Steve followed Carlos to two wheelbarrows loaded with bags.

Steve whistled. "Well, this should be fun."

Carlos grinned. "Why do you think I picked you?" He jerked a thumb back at the rest of the group. "I'm pretty sure anyone else would have a heart attack if they even tried."

"Not sure *I* won't."

Carlos laughed. "Well, I'll be sure to call the paramedics." He extended his hand. "Didn't catch your name."

"Uh, Steve."

Carlos gave his hand a firm shake. "Good to meet you, Steve. Now let's get to work."

Over the next two hours, Steve and Carlos filled wheelbarrows and moved them over to the wall of sandbags. They'd add their loads to the wall, then head back for another one. Slowly, the wall built up.

The whole time, Carlos kept up a constant flow of conversation. And despite Steve's attempt to keep the man at arm's length, Carlos's enthusiasm was infectious. Steve found himself relaxing and enjoying the man's company.

After the last sandbag was moved, Carlos swiped them two waters from the stand someone had set up for volunteers. He handed one to Steve, then leaned back against the bridge. "Well, that was some damn fine work. If you hadn't come along, it would have taken me forever. So thanks."

"No problem."

"So, what do you do for a living, Steve?"

"Um, I just started over at Mel's while I look for something."

"Hey, times are tough. I manage the lumberyard over on the mainland. If you're looking for work, you should come by after the storm. We're always looking for hard workers, and that's definitely you."

"Yeah. I might do that. Thanks."

A squad car pulled up. Keith stepped out, pulling his belt up over his stomach.

Steve's good mood vanished. *Shit.*

Keith looked around for a minute before spying Steve. Then he headed over.

Carlos watched Keith approach. "Wonder what he wants."

"Pretty sure he's not here to move sandbags," Steve muttered.

Carlos chuckled.

"Hey, Carlos," Keith said.

Carlos nodded. "Chief."

Keith nodded toward Steve. "I see you're getting to know Millners Kills' most famous resident."

Carlos glanced over at Steve, a question on his face.

Keith feigned surprise. "Oh, that's right. You weren't here when Steve killed the Granger girl. Killed her right in her own kitchen."

Steve struggled to keep a rein on his temper. *Bastard.* He started to step around Keith, but Keith shot out an arm. "Where do you think you're going?"

Steve stared him down. "What do you want, Keith?"

Keith's face turned red. "That's 'Chief' to you."

"Um, I'm just going to go," Carlos said, beating a hasty retreat. He cast a glance over his shoulder at Steve.

Well, I guess that friendship's over before it began.

"Is there a problem here?" Jack asked, materializing behind Keith.

Keith glanced back at Jack and lowered his arm. "No problem. Just making sure your brother here is behaving himself."

Jack smiled. "Why, Chief, you wouldn't be harassing my brother without cause, now would you?"

Keith smiled in return. "Just saying hello."

Jack's eyes were hard. "Well, isn't that nice. Come on, Steve. We need to get back and board up those windows."

Steve stepped around Keith, his anger boiling.

Jack grabbed his arm, keeping his smile in place. He leaned down. "Not a word, Steve."

CHAPTER TEN

THE IMAGE of Keith's slimy little smile stayed in Steve's mind for the whole drive back to his grandmother's house. "It's always going to be like this," he growled.

Jack pulled in to the drive and turned off the engine. "Keith is a small-minded asshole. You can't paint the whole town with his brush."

Steve groaned. "Jack, you're an optimist. But reality needs to take precedence here. As long as I stay here, Simone Granger's death is going to follow me. Keith is going to make sure of it. As soon as I can, I'm getting out of here. If I'm really going to start over, it's going to have to be somewhere else."

Jack stared at him for a moment, then looked away, gripping the steering wheel tightly. "And what about Grandma? You're just going to leave her?"

Steve leaned his head back against the headrest with a sigh. "No, of course not. But I don't see how having me around is going to help. She's going to be looked at as a pariah, just like me."

"So you'll leave her to go through that alone? You don't know what it was like for her—for me. We lost friends. People stopped talking to us. I begged her to move off this street, but she wouldn't do it. I know you went through a lot. But so did we. So you damn well can't leave—not after all she's been through."

Even more guilt weighed down on Steve's shoulders. God, he was sick of it. During the trial, he'd watch his grandmother age before his eyes. And every time he thought about her alone in this house, in this town, it made him feel worse. He'd thought that when he got out he'd feel less guilty for what he'd put her through. But he'd been out for less than twenty-four hours, and already the guilt was threatening to eat him alive.

"Jack, it's just—" Steve sighed. "I don't know. I thought it would be easier when I got out. But if anything, it's harder."

Steve stared out the window. In prison, he'd known what the rules were. He'd known how to behave. But here? He felt like the ground kept shifting under his feet.

"It might be," Jack said softly. "But you're not going through it alone. We're here. We'll go through it together. And you need to give yourself some time. Now come on, we need to get the house ready for the storm." He got out of the car.

Steve watched him go, needing a minute to calm down. He knew Jack was right, but, damn it, it wasn't fair. He hadn't expected people to forgive and forget, but he *had* hoped maybe he could have a little peace—maybe a chance at a life.

He pictured Carlos's face after Keith had mentioned the Granger case. No, he was never going to have a chance at a life in Millners Kill. Keith would make sure of that.

Steve stared out the windshield. He hadn't killed Simone, but he'd done the time. And now it looked like he was going to *keep* doing time for a crime he hadn't committed. Meanwhile, Simone's real killer was out there somewhere, living his life freely, without the taint that stuck to Steve.

Steve slapped his palm against the dash. "Fuck!"

His hand stung. And there was a small dent in the dashboard, and he still didn't feel any better. *The story of my life: all I seem to be able to do is cause myself and those around me more pain.*

CHAPTER ELEVEN

JULIE GRANGER TURNED off Main Street. She'd stopped by the supermarket on the mainland before heading over the bridge to Millners Kill. It had been an eight-hour drive to get here, and once she got to her parents' house, she wanted to be able to stay there and not have to run back out for anything. And she was pretty sure her parents' cupboards were bare. They had moved to Charleston, South Carolina six months ago, so even if there *was* anything left to eat in the house, she didn't think she'd want it.

She hit a pothole and some of the groceries in her back seat spilled to the floor. "Damn it."

"What's wrong?" Her friend Leslie asked from the car phone. Leslie and Julie had been on the phone together for two hours. The two of them had met in med school and had become instant friends. They'd been thrilled when they'd both landed the same residency program at SUNY Stony Brook. Leslie knew more than anyone how hard this trip home was going to be.

"Just dropped all my groceries across the back of the car."

"Pothole?"

"Yup."

"You know you're supposed to drive around those, right?"

Julie laughed. "I have never heard that before."

"Well, I'm here to help. But you will be back in three days, right?"

"Yes, yes, I'll be back." Julie paused. "How's Dr. Santorina?"

Now it was Leslie's turn to hesitate. "He's, well, slightly less cheerful than his normal dour self. So just make sure you're back."

Julie cringed. She'd requested and been granted time off from her residency, but Dr. Santorina viewed her as his star pupil, and he was not happy. He wanted his students to be focused on medicine twenty-four seven. A life outside of medicine was not a consideration in his program.

But Julie knew this would probably be her last chance to go home. By some miracle, her parents' realtor had found a couple who was interested in their house. Her parents had been trying to sell their house for over a year now, with no success. Millners Kill was a small market, making it a tough sell to begin with, but when your house came with a history of murder, it made it near impossible. Julie hadn't thought it would ever sell.

But then along came the Phifers—professors moving into the area from the Midwest. They would take ownership in December. In less than three months, Julie's childhood home would belong to somebody else.

Julie had mixed feelings about that.

"Jules?" Leslie's voice called through the car's speakers.

"Sorry. Yes, I will be back." She turned onto her street. "Look, I'm almost there. I'll call you in a few days when I'm heading back. Okay?"

"Okay. But if you need me, you call, all right?"

Touched, Julie nodded. "I will."

"Okay. And while you're there, try to have a little fun, okay?"

"I will," Julie said, although fun was not exactly on the

agenda. They said goodbye just as Julie spied the familiar blue and white Dutch colonial with black shutters. She felt a combination of excitement and fear. *Home.*

She pulled into the drive and under the carport, then turned off the engine. She sat there for a full minute, working up her courage. She hadn't been back here for two years. And the last time she'd only stayed for two days.

The house itself looked like it was in good shape. Her parents had paid a landscaping company to keep the yard looking presentable. Julie glanced in the rearview mirror and saw the "For Sale" sign swinging in the wind.

She felt torn about the decision to sell it. True, she had barely been able to force herself back here since she'd left for college, but it was still home. Even if she didn't want to be here, she still wanted the option of being able to come here.

She shook her head and opened the car door. *And* that's *completely unselfish.*

She pulled her suitcase and air mattress out of the trunk then carried them to the side door, bouncing the suitcase up the three steps. When she unlocked and opened the door, stale air came back at her. It no longer smelled like home.

She placed the case and mattress inside the door, then headed back to the trunk and debated for a moment whether she should take out her supplies for boarding up the house. She shook her head and closed the trunk. First she needed something hot to eat and drink. Then she'd face getting the house ready for the storm.

She grabbed the two bags from the back seat, gathering up the spilled groceries, then headed into the house, nearly tripping over the air mattress as she entered.

"Shit."

The two grocery bags tipped precariously for a second before she got everything under control. *Oh, I'm such a klutz.* Shaking her head at her clumsiness, she walked into the kitchen and put the bags down on the counter. She was careful to not look over toward the breakfast nook.

She'd just put the milk, margarine, and eggs in the refrigerator when her cell rang. She glanced at the screen before answering. "Hi, Mom. Don't worry. I arrived safe and sound."

"Oh, thank God. Now honey, I don't want you to worry, but I need you to get back in your car and leave again."

Julie rolled her eyes. Her mother was always dramatic.

Julie pulled the spaghetti and sauce out of the bags and placed them in the pantry next to the fridge. "Mom, I'll be fine. I'm sure the storm won't be that bad. If it was, they'd evacuate. So don't worry. As soon as the storm is over, I'll button up the house and head out. I have to get back to the hospital, anyway."

That was an understatement. Although they'd agreed to the time off, they hadn't exactly been thrilled about a second-year resident taking it. But she needed to come back here and put to rest some old demons before she could move on. And this could be her last chance to do that.

Her father's voice came on the line. "Julie, this is your father."

Julie tried not to laugh. Her father always introduced himself when he got on the phone. As if, after twenty-six years, she wouldn't recognize his voice. "Hi, Dad. Tell Mom I'll be—"

"Julie, this isn't about the storm. There's been a development."

Julie felt a chill begin at the base of her spine. "Dad, what's going on?"

He paused. "It's Steve Kane. He was released yesterday. He's in Millners Kill."

Julie gripped the counters. Her vision wavered for a second. *Steve.* "But I thought he wasn't getting out for another few months."

Julie could hear the anger in her father's voice. "His release was part of some plan to reduce prison overcrowding. Those with good behavior were released earlier. Good behavior." Her dad scoffed.

Julie knew he was about to go off on a tirade. She'd heard it every time Steve's name came up. "Okay Dad, calm down. Are you sure he's actually in town? Just because he got—"

"I called the police department. He's in town. He'll be working at Mel's Diner."

Julie flashed on a memory of her and Steve sitting in one of Mel's booths, arguing over who got the next song choice on the jukebox. Steve had let her choose. Fact was, he almost always did.

She shoved the memory away and the confusing feelings it brought with it. "Okay. But there's no reason he would come see me. And no reason he would even know I was in town."

"Criminals always go back to the scene of their crime. You need to get out of there—"

"Dad." This time Julie cut him off. "I'm not a little girl. I can handle myself. You know that—you're the one who taught me. And I just drove eight hours. I'm not getting back in the car. Not tonight. Look, I promise I'll be careful and I'll stay away from him."

"And if you see him anywhere near you, you call the cops. And you call us every few hours."

Julie sighed. "I'll call you twice a day until I leave town, okay? And if I see him, I'll call the cops, *if* the situation warrants it."

"Julie—"

"Dad, I love you. But I'm a grown woman." She softened her tone. "I'm not a teenage girl. You don't need to worry about me."

Her father paused. "You don't still... You don't still think he's innocent, do you? Because the courts convicted him. He killed Simone."

Julie swallowed. She'd accepted that, mostly. But it was still hard to believe that the Steve she'd been best friends with since kindergarten was the same monster who had brutally stabbed her sister to death.

So Julie did what she did every time she talked to her parents about Simone's murder: she lied. "Yes, Dad. I know he killed her."

CHAPTER TWELVE

STEVE NAILED the last board over the windows at the front of his grandmother's house. The boards were probably overkill, but Steve felt better doing something.

Jack had helped him shore up most of the house, but he'd left a while ago. He said he still had some things to button up at his own apartment, but that he'd be staying with Steve at their grandmother's starting tomorrow.

Grabbing his hammer and a box of nails, Steve headed into the house, put his tools in the closet by the back door, and looked around. He wasn't sure what to do. He didn't want to watch TV. There was only storm coverage on, anyway. A book wouldn't hold his interest right now. And his grandmother seemed determined that he never feel even the slightest pang of hunger, so food wasn't an option. He rubbed his hands together. Sit down? Go upstairs? Do a puzzle? Nothing appealed to him.

I'm going stir crazy, Steve realized with a shock.

After all his time in prison, he thought he'd be used to staying inside, but with the opportunity now to be outside, he found he was practically climbing the walls. He needed to get out and walk.

He grabbed his sweatshirt and headed for the door. "Grandma? I'm going for a little walk."

He heard his grandmother moving about upstairs. "Hold on a sec," she called. A few seconds later, she bustled down. She walked to the closet by the front door and pulled out a dark green jacket with a hood.

Steve stared at it for a moment. "Where'd you find that?"

"Your mother put a bunch of your father's things away after he—" She paused. "After he left."

You mean abandoned us, Steve thought, but he didn't correct her. His grandmother had loved his dad like he was her own. She had never believed that he had just left. She always thought there must be a good reason for his absence—not that she had ever come up with a convincing one.

Steve realized with a shock that she had the same faith in him —a complete, blind faith.

"Here." She handed him the jacket. "It's probably going to rain any minute, and that sweatshirt won't be enough."

Steve hesitated. If it had been anyone's but his dad's, he would have simply taken it with his thanks. But his dad always brought up conflicting emotions in him. He'd loved his dad. His dad had been his best friend. And then, one day, he just didn't come home.

For years, Steve thought that he himself was responsible— that he had done something to make his father go away. He'd tried his hardest to be the best son ever. Then his mom had gotten sick, and she'd gone away too. And then he was charged with murder. Apparently, being good hadn't done much for him.

Steve pulled himself from his thoughts. His grandmother stared at him expectantly. He reached out and took the jacket. "Thanks, Grandma."

She kissed him on the cheek before heading back to the kitchen. "Don't be too long. Dinner will be on the table in an hour. Oh, and Declan's coming to dinner. He wanted to welcome you home."

Steve wasn't really surprised that Declan was coming over. Actually, he was surprised that Declan hadn't stopped by or called already. "Is Jack coming?"

"No. He wanted to, but he needed to finish some work up tonight so he could have the next few days off."

"Oh," Steve said, feeling disappointed. But he shook it off. He couldn't expect Jack to drop everything just because his little brother was back.

Steve pulled on the jacket and sniffed the collar. It smelled like his grandma's house. Disappointment filled him. He didn't know why he'd thought it would smell like his dad all these years later.

He let himself out of the house, then pulled up the hood as the wind blew hard against him. Tossing a mental coin, he turned right. He had thought the walk would ease some of the tension in him, but if anything, it increased it. He wasn't used to wide open spaces and few people. Each time a car drove by, his heart rate picked up. Each time he saw a person, he scanned them for a threat.

Get a hold of yourself. You're not inside anymore. This is Millners Kill. Nothing happens here.

But the thought of Simone's murder countered that attempt at logic. Of course, that had been ten years ago. The killer, whoever he was, had gotten away with it, but he hadn't made a move since then.

A group of kids cycled past him and Steve forced himself to unclench his fists. Just kids. At the end of the street he turned right. He took some deep breaths and released the tension in his shoulders. He tried to focus on the houses and changes that had occurred around him. Some had been renovated, some had been painted, but most looked the same. When he reached the end of the street, he kept going. And again at the next street. He turned now and then, not by any conscious choice, not with any clear destination. And he found that by focusing on the houses he was able to actually enjoy himself. He still tensed when cars came around, but he couldn't expect too much on his first day.

He passed the Neimans' house, where a couple of kids played on the lawn. He walked past the Forresters' house, where Mr. and Mrs. Forrester were out, walking around their house, making sure everything was buttoned up. They glanced over at him, but Steve looked away quickly before they got a good look at his face. They'd always been nice to him. He didn't want to know what they thought of him now.

He made it all the way to the elementary school. The playground was empty, its giant metal spider and monkey bars sat abandoned, unused. But the swings blew as if invisible children were at play. He smiled. He'd really liked this school, especially the playground.

He glanced at his watch. With a shock, he realized that forty-five minutes had passed since he'd left his grandmother's house. He'd need to head back right away if he was going to make it back in time for dinner. He hurried past the elementary school and turned onto Tulip Lane. Two more lefts and he'd made almost a complete circle. He reached his block, coming in from the other side.

His shoulders ached from moving the sandbags earlier, but he enjoyed the feeling. It had felt good to do manual labor. Plus, hauling those bags of sand had helped out the town. His brother had been right about that. Maybe he was right about the rest too.

In fact, until the chief had shown up, Steve had actually been able to relax a little. And he and Carlos had gotten along really well. The chief had ruined all that, of course, but now that Steve thought about it, he realized that today had shown him that maybe he really *could* have a normal life. At least, outside of Millners Kill.

Steve smiled, feeling a sense of possibility for the first time in ten years. *Maybe I can do this.*

"Hey."

Steve tensed and glanced around, not seeing anyone.

"Hey. Up here."

Steve looked at the tree branches above him. The kid in the red fleece from earlier was crouched on a branch up near the top. Steve paused, unsure what the hell was going on.

"You okay, kid?"

The boy shook his head, his eyes wide. "I can't get down."

Steve looked around. "Um, should I get someone?"

The boy shook his head again, and Steve could hear the tears in his voice. "No. If my brother finds out—" The boy didn't complete the rest of the sentence, but Steve got the drift. He looked around again. No one. *Oh crap.*

"Okay, I'm coming up." Steve grabbed the lowest branch and pulled himself up.

It had been almost twenty years since he'd climbed a tree. He didn't remember it being this difficult or scary. Then he realized why: it was easier to climb when you were small and completely unaware of gravity. The wind pushed and pulled at Steve as he climbed higher. He swallowed, glanced down, and wished he hadn't.

"Careful," the boy called out as Steve's foot slipped.

Heart pounding, Steve held tightly to the branch above him. Giving himself a moment, he looked up at the boy. "What are you doing up here, anyway?"

"My brother and his friends said I was too small to climb it."

Steve nodded. Boys and their stupid dares. "Well as far as I can tell, you did climb it. They didn't say anything about climbing down, did they?"

The boy shook his head, and a smile broke across his face. "No, they didn't. You won't tell, will you?"

Steve started to climb again. "Your secret is safe with me." He pulled himself up to the branch the boy was on. "What's your name?"

"Micah."

"Hi, Micah. I'm Steve."

"I know. Everybody knows who you are."

Steve sighed. *Oh, good. My return is already common knowledge.* "Well, why don't you inch back this way and we'll get out of here?"

Micah slid himself carefully toward Steve. Steve reached out his hand when Micah was close and pulled him over. Micah threw his arms around Steve and hugged him tight.

Momentarily stunned, Steve went still. Then his arms closed around the trembling boy. He patted him on the back. "It's okay. You're all right now."

Micah nodded into Steve's chest but didn't seem inclined to let Steve go.

Steve patted him on the back one more time before pulling him away. He looked into pale green eyes that stared back at him from a mixed-race face. Mocha skin and a slight slant to his eyes suggested a black and Asian heritage.

"Okay, Micah. Why don't you hop on my back and we'll get out of here?"

Micah carefully climbed around Steve, placed his arms around Steve's neck, and squeezed tight.

Steve tapped Micah's arms. "Maybe loosen up just a little bit."

"Sorry," Micah mumbled, and he released some of the pressure on Steve's neck.

"Here we go." Steve stepped down to the next branch, careful to keep his weight forward. Luckily, the wind died down just then and the climb down was uneventful. Less than two minutes later, Steve stepped onto the ground. He knelt down and Micah clambered off.

"All good," Steve said, standing.

Micah looked up at him. "Thanks. You're nice."

Steve nearly laughed. If only the rest of the town were so easy to convince. He pictured everyone in town getting caught in a tree. Steve could go around and rescue them all one by one and everyone would like him again.

"You're not so bad yourself," Steve said.

Steve turned to go, and Micah fell in step next to him. "How come you killed that girl?"

Steve glanced down in surprise, stunned yet again. "Um, I didn't."

Micah nodded his head so hard Steve worried it might roll off his shoulders. "That's what I thought. You're too nice. My brother and his friends said you were real dangerous. Said you would kill someone as soon as look at them."

Great. "So how come you're talking to me?"

Micah shrugged again. "You don't look like you killed anybody."

"Yeah? And what do people who kill people look like?"

Micah paused for a moment. "I guess they have blood on them."

"What if they killed the person a long time ago?"

Micah looked at him, uncertain. "I guess they look mean. And you don't look mean."

Steve smiled. If only the jury had thought the same way. Steve wasn't sure what to say to the kid, so he stayed quiet. Micah didn't seem to mind. He babbled on about the kids at school, his mom's meatloaf, which apparently he hated, and the fact that his dad worked too much to come see him and his brother very often.

Steve stopped in front of his grandmother's house and looked down at Micah. "So I told them that I could too climb that tree," Micah said.

"Well, you did."

Micah beamed. "Yeah, I did." Then his smile slid away. "You won't tell anyone I didn't climb down, will you?"

Steve shook his head. "Nope. Not a soul."

Micah's smile returned. "Thanks. See you later." Micah ran back down the street.

Steve watched him cross the street and go up a path four houses down. He shook his head. *Cute kid.* He smiled as he thought about Micah's non-stop conversation. *Well, at least not everyone in this town hates me.*

CHAPTER THIRTEEN

THE WIND SHOOK Declan's car as he pulled into the parking lot at Mel's diner. He turned off the engine, leaned on the steering wheel, and stared up at the darkening sky before turning his attention to the water in the distance. Along the shore, trees swayed violently. Water plumed in the air in angry bursts.

A feeling of dread settled in the base of his stomach. *Oh, this is not going to be good.*

A patron from the diner opened the door and fought the wind to her car. Declan had promised Bess he'd bring dessert, and he thought one of Mel's lemon meringue pies would be just the thing. So he'd called earlier today, and Mel promised to have one ready for him.

Steeling himself, he pushed open the car door. The wind immediately wrenched it out of his hand. When he stepped out, the wind practically blew him over. It took him a few long seconds to wrestle the car door shut again. Then he hurried over to the diner entrance, his unzipped jacket snapping in the wind.

The bell above the door jangled as he pushed through. He

paused for a moment to catch his breath and smooth down his hair. *Man, that wind got fierce.*

Only a few of the tables were taken, and a few of the stools. Mel's was usually busier at this time. *Everyone's probably home getting ready for the storm.*

Mel appeared from the kitchen, pushing through the doors behind the counter, a plate balanced in each hand. Catching sight of Declan, he smiled. "Hey, Declan. How you doing?"

Mel was pushing sixty and had owned the diner for the last thirty years. He was about five ten and had a strong build—a remnant of his Navy days. He used to keep his hair cut close, too, but nature had taken care of that for him now. His bald head gleamed in the diner's bright lights.

Declan walked over and took a seat at the counter. "I'm good."

Mel dropped off the plate farther down the counter before coming back to stand in front of Declan.

"How are *you* doing, Mel?" Declan asked.

Mel shrugged, picking up the coffee pot from the burner behind the counter. "Can't complain. We were pretty busy for most of the day although it's slacked off some. Coffee?"

Declan nodded, flipping over the cup in front of him. Mel filled it up. Declan smiled as the smell reached him.

Mel replaced the coffee pot back on the burner. "I'll grab that pie for you as soon as I get these orders out."

Declan took a sip and sighed, feeling the warmth course through him. The storm had brought a big dip in the temperature, and Declan hadn't been prepared for it. "Take your time. I'm enjoying my coffee."

"It'll be just a few." Mel hustled back into the kitchen.

Declan looked back out the window. *Did the bridge just move?* He narrowed his eyes and stared before shaking his head. *Must be the storm playing tricks with my eyes.* He took another sip. *Well, at least Steve's first day went well.* When he'd spoken with Bess, she'd made it sound like everything was perfect. And while Declan seriously doubted that raging optimism, it did mean there probably hadn't been any huge issues.

He felt a little weight lift off his shoulders at the thought. He knew Steve was a man, but Declan just wanted his transition to be as bump-free as possible.

The bell above the door jangled again. Russ pushed through, stopping in the entryway to look around. Catching sight of Declan, he nodded with a smile and headed over.

Declan returned the smile, inwardly shaking his head. Russ never seemed to understand that town cops and state cops were supposed to butt heads. Declan had asked Russ about it one day, and Russ had looked completely confused. "Why would I do that? You're trying to help and I'm trying to help. As far as I'm concerned, that's all that matters."

Not for the first time, Declan hoped that Russ would consider running for Chief sometime in the near future. The town could use some of his open-mindedness.

Russ took a seat next to him. Declan took one look at him and reached over the counter for the coffee pot. Russ flipped over the cup in front of him.

Declan poured him a cup. "You look like you could use it."

Russ poured a small mountain of sugar in it and added a dash of milk. He took a sip with a grimace. "God, I hate coffee."

Declan let out a laugh. "So why do you drink it?"

Russ shrugged. "I'm a cop. I'm pretty sure we're required to drink it."

"How's it going?"

Russ shook his head. "It's crazy. People are losing it. Mrs. Beale over on High Street accused the Schroeders of stealing her mums."

"Did they?"

"Well, seeing as the Schroeders moved away twenty years ago, I doubt it. Mrs. Beale suffers from dementia. Her kids were supposed to come back to town and grab her before the storm, but unsurprisingly they didn't. Luckily her neighbors agreed to take her in. She's been fine for the most part, but the storm's setting her off." Russ paused. "And just about everybody else."

"Storms will do that."

"Oh, there's also a missing teenager."

"What? Who?"

"Elise Ingram. She never showed up home after work."

"Any ideas?"

"She's run away before and has a boyfriend over on the mainland. But her friends say she was supposed to meet up with them and never showed. That's not like her."

A missing teenager just when Steve shows up in town. *Damn it.* But Declan also knew that with a missing teenager, it was usually a case of simple running away, not some sort of abduction. "What are you guys doing about it?"

"The regular—calls to the boyfriend, a BOLO. But she's eighteen. We can't really do much more than that, at least not yet. And with the storm..."

Declan shook his head. "I'm surprised the governor didn't call for an evacuation. With the reports, it looks like it might even be worse than originally forecasted."

Russ shifted his eyes away and stared at his cup.

A feeling of dread began to build inside Declan. "Russ? The governor *didn't* order an evacuation, did he?"

Russ sighed. "It wasn't an order so much as a strong suggestion—at least that's how the chief is taking it."

"The chief? Why is he calling the shots? What about the mayor?"

"Mayor Do-Nothing? He's out of town. As soon as he heard about the storm, he took off with his family. Left Keith in charge."

"Oh, for God's sake. Is Keith at least going to tell the town?"

"I don't think so. I tried to talk him out of it, but you know how he gets."

Mel bustled in from the kitchen, two more plates in hand, a pie box dangling from his fingertips. He dropped the plates off at another table and headed back to Declan. "Here you go. Hey, Russ."

"Hey, Mel."

"What do I owe you?" Declan asked, pulling his wallet from his back pocket.

Mel waved his money away, his cheeks growing redder. "It's on me. Tell Bess I said hello."

Declan had always suspected Mel was a little sweet on Bess. Looks like he was right.

Declan slid off the stool. "I'll do that. And thanks." He turned to Russ. "Be careful out there. And if you need anything, you give me a call."

"Will do," Russ said, grimacing as he took another sip of coffee.

Declan headed for the door, his thoughts heavy with the upcoming storm. Keith was an idiot. When he pushed open the diner door, a gust of wind nearly tore the pie box from his hands. He cradled it to his chest like a football as he made his way to the car. *Damn, that wind's getting really strong.*

The wind almost yanked the passenger door from his hand as he opened it. He carefully placed the box on the floor, then wrestled the door shut. He walked around to the driver's side, shaking his head. *If this is the pre-storm, the actual storm is going to be a monster.*

A groan of metal snapped his attention to the bridge. *What the hell was that?*

He peered at the old bridge, and there was a sinking feeling in his chest. Was he seeing things, or was the bridge actually shaking? He watched for a long minute until the wind gusted again. This time he knew it wasn't a trick of the light. There was definitely a tremor in the metal.

God damn you, Keith, Declan cursed as he pulled out his phone. There had to be a way to go over Keith's head. It was already past five o'clock though. He glanced at the darkening sky and at the bridge as he dialed.

The bridge gave another shudder.

Declan listened to the call ring out. *Come on, someone pick up.* But he knew that even if someone did pick up, it might already be too late.

CHAPTER FOURTEEN

THE SMELL of lasagna greeted Steve as he walked in his front door. His grandmother's cooking was so far the one thing that had thoroughly lived up to, if not surpassed, his memories. He tossed his jacket over the banister, then backtracked and hung it in the closet.

Walking into the kitchen, he took a deep breath. "Now that smells delicious."

His grandmother placed the silverware on the table. "Wash your hands. It'll be ready any minute."

"Yes, ma'am," he replied, turning around.

As he headed toward the bathroom, the phone rang. Spying it on the table next to the stairs, he called out, "I'll get it."

"No, Steve. I—"

Steve picked up the phone. "Hello?"

"Murderer," a voice hissed. "They should have put you to death. If they won't do it, I will." *Click.* The call was disconnected.

Steve pulled the phone from his ear and stared at it. Slowly he turned to his grandmother, who was wringing a potholder in her hands. "Now, Steve—"

He cut her off. "How often have you been getting these?"

She wouldn't meet his eyes. "Not very often."

He knew she was lying. She lied so badly even a child could tell. "Grandma, have you been threatened?"

"Steven James Kane, you listen to me. I don't care about a bunch of redneck idiots. I care about you. I can handle a few phone calls. You've had much more to—" The rest of her words were choked off, and there was a tremble in her chin. Taking a steadying breath, she continued, "You've had to endure more. And I would endure tenfold these calls to have you home. So you just go wash your hands and get ready for dinner and forget about that."

Steve looked at his grandmother, the strongest woman he knew. A feeling of tenderness washed over him. "I love you, Gran."

She smiled back at him. "I love you more."

He grinned at the familiar exchange, but then his smile faded. "But I don't like you having to put up with these calls."

"The Lord doesn't give us any more than we can handle," she declared before heading back into the kitchen.

Steve watched her go, noticing her shoulders were a little more bent—her gait a little slower than he remembered. *I'm not so sure about that*, he thought.

The idea of someone threatening his grandmother... Steve took a deep breath. No. He wouldn't let anyone hurt her. He'd talk to Jack and Declan. Make sure they knew what was going on.

CHAPTER FIFTEEN

AN HOUR LATER, the phone call was still on Steve's mind, but he thought he had put on a good show in front of his grandmother. He leaned back in his chair and patted his stomach. "That was delicious."

Declan grinned at him. "Which serving? One or two?"

Steve pretended to ponder the question for a moment. "I'm going to go with two. It seemed to have a little more time to settle."

Declan laughed, pushing his chair back. "Bess, it's a good thing I don't come into town more often. Eating like this, they'd have to roll me into my car."

Bess smiled. "You could do with a little fattening up. And any time you want a home-cooked meal, you just stop by."

Steve stood up and started collecting the plates, but Bess shooed the two men toward the living room. "You two go chat. I'll get the dishes."

"Gran..." Steve said.

She fixed both of them with the look. "Out—both of you. Shoo."

Declan grinned at Steve before heading for the living room. "*I* know better than to argue with her."

Shaking his head, Steve followed.

Declan took a seat on the couch. Steve sat on his grandfather's old recliner. Through the window, he could see the wind whipping through the trees. The rain had begun about an hour ago.

"It's started," he said.

"Yeah." Declan sighed.

Steve looked over at him. "Want to tell me what's on your mind?"

Declan leaned back. "The governor ordered us to evacuate. Keith decided to ignore the order."

"You're kidding." Steve shook his head. Of course Keith overrode the evacuation order. That was just like Keith. "Is it really going to be that bad?"

"I was at Mel's before I came here. Took a look at the bridge. It was already groaning. I'm a little worried."

"From the look on your face, I'd say you're more than a little worried."

"True. There was a deputy at the diner. I asked him to see if they could position someone at the bridge. It's going to be closed until after the storm. I don't think anyone should try crossing that thing."

Steve nodded, not knowing what to say. There was nothing he could do about the bridge that was for sure.

But there *was* something he might be able to do about the phone calls. He glanced back at the kitchen and saw his grandmother bustling about. He leaned toward Declan, his voice low. "There's something worrying me too."

Keeping his voice equally low, Declan leaned forward. "What?"

"Grandma's been getting some nasty calls. I know it's probably just a bunch of cowards, and nothing will happen, but—"

Declan nodded. "I know someone in Millners Kill's police department who's, well, not an asshole. I'll talk to him. See if he'll do some drive-bys."

Steve felt some relief. "Thanks. I appreciate that."

Declan nodded, but his face was still tight.

"What is it?" Steve asked.

"Listen, when people realize the bridge is closed, they're going to get a little panicked. It might be good for you to lay low, just until things calm down."

Steve looked at him for a long moment. "Wasn't really planning on throwing a party. I'm guessing you mean just stay away from people as much as I can?"

Declan blew out a breath. "Look, as long as things stay calm, it won't be a problem. But—"

"But you don't think the police will exactly be running to my rescue if the town turns against me."

Declan nodded. "Something like that. So just to be safe, maybe stay inside as much as possible, okay?"

Steve nodded, picturing a mob of angry people trying to get to him—and his grandmother getting caught in between them. He gripped the sides of the chair. "Okay."

Declan's cell phone chimed, and he glanced down at the screen. "Got to take this." He walked over to the front windows.

Steve couldn't overhear the conversation, but Steve could tell he was getting more agitated by the second. *Uh-oh.*

Declan stalked back into the room. "God damn idiot."

"I'm guessing Keith."

Declan gave an abrupt nod. "He pulled the deputy off the bridge. That guy is going to get somebody killed. I'm heading over there now. Keith needs to understand how important this is."

"Go. Give him hell."

Declan gave Steve a smile. "I'll go say goodbye to your grandmother first."

Steve's thoughts were dark as he watched Declan head to the kitchen. If the bridge went, they'd all be stuck here for God knew how long. And he'd be stuck trapped with the assholes who were making those calls.

He shook his head. *No sense borrowing trouble,* he thought, using one of his grandmother's favorite phrases.

He heard the back door close and got up to watch Declan back out of the driveway. Declan practically peeled away, he was driving so fast. Steve watched him go, his dread growing. *It'll be all right.*

But then he noticed another car drive slowly by the house. He'd seen it earlier today as well. *Probably just someone from the neighborhood,* he thought. But he couldn't shake the feeling that the person driving the car seemed awfully interested in his grandmother's house.

CHAPTER SIXTEEN

DECLAN COULD SEE the bridge lights up ahead. "God damn it."

The rain was still coming down, but it had eased up some.

He pulled up in front of the bridge entrance, using his car to block one of the two lanes leading onto the bridge. When he got out, Russ hustled over from his cruiser, which was parked next to the bridge.

Russ put up his hands. "I'm sorry, Declan. The chief pulled me off."

Declan swallowed down his annoyance. *It wasn't Russ who was being an ass.* "It's okay. It's not your fault."

The bridge groaned. Declan whipped his head around, his stomach plummeting. He couldn't leave this to Keith. He turned back to Russ. "Russ, call your chief. If he doesn't get some blockades up, I'm going to have him suspended from duty pending a review of his actions."

Russ gulped, looking like a beached fish. "Um, okay. I'll call him."

"Give me your keys."

Russ handed them over.

Declan ran over and hopped into Russ's squad car. He could already see a car approaching, heading for the bridge. He quickly drove Russ's car over and parked it next to his own, blocking both lanes leading onto the bridge.

Then he pulled out his own cell and dialed the state police. After quickly explaining the situation, he got the officer to agree to blockade the bridge from the other side. Declan disconnected the call and let out a breath. At least he didn't have to worry about people crossing from the mainland.

When he looked up from his phone, Russ was leaning into the car that had approached. Russ stepped back, and the car did a three-point turn and headed back the way it came. But another car was headed toward them now.

Russ came over to stand next to Declan. "That's the chief."

Declan nodded but didn't say anything. The Jeep jarred to a stop, the back end fishtailing a bit on the wet surface.

Keith hiked himself out, covered from head to toe in bright yellow rain gear. He marched over to Declan. "Just what the hell do you think you're doing?" he barked.

"What am I doing?" Declan's temper exploded. "The governor ordered you to evacuate. You ignored that order. You have placed everyone in this town in a very dangerous situation."

Keith snorted. "Bunch of terrified paper pushers. We can handle a little rain." He turned to Russ. "Move your cruiser."

"God damn it, Keith!" Declan yelled. "Look at the bridge. It's unstable. You knew that before the damn storm. With the wind, it's not safe. Anyone who goes across that thing is risking their life."

"It's fine," Keith said. "It's been here for decades. It'll survive—"

A metal screech tore through the air. All three of them turned to look at the bridge. It swayed for a moment before going still.

Declan looked back at Keith, whose face had gone white. "Still think the bridge is just fine?"

Keith glared at him. "I won't have the state police coming in and taking over. You don't have any cause—"

Declan took a step toward him. "You want *me* to take over? Because I assure you, I could make a few calls and have you side-lined. The bridge is closed until the storm has passed. God willing, we can open it back up after the storm."

Keith tried to stare him down. Declan didn't flinch.

Finally Keith looked away. "Fine. I'll close it. But as soon as the storm passes, it's getting opened back up. And I'll make sure everyone in Millners Kill knows you're the one who stranded them during the storm."

Keith stomped back to his car, calling back over his shoulder, "Russ, put up a blockade."

"Yes, sir, Chief," Russ said, saluting the chief behind his back.

Declan smiled in spite of himself. But his thoughts quickly darkened again. Panic was going to set in once people realized that Millners Kill was now officially cut off.

It'll be okay. As long as everything else stays calm, it'll be fine.

CHAPTER SEVENTEEN

STEVE SAT in his grandfather's recliner, a baseball bat next to him on the floor. They'd gotten a few more threatening phone calls after dinner. He'd finally ended up unplugging the phone.

And after his little chat with Declan, who had told him the bridge was going to be closed until after the storm, Steve planned on staying down here for a little while—just in case.

A soft knock at the back door woke him just as he was drifting off. At first he didn't recognize it, thinking it was just the house creaking. But then it got a little louder. Steve glanced at the cable box—9:30 p.m.

Outside, the wind howled, and the rain had picked up speed. Whoever was at their door was awfully determined, coming out on a night like this.

Steve grabbed the bat from next to the recliner and gripped it tightly, although he was pretty sure that if anyone meant him or his grandma harm, they wouldn't knock first. He walked to the door, flipped the switch that illuminated the back steps, and peered through the yellow curtain on the door.

A woman around his age stood there, blinking in the light on the covered back porch. Soft, wavy brown hair fell over her shoulders and halfway down her back. She was looking back behind her when Steve peered out, but then she turned and faced the door.

And Steve got his first good look at her. The breath left his lungs. *Julie.*

His hand trembling, he rested the bat against the kitchen cabinets before unlocking the door. Steeling himself, he opened it.

"Julie. Hi."

"Steve."

They stared at each other for a moment, neither seeming to know what to say. Steve finally got a grip on himself and took a step back. He gestured toward the kitchen. "Do you want to ⸺"

She shook her head, taking a step back.

Of course she doesn't want to come in, you idiot. She thinks you killed her sister. Self-conscious, Steve put his hands in his pocket. "Okay. Um, what can I do for you?"

"Could you come out here?"

Steve hesitated, peering into the dark. It was quiet. If she'd brought someone with her, he couldn't see or hear any sign of them.

"Sure." He stepped out and closed the door behind him.

Hands back in his pockets, he looked at her before his eyes cut away. The words slipped out before he could catch them. "I didn't kill her, Julie."

She gasped, and he cursed himself. Why the hell had he said that? He'd promised himself after he'd gotten locked up that it didn't matter. It was done. He'd been found guilty. It didn't matter if he did it or not, and he was done trying to get people to believe him. But he'd always wanted to say those words to Julie. And have her reply, "I know."

But this wasn't one of his daydreams.

There was a tremble in her voice when she spoke. "That's not why I came here."

Steve waited for her to say more, but she just stared past him. Finally, he broke the silence. "Why did you come?"

For the first time, she looked him in the eyes. "I don't know. I heard you were back. I didn't want to just run into you." She gave a small laugh. "I thought this would be easier."

"Not so much, huh?" Steve said softly, feeling the gulf that existed between them now.

She shook her head. "No. Not so much." She paused. "I loved her, Steve."

"I know."

"I loved you, too."

He didn't know what to say to that. He wasn't sure he could say *anything* to that. His throat felt tight. He took a breath.

"Just do me a favor, okay?" Julie asked.

He nodded. "Anything."

"Stay away from me. I'm here for a few days and then I'm gone. And I don't want to deal with any drama, okay?"

Without waiting for an answer, she turned and walked away.

CHAPTER EIGHTEEN

STEVE WATCHED Julie walk around the side of the house in the rain and disappear. More than anything, he wanted to run after her. Beg her to believe him. But he didn't. He just watched her go.

He sat down on the old lounge, not caring about the rain that was coming in through the sides of the porch. *My God—Julie Granger.* She looked good. The promise of beauty had been there when she was younger, but it had been fully realized at some point while he was away.

His childhood was defined by his friendship with her. They'd met in kindergarten, and from day one, they'd been best friends, always in and out of each other's houses. They'd had tons of sleepovers, although Julie's parents had ended those when they'd become teenagers. But it had never been romantic between them —not, at least, until that last year. He'd begun to notice how good she looked in jeans, how well she filled out her shirts. But he'd been too terrified to do anything.

And then Simone had been killed.

Julie had actually come to him the morning they'd found Simone. Tears had poured down her cheeks. "She's dead, Steve. Simone's dead."

Steve had been shocked. His grandma had overheard and ushered the two of them into the living room, wrapping a blanket around them both. Steve had held Julie while she cried her heart out.

And he'd cried with her. Simone had always been nice to him. And Steve had gone out of his way to be nice to her as well. She had become like his big sister.

He still remembered the shock on Julie's face when Keith came to his grandmother's house and arrested him two months later. He and Julie had been putting together a puzzle in the living room. As Steve was taken away in handcuffs, Julie had opened her mouth, but no words came out. Yet as soon as the door had closed behind him, he'd heard her heartbreaking screams.

She hadn't spoken to him again since that day—not once. At the trial, she wouldn't even look at him. She hadn't been there the day of the sentencing. And now here she was. Just one block over.

But she might as well be on the other side of the planet.

Somewhere down deep, Steve had always harbored the belief that she knew he couldn't harm Simone. Outside of his family, Julie had been the one that knew him the best. In fact, she probably knew him better than even his family did.

His gut clenched. Now he knew the truth. Julie thought he killed Simone.

He was surprised at how much that knowledge hurt. He'd told himself years ago it didn't matter what anyone thought. But it did.

It mattered what Julie thought.

Steve dropped his head into his hands. He felt the tears build at the back of his eyes. He hadn't let himself cry since the verdict. But for just tonight, he'd let himself feel the loss of his one true friend.

CHAPTER NINETEEN

JULIE LET herself in at the back door of her parents' house, then closed it behind her, turning the deadbolt and pulling the chain. Leaning heavily against the old oak door, she ran her hands through her hair.

Why did I do that?

She should have just kept her distance. But when her father had told her Steve was back, she'd felt this undeniable pull. She'd had to see for herself who he was. To see the monster that she had somehow missed in their years growing up together.

She walked over to the kitchen table and sat. Resting her head in her hand, she looked around the kitchen. It had been entirely remodeled after Simone's death.

She remembered that morning like it was yesterday. Her mother's keening wail had pulled her from sleep. Julie had stumbled down the stairs, fear making her whole body shake. She'd stood in the kitchen doorway, unable to step inside. Her mother and father were crouched low over Simone, blocking her view, but Julie could see the blood—splashed across the walls, the blinds. A giant pool of it soaked the bottoms of her parents' robes.

Julie must have made a sound because her father turned. He yelled for her to go to her room and stay there. Terrified, she fled up the stairs, but the image of the blood stayed with her, working its way into her dreams. For a few years, it had even invaded her waking life.

Julie dropped her head into her hands. *Maybe I shouldn't have come home.*

Her parents had finally agreed to sell the house a year ago. Learning about Steve's impending release had been the final push. But Julie had never understood how they could have stayed in the first place. She hadn't been able to set foot in that kitchen for over a year after her sister's death, even after it had been remodeled and all traces of Simone were gone.

But now, as she looked at the sleek dark cabinets, she understood why they had stayed. They had wanted to be close to Simone. And this house was as close as they could get to her.

Julie looked out the window as a light turned on three houses over—Steve's grandmother's kitchen light. When they were kids and Steve stayed at Bess's house, they would use the kitchen lights to send Morse code messages to each other. Julie remembered sitting at the kitchen table, writing out dashes and dots.

She stared at the long light. There was no message in it tonight.

Years ago, she'd accepted that Steve had killed her sister. At least, she thought she'd accepted it. And guilt had eaten at her ever since. After all, it was Julie who had brought Steve into their home. Granted, they'd been kids when they met, but she blamed herself nonetheless.

The prosecution said he'd been obsessed with Simone—and that when Simone rebuffed his advances, he'd lashed out and killed her. Julie had let them convince her, but the doubts lingered. He'd been nice to her sister, sure, but Steve had been nice to everyone. Had she really misjudged him that badly?

And when she saw him tonight, all those old doubts came flooding back. It was easy to paint him as a monster when she wasn't looking in his eyes.

He'd changed since she saw him last—there was no doubt about that. He was tall and really muscular. He looked tough, hard—but after ten years in prison, he'd have to be. But what had surprised her—and unsettled her—was that she could still see Steve, her friend, in his eyes.

Julie stood up and headed for the stairs. It didn't matter. He was responsible for his sister's death. Kind eyes didn't change that fact.

It was time for her to put all of this behind her. She'd ride out the storm, fix whatever needed to be fixed afterward, and then beat a fast path out of town. Her life in Millners Kill was over.

Just like Simone's was.

DAY 2

"Morning, upstate New Yorkers! This is Billy the Kid on KLNQ. It's started. Rain has hit most of our area this morning, and those lucky few who haven't been hit yet will certainly be hit by the afternoon. Hope you've got your supplies in and maybe a rowboat handy, because it's too late to leave now!"

CHAPTER TWENTY

WHEN STEVE WOKE UP, he was disoriented for a minute as he looked at the sloping ceiling, blue walls, and white curtains. Then he heard the sound of Frank Sinatra drifting up the stairs and smelled the undeniable scent of cinnamon rolls.

I'm home, he thought with a pang.

He glanced at the clock: four a.m. He hadn't set the alarm. Four a.m. had been his wake-up time in Auburn. His system was primed for the early rise. Which was perfect because it gave him an hour before he was due at the diner.

He rolled out of bed and dropped to the floor. He cranked out a hundred push-ups followed by a hundred sit-ups—his morning routine while inside. Then he sat on the floor, his back against the bed.

This had been his room since he was ten years old. His grandmother had carefully packed away most of his old teenage stuff, leaving only a few of his things out: his soccer and swimming trophies, some of his favorite books. He was glad she had put the other stuff away. He didn't think he would have been able to face his old room, his old life. And she—or more likely, Jack—had picked up some clothes for him as well. He liked his room this way—a couple of mementos, but a fresh start.

The conversation with Julie flashed through his mind. He had really missed her. She'd never written him, never visited, but she'd kept him company nonetheless in his mind, helping him pass the interminable hours. He'd replayed all their board games, listened in on all their old conversations, and when it didn't hurt too much, he'd even let himself daydream about what his life could have been with her.

And now, even though she was one street over, she felt farther away than ever.

He pulled over the box his brother had left for him. He'd opened it yesterday, but hadn't yet removed the contents. He re-read the note attached:

STEVE,

Sorry I couldn't be there your first night home. But in case you thought I had forgotten you, I got you a little coming home present.

The best big brother ever,

Jack

STEVE SHOOK HIS HEAD. He opened the box again. It was jam-packed with Twinkies. When Steve was a teenager, he'd been crazy about them, and for the first year he'd been away, he'd even dreamed about them. He smiled as he gazed at the familiar packaging.

The box also contained his old pocketknife. Jack must have held on to it for him. A relic from another life.

"You going to sleep all day?" his grandmother yelled from the bottom of the stairs.

Steve smiled. She always knew when he was awake. "I'm

coming," he yelled. He pulled on his jeans and slipped the knife in his pocket, then hustled down the stairs to the kitchen. The smells of breakfast assaulted his nostrils—eggs, bacon, pancakes and of course the cinnamon buns—and he nearly swooned. When he'd gone to sleep last night, he hadn't expected this. He figured he'd slip out of the dark house while his grandmother slept.

He walked over to his grandmother, who stood at the stove. Putting his hands on her shoulder, he kissed her cheek. "I don't deserve you."

She patted his hand. "Yes, baby, you do. Now start eating before this gets cold."

Steve took the plate she handed him. "Yes, ma'am."

His grandmother took her own plate and sat across from him. Steve was about to dive in, but Bess's silence stopped him. He looked up. She was giving him the look—again.

He nearly smiled. He'd even missed the look. He placed his fork and knife on his plate and took her hand.

With a nod, she closed her eyes. "Bless us, O Lord, and these your gifts, which we are about to receive from your bounty. Through Christ our Lord. Amen."

"Amen," Steve echoed, picking up his utensils.

His grandmother let him eat in silence, and Steve appreciated it. He had been dreaming about one of his grandmother's breakfasts for ten long years, and now he savored every bit.

Finally, he leaned back from the table and patted his stomach. "Now *that* was delicious. And Declan's right: if I keep eating like this, I won't fit through the door."

She smiled, a coffee mug in her hand. "I'm glad you liked it. You could use a little fattening up, too."

Steve rolled his eyes with a smile.

"Jack said he's going to stop by today," his grandmother said, sipping her coffee.

Steve nodded. "Yeah. He told me."

"He's real happy you're home again."

"He the one who talked Mel into hiring me?"

She looked away. "No, honey. Mel did that all on his own."

Steve sighed, wishing she wouldn't bother trying to lie. He pushed away from the table and took his plate to the sink. But when he turned on the water to wash it, his grandmother gently pushed him aside.

"Go take your shower, sweetie. I don't want you late on your first day."

He set the plate down in the sink. "Okay, I'm going."

He kept his tone upbeat, but fear bounced around his brain. Mel hadn't volunteered to hire him, he knew that much. How was Mel going to react when he saw him? How was *anyone* going to react when they saw him?

He took a deep breath as he headed for the stairs. He'd faced down the inmates at one of the country's oldest prisons. He could handle the residents of Millners Kill.

CHAPTER TWENTY-ONE

WITH A NEON SIGN rimmed in white and red, Mel's Diner—named after Mel himself, although everyone thought he'd named it after the old TV show—stood at the end of Main Street about two hundred yards from the bridge. As Steve jogged down the sidewalk toward the diner, careful to avoid the giant puddles that pooled there, he saw that sawhorses now blocked the bridge—along with a sign announcing that the bridge was closed.

Steve smiled. *Go Declan.*

He stopped across the street from the diner and was surprised to feel a pang of homesickness just looking at the place. He'd worked there from the time he was eleven until he was sixteen. He'd started as a busboy and worked his way up to a short-order cook. Mel had said he was a natural.

Dodging the early morning traffic and the waves of water they created on the rain-drenched street, Steve crossed and stood for a moment at the door. He blew out a breath. *You can do this.*

He pulled open the door. The bell above it jangled.

Mel came out of the kitchen drying his hands on a towel. He still looked the same: white shirt and white pants with a white apron over it. The only splash of color was the St. Christopher's necklace he always wore. Steve and Julie used to joke that with his bald head, thick arms, and round stomach, if Mel was a dog he'd be a bulldog.

The thought of Julie brought back memories from last night. Steve shoved them aside. *One difficult re-acquaintance at a time.*

"We're not open yet, but if you—" Mel stopped short and took a step back, his eyes widening. "Steve."

Steve shifted his feet. "Um, I thought I was starting this morning."

Mel shook his head. "Right, right. You are. Sorry, with the storm coming I just forgot. Um, come on around back."

Steve nodded, feeling the tension in the air. He wasn't sure how to make it go away. Assure Mel he hadn't killed Simone Granger? Assure him he wouldn't harm any customers? But he knew from experience that his words would have no effect. They never did. So he silently followed Mel through the kitchen doors.

Mel nodded toward the food prep area. "Okay, so for the morning, the main priorities are getting the griddle up and running and prepping for the lunch crowd. Breakfast is mainly eggs, bacon, and pancakes. For lunch, you'll need to prep—"

"The tomatoes, pickles, and lettuce. I remember."

Mel nodded. "Good. Well, I'm going to put on the coffee. Everything's where it used to be."

Steve grabbed a white apron off the hook to his right and tied it around his waist. "Sure. No problem."

Mel headed for the dining area, but then turned back. "Steve, it's probably best if you stay in the back today. At least until people get used to you being back."

Steve's back stiffened. "Yeah. You're probably right."

Mel watched him for a minute, and Steve knew he was struggling with whatever he was going to say. Mel finally looked him in the eye. "Look, I don't know if you did what they say you did. I gave you this job for your grandmother. It about killed her to see you get locked up. If you're thinking of doing anything stupid, just remember her. She doesn't deserve any more grief in her life."

On that they agreed.

"I know."

Mel nodded. "All right then. Let's get to work."

Steve went over to the fridge and started pulling out supplies, but the memory of his grandmother heartbroken after the verdict stayed in the forefront of his mind. Jack had looked equally devastated. They'd been through so much.

But then, so had he. He might not be able to control any of what had happened before, but he was sure not going to let them get hurt again because of him.

But Steve put all those thoughts out of his mind and focused on the job at hand. *One thing at a time.* After a few fumbled starts, Steve soon got the hang of things and fell back into the old, familiar rhythm of the diner. It went pretty well, everything considered. In fact, the only fly in the ointment was Mel's waitress, Wendy. She had been decidedly cold if not downright hostile.

For the umpteenth time that morning, Steve placed a plate on the window and rang the bell. "Order up."

Wendy came and picked it up, careful not to make eye contact with him. Steve had overheard her complaining to Mel about having to work with a murderer. Steve really hoped he didn't get fired. He needed this job. One of the conditions of his parole was employment. It was a tough job market, and that was before you added the ex-con line to the resume. He'd met a few guys inside who'd been yanked back in when they'd lost their jobs. Steve couldn't even think about that possibility.

Shawn, who'd worked with Mel forever, had shown up to take care of the lunch crowd about an hour ago. Shawn was rail thin, with a full head of pure white hair, dark skin, and a big smile. He and Mel had met in the Navy. In fact, Shawn was the one who'd convinced Mel to move to Millners Kill when their tours were up.

Steve had been scheduled to leave when Shawn took over, but the diner had gotten slammed—everyone must have realized this was probably their last chance to get out and about before the storm hit—so Steve stayed to help. Still, heeding Mel's words, he made sure to stay away from the kitchen window. He even kept his back to the dining area as much as possible when working. And it seemed to have worked. No one had given him a second glance.

Eventually, things settled down, and the diner started to clear out. Shawn leaned back against the counter and wiped his hands on a towel. "Well, I think that's the end of the rush. Thanks for sticking around."

"Sure. Actually, I enjoyed it." And it was true. It was nice to be working—and not thinking.

Shawn nodded. "I ever tell you about my time inside?"

Steve looked back, surprised. "No. You never mentioned it."

"It was back when I was eighteen. Stupid shit. Friend decided to rob a store. I drove the car. I didn't realize what was happening." He paused. "Ah, hell, I probably did. I just didn't think too much about it. Anyway, we got caught because we were a couple of idiots. I spent four years inside."

"Where?"

"Auburn. When I got out, I had a chip the size of a boulder on my shoulder." He shook his head. "Took a while to get that off. Navy helped with that. One day, though, I just realized that all the bad things happening to me, I'd really done to myself. My life wasn't going to get better on its own. I had to make that happen. Wasn't easy, but I did. You can too."

Steve took a good long look at Shawn. He'd never realized

Shawn had been locked up. Shawn was married, had been for years, even had a couple of grandkids. Steve felt a little kernel of hope.

Shawn stuck out his hand. "Just keep moving forward, kid. You'll get there."

"Yeah, I will. And thanks." Steve shook Shawn's hand before untying his apron and hanging it on the same hook he'd taken it from nine hours ago. He was about to head out when Mel appeared from the hall that led back to his office. He wasn't smiling.

"Steve, can I talk to you for a minute?"

A pit formed at the bottom of Steve's stomach. *Oh, no, no, no. I can't get fired. I can't go home and tell Grandma I got fired.* But despite the storm of emotions running through him, he kept his face a mask and his voice even. "Sure."

He followed Mel down the back hall to his office, which was located across from the storeroom and next to the back exit.

"Close the door," Mel said as he took a seat behind his desk.

Steve closed the door and sat on one of the folding chairs in front of Mel's ancient desk. "Look, Mel, I know Wendy's not happy I'm here—"

Mel waved his words away. "Oh please. That girl is always complaining. If I could find another waitress, I'd let her go in a heartbeat."

"So, you're not going to fire me?"

Mel's surprise was evident. "Fire you? Is that what you thought? No. You did a great job. And I appreciate you sticking around to help out Shawn. No, actually I wanted to see if you want some more hours. Shawn wants to spend some time with the grandkids. So I need someone to fill in on Saturdays. I know I already have you scheduled for Monday through Friday, but—"

"Yeah. Absolutely. That would be great."

Mel smiled. "Good, good. Takes a load off. Oh, and I meant

to tell you, we're going to be closed for the next two days because of the storm. Okay?"

Steve felt lightheaded with relief. He wasn't getting fired. "Yeah. No problem."

Mel stood and extended his hand. "You did good today. Keep it up."

Steve took Mel's hand. "I will. And thanks."

CHAPTER TWENTY-TWO

DECLAN'S STOMACH GROWLED, and he swallowed down another yawn as he stretched. He'd headed straight to the elementary school when he'd woken up. Last night, he'd gotten it designated as an emergency shelter.

Declan had taken over the principal's office. He'd been on the phone most of the morning, trying to see what options were available to get supplies into Millners Kill if the worst happened.

The news wasn't good.

Choppers couldn't fly if the wind was really kicking, and the boats wouldn't be able to cross the surf. Even when the storm calmed down, the choppers would be delegated on an as-needed basis, and supply runs would rank far below medical needs.

Which was their other problem. With the bridge closed, they had no access to the hospital on the mainland. Right now the school nurse was in the cafeteria with a few volunteers, turning it into a makeshift hospital, and she had gotten at least one doctor in town to agree to come down when needed—but it was hardly ideal, and they weren't equipped for a real medical emergency.

Declan let out a yawn that threatened to break his jaw. He hadn't slept well last night. He kept imagining the bridge going. And he worried what would happen to the town's mood. Caged people did not always behave rationally.

When he'd stopped for coffee this morning, the only thing anyone was talking about was the bridge closing. Well, not the only thing. A few people mentioned Steve's name. Declan didn't like the tone those latter conversations had taken.

His stomach growled again, reminding him that breakfast had been a long time ago. And a simple bagel and cream cheese wasn't much of a breakfast to begin with. He knew he should have something healthy, but honestly? He wanted something full of fat and bad for him. It was that kind of day.

He remembered seeing vending machines near the gym. He headed out of the lounge in search of one when Mrs. Poole, the school nurse, called out to him.

"Declan?"

He tried not to groan. He just wanted five minutes where he didn't have to talk to someone. But he slapped a smile on his face and turned. "Hi, Mrs. Poole. How's the med center coming?"

"Good. I wanted to let you know that we have it up and running. Now, if we get anything serious, we'll be in trouble. But for little things, we'll be good to go."

Declan flashed on Julie Granger. He'd heard she was back in town, and she was apparently a second-year medical resident, if the town gossip was correct. Maybe he could get her to come help out.

"Thank you. You've been a godsend."

A blush spread across Mrs. Poole's cheeks. "Just doing what needs to be done. I'm going to head home for a bit, if that's okay—make sure everything is all right there. But I've arranged to be here for most of the time for the next two days, along with a few other volunteers. And my sister, who's also a nurse, will be here when I'm not. And Dr. Robbins will be here whenever we need him."

"That's great. Thank you for everything."

She smiled at him and headed for the parking lot.

Declan turned, feeling a little better. The storm had officially begun this morning, but the rain had already come down hard last night. And the wind had been ferocious. *But at least the medical angle was being handled.* He smiled, imagining the bag of Cheetos he was going to wolf down.

"Declan."

Oh, come on.

Russ came running up the hall toward him.

Declan's irritation disappeared when he saw the worry on Russ's face. "Russ? What's going on?"

Russ looked around before speaking. "I thought you should know. Chief is bringing in the Donaldson kid."

Declan paused, trying to remember who that was. "Darrell?"

"No. The younger one—Micah."

"Micah? He's what, eight?"

Russ shook his head. "Six. Micah was seen talking to Steve. Chief wants to find out what they said."

"Why? Is the kid hurt?"

Russ shook his head. "No. Someone just reported that Micah was seen walking with Steve."

Declan's gut clenched. God damn it. Hearing a kid was being questioned about Steve was not going to calm the fears that were already cropping up in town. And what the hell was Keith thinking? There were ten million things they needed to prep for the storm. There wasn't time for this crap.

But Declan would have to make the time. "Okay. I'll head over there."

Russ hesitated. "Just... Could you not mention that I told you?"

Declan smiled. "No problem."

The relief on Russ's face was palpable. "Thanks."

Declan turned to go before turning back to Russ. "How come you *are* telling me this? I mean, I know you're a good cop, but it's almost like you're looking out for Steve. In fact, I think you're the only one in the police department who seems to give a damn about him."

Russ looked around again; there was still no one nearby. "I was friends with Steve back in high school," he said. "Not best friends or anything, but we had some good times. When he was arrested, I believed he'd killed Simone. After all, the cops said he did, and the courts did too."

"Something change that?"

"When I joined the department, I looked at the old case work and..." He stopped. "Look, this stays between us, right?"

Declan nodded. "Right."

"Well, the chief—he likes to cut corners. And when I looked at the investigation, there were a lot of red flags. But the chief never investigated any of them. As soon as they found those clothes in Steve's closet, it was game over. I thought reading the file would put to rest any doubts I had. But it just created more."

"So you don't think he killed Simone?"

"I honestly don't know. But I do think there are a lot of questions that still need to be answered."

"I know what you mean."

Russ paused. "Do you think he killed her?"

"I know that, given the right circumstances, anyone can kill. But I don't think those were the right circumstances for Steve. So no, I don't think he did."

"Yeah, I know," Russ said, although Declan had the distinct impression the words weren't for his ears.

"I better go," Declan said. "But can you just go keep an eye on Steve? I don't like the mood this town is in. He should be heading home from work any minute."

Russ nodded. "Yeah. I was actually planning on it. But remember, when you talk to the chief, you didn't hear anything from me."

"You got it."

Declan ducked back into the main office and shrugged on his jacket before jogging to the school's main doors. Outside, he could barely make out the parking lot through the rain whipping against the windows. Declan groaned. *And this is just the beginning.*

He discounted driving almost immediately. He could see the lines of water running along the road. And the station was only down the street. *It'll probably be faster to go on foot.*

Preparing for a wet run, he pulled up his hood with a grimace before dashing out into the storm. The rain was coming down in sheets. He was soaked in the short run to the police station. As he stepped into the foyer, water dripped off him, forming a puddle on the floor.

Dee raised an eyebrow. "Need a towel?"

He grinned. "That would be nice." He started to walk toward her.

She put up a hand. "I'll bring it to you. I don't need my whole station soaked." Dee rounded the desk and pushed through the doors. She tossed him a white towel.

Declan caught it one-handed. He wiped down his face, pulled his jacket over his head, and hung it on the coatrack by the door. Another pool of water started to develop under it.

Declan dried his boots off the best he could before heading over to the desk. He held up the towel. Dee pointed to a bin just outside the swinging doors. He tossed it inside.

"Where's the Donaldson kid?" Declan asked.

Dee raised an eyebrow. "How'd you hear about that?"

Declan shrugged. "Small town."

She huffed and hooked a thumb toward the back. "Yeah, sure. Interrogation room."

This time it was Declan who raised his eyebrow. "Interrogation?"

She nodded, although she wouldn't meet his eyes. "Chief's orders."

Declan pushed through the doors. *Great—a six-year-old in an interrogation room. That's not intimidating.*

As Declan headed toward the back room, he saw a good-looking black woman sitting beside a mountain of a man in the chief's office: Michone Donaldson and her brother, Reggie Tully. Michone was Micah's mother, and Reggie his uncle. Micah's father was off somewhere in Pennsylvania with family number two.

Declan's temper began to rise. If Micah's mom and uncle were in the chief's office, it meant the kid was on his own without any adult representation. And Declan was damn sure Keith hadn't bothered to get the kid any kind of legal representation. *That bastard.*

He paused just outside the interrogation room, trying to rein in his anger. He took a deep breath, then pushed open the door.

"Micah, I'd just like—" Keith cut off in mid-sentence, staring at Declan. "What the hell are you doing here?"

"Well, I heard you were having a chat with Micah here, and I wanted to see if you need my help."

"I don't." Keith gestured toward the door.

Declan ignored him. He pulled a chair out from the table, placed it at the end, and took a seat. Now he could see both Keith and Micah at the same time. He smiled at Micah. "Hi, Micah. How you doing?"

Micah looked down at the tabletop. "I'm okay."

The chief glared at Declan. "I appreciate your interest, but I've got this under control."

Declan gave Keith a friendly smile. "Don't worry, I'm just observing. You go right ahead." He sat back in his chair.

Keith eyed Declan a moment longer, but Declan showed no sign of moving, so finally the chief grunted and turned back to the boy, a giant smile on his face. Declan knew Keith was trying to appear friendly, but in Declan's opinion, it only made him look creepy.

"Now, Micah," Keith said, "you were saying you spoke with Steve Kane the other day."

Declan narrowed his eyes but held his tongue.

Micah darted a glance at Keith before his gaze returned to the table. "Um, yeah."

"What did you two talk about?" Keith asked.

Micah just shrugged.

Keith leaned forward, his voice hardening. "Now Micah, you know when the police ask you a question, you need to answer."

Micah started to shake.

Declan could have throttled Keith. He was about to interrupt when Micah's soft voice whispered, "It's a secret."

Keith grinned and tried to tap Micah's hand, but Micah pulled it away.

"Well, that's all we need," Keith said. "You stay here a minute, and your parents will be right in."

Keith headed out the door, and Declan stared after him. What the hell was that all about?

Declan reached over and squeezed Micah's hand—he noticed that Micah didn't pull away from *him*. "You did fine. I'll be right back."

Declan followed Keith out, closing the door behind him. He caught up with Keith and stepped around him, forcing him to stop. "What the hell was that?" he asked.

Keith smirked. "That was called investigating."

"And *what* is it exactly that you think you just found out?"

Keith took a step back, the smirk on his face growing wider. "What, you don't know? A secret?" He did air quotes. "We all know what that means."

Declan stared at him dumbfounded. How the hell could anyone elect this guy to office? "So, what? Steve's not just a murderer now, he's a sexual predator as well?"

Keith shrugged. "He's been in prison. You learn a lot in prison."

Declan bit down an angry retort. "First off, whatever you think you just accomplished in there, you didn't. You need to get the boy to say what the secret is—not just assume. And second, why isn't his mother or uncle in there with him?"

"I told them they didn't need to be. I didn't want to traumatize the kid."

Declan pictured Keith looming over Micah. "Are you kidding? You just questioned a minor alone in an interrogation room." Declan took a breath. He took a step toward Keith. "You say nothing about sexual assault, do you hear me? Not until there's proof."

"You don't get to—"

Declan spoke through gritted teeth. "If you breathe a word of this, I will have your badge stripped so fast it will make your head spin. Then *I* will hire the lawyer for Steve to sue this town, and you personally."

"This is my case. I can—"

"Case? There is no case. You have nothing."

Keith spluttered. "You can't come in here and—"

"I just did. And if you don't like it, feel free to call the state and complain—although everybody's a little busy with the storm right now. It might take a few days for them to get back to you."

"You're making a huge mistake here," Keith snarled.

"No. This *town* made a huge mistake electing *you*."

Keith narrowed his eyes. "Screw you, Declan."

Declan turned away. "No thanks. You're not my type."

CHAPTER TWENTY-THREE

STEVE STOOD at the back door of the diner staring out at the rain. It was as if someone was pouring water from a never-empty bucket. It just wasn't letting up.

Should have grabbed Dad's jacket, he thought as he glanced down at his sweatshirt. He was going to be soaked before he made it to the end of the parking lot.

After his talk with Mel, the diner had gotten swamped again, and Steve had stayed around to help. He didn't mind, but the rain had only gotten heavier in the last hour.

He watched the rain for a while, thinking about what Shawn had said earlier. It had gotten him thinking about where his life was heading. And where it *could* have gone—which meant Julie.

He couldn't get her out of his head. She was a giant one of his "what ifs." What if he had told her how he felt years ago? What if he hadn't been arrested and sent away? Would they be living their lives together?

He shook his head. Or was he just romanticizing a childhood crush because it was the closest thing to a romantic relationship he'd ever had?

Outside, the rain showed no signs of slowing. He sighed. It was going to be one really soggy walk.

Mel walked over and eyed him. "You only got that sweatshirt?"

"Yeah. It's okay though."

"Hold on." Mel ducked back into his office, then came back holding out a dark green rain poncho. "Some customer left it weeks ago and never picked it up. His loss is your gain."

Steve hesitated, not wanting to owe Mel anything. But he shook off the thought. This wasn't prison. It wasn't tit for tat. He reached out and took the jacket.

"Thanks."

"You did real good today. Haven't missed a beat." Mel paused. "Look, I changed my mind about tomorrow. I'm going to open up, what with everyone stuck in town. Shawn's not going to be able to make it in though, so I could use you for the whole day, if you're up for it."

"Yeah. No problem."

Mel smiled. "Great. See you in the morning." He clapped Steve on the back and headed back to the front counter.

Steve watched him walk away. It was almost like old times.

Feeling lighter than he had since he'd arrived back in town, Steve pulled the poncho over his head and opened the back door. Rain pelted him in the doorway. He could swear the rain was coming in sideways.

He pulled up his hood, ducked his head, and stepped out. Wind and rain tore at him, but the poncho at least kept his chest and the top part of his jeans dry. His sneakers, though, were soaked within seconds.

But as his feet squished along in his soggy sneakers, he smiled. There was something wild about a storm—and something freeing.

He paused at the end of the parking lot. He should head

home. But to be honest, he was enjoying himself. Besides, with the rain lashing down, the few people who were out were rushing by, their heads down. No one paid him any attention. For the first time since he'd been released, he could walk around without worrying about people's prying eyes.

Feeling freer than he had in ten years, Steve smiled and headed for the water's edge.

He could see the bridge shaking in the torrent. As he got closer, he could hear the groan. *Holy crap, that thing really is going to go.* He noticed that they'd switched out the sawhorses for rope. Good call. The sawhorses would never survive the wind.

Steve stood at the divider's edge. The water looked like it was battling itself. Waves swelled and crashed, sending up plumes of water. More waves slammed into the bridge, causing it to tremble. It was violent and explosive. Steve couldn't look away. It was incredible.

The blare of a car horn sounded behind him. Steve turned.

A red sedan, going way too fast for the road conditions, cut in front of an SUV. The SUV driver slammed on their brakes, but the tires had no traction on the rain-covered street, and the SUV fishtailed, hydroplaning directly past the spot where Steve stood. He was close enough to see the terrified female driver's face and the small child strapped into the car seat in the back. As Steve watched in disbelief, frozen in place, the SUV careened straight onto the bridge, cutting through the rope like it wasn't there and skidding into the guardrail.

For a second, Steve thought the rail would hold—but then, with a screech, it tore away from the bridge.

The car tumbled over the side into the waters below.

Steve sprinted to the spot on the bridge where the car had gone over, yanking his poncho off and throwing it aside as he ran. He saw other people running for the bridge as well, but he was the closest.

The SUV had fallen right side up but it was sinking fast. For just a moment, doubts crowded Steve's mind. He hadn't swum in a decade.

Then he pictured the small face in the back of the car.

Holding his breath, he jumped.

CHAPTER TWENTY-FOUR

DECLAN WALKED BACK DOWN the hall of the police station, trying to cool down. He'd lost his temper, and that wasn't good. Keith could, and *would*, make things difficult for him from this point on. Of course, Keith hadn't exactly been going out of his way to help Declan before now, so Declan probably hadn't lost too much.

Declan stopped at the vending machine and looked at its contents with a sigh. No Cheetos. He settled for two cans of fruit punch and a bag of pretzels. Then he made his way back to interrogation and nudged open the door. Micah jumped up like he'd been shot.

Declan cursed Keith again. *Goddamn it.* The poor kid was terrified.

Declan forced himself to smile. "Hey, Micah." He held up the juice and pretzels. "I thought you might want a snack."

Declan placed one of the cans of fruit punch in front of Micah. Taking a seat across from him, he opened the other can and took a sip. "Ah. I needed that."

Micah slowly took his can, opened it, and took a careful sip.

Declan opened the bag of pretzels. He took one out, tossed it in the air, and caught it in his mouth. He offered the bag to Micah.

Micah shook his head.

Declan took a few pretzels from the bag before placing it in the center of the table. "Well, it's here if you change your mind. How's school going?"

"Okay."

"I heard your school is putting on *Mary Poppins*."

Micah nodded.

"Are you going to be in it?"

"I'm going to be a dancing penguin."

"Really? That's great."

Declan reached over and nudged the pretzel bag closer to Micah. Micah's little hand dug into the bag this time, coming away with three pretzels. "Thank you."

"No problem."

Declan was content to let them sit and eat pretzels until Micah was comfortable talking. It only took about two minutes.

"That other guy's not very nice," the boy said.

Out of the mouths of babes. "Well, he's trying to make sure nothing bad happens to the town."

"And he thinks Steve might do something bad?"

Declan nodded. "Yes, he does."

Micah took a sip of fruit punch. "I don't think he would."

"Why not?"

Micah shrugged. "He's nice."

"So you talked to him?"

Micah nodded his head. "Yeah. He's my friend."

"How'd you guys become friends?"

Micah opened his mouth, then shut it. His gaze returned to the table.

Declan leaned forward. "You know, Steve's a friend of mine too."

Micah looked up at him through thick lashes. "He is?"

"Yup. In fact, I've known Steve since he was a baby." Declan paused. "And I'm guessing him being your friend has something to do with your secret."

Micah nodded.

"Seeing as I'm friends with Steve, how about if you tell *me* this secret? I promise not to tell."

"Do I have to?"

"Well, Steve actually might get in trouble if you don't."

Micah chewed on his bottom lip.

Declan felt bad pressuring the kid, but he really needed to find out what the kid was talking about.

"You won't tell my brother or the kids at school?"

Declan held up his hand. "Scout's honor."

Micah giggled. "You're not a Boy Scout."

"Am too. Or at least I was."

Micah hesitated.

Declan stayed quiet, not wanting to interfere with whatever debate was going on in the kid's mind.

Finally, Micah spoke. "Steve got me out of a tree."

Declan looked at Micah, not sure he'd heard him right. "What was that?"

The words burst out of Micah's mouth. "Darrell and Zeke said I was too small to climb the big tree by Roy's house. So I climbed it, but I wanted to do it when no one was looking. So I did. I made it all the way up. But then I couldn't get down. Steve climbed up and got me down. He promised not to tell anybody. And he said I did climb the tree. And I did. I just didn't climb down. So it's okay to say I climbed it, right?"

Declan's mind whirled, trying to keep up with the boy. "So you climbed the tree. Why was that a secret?"

Micah looked exasperated. "Because I didn't climb down, only up. I didn't want anyone to know." He looked at Declan expectantly.

Declan struggled not to laugh—all this because Steve had rescued a kid from a tree.

"So, you won't tell anybody, will you?" Micah asked.

Declan went to nod his head, but caught himself. "Well, I have to tell the chief, but that's it. Okay?"

Micah seemed to consider this for a moment. "Okay. But make sure he doesn't tell anyone, all right?"

"You got it." Declan stood up. "Come on. Let's go get your mom and uncle."

Micah hopped out of his chair, and the two of them walked down the hall. Declan struggled not to laugh out loud. *A tree—all this because he climbed a tree.*

CHAPTER TWENTY-FIVE

THE SHOCK of the cold water immobilized Steve for a moment. Then he righted himself, kicked for the surface, and broke through. Waves crashed down on him, pulling him away from the car. He started to swim toward the SUV, which had landed right side up. It hadn't sunk all the way yet. Steve fought the waves to reach it, but they kept tossing him back.

Taking a deep breath, he dove, hoping swimming under the water would be easier. It was. He had to surface once more, but on his second dive he reached the car. The water had now almost reached the roof.

Steve dove under again. His hand found the door handle. He yanked, but the door didn't budge. Locked, or maybe just stuck. He remembered once hearing something about not being able to open a car door underwater—water pressure or something. You were supposed to roll down the window. He banged on the glass, but it was too dark to see anything, to communicate with the driver.

He swam back to the surface and gasped for breath. The water was dribbling over the roof now. The car was going under.

Then Steve spotted it: a sunroof. It was closed, but a jagged crack ran across the glass. If he had something to break it with...

He remembered the pocketknife, still in his jeans pocket from this morning. *Thank you, Jack.*

Steve climbed onto the roof. Fishing his knife from his pocket, he slammed the hilt of the knife into the glass. It spider webbed. He hit it again. And again. It fragmented. He kicked the glass through, and a thin stream of water began pouring through the opening.

Steve lowered himself in, crouching on the divider. The driver was unconscious. She was in her early thirties, with dark hair. He unbuckled her seatbelt, then pulled her toward the opening.

Standing on the divider between the seats, he got her shoulders out. Water was now gushing through the opening, trying to press them both back inside the car.

"Give her here!"

Russ Nash appeared in the water next to the car, a rope attached to his belt. He was ten years older than the high school friend Steve had once known, and he was wearing a policeman's uniform, yet Steve recognized him instantly. But he didn't have time to think about what Russ Nash, of all people, was doing here next to a sinking SUV. He just dragged the woman out through the sunroof and pushed her toward him.

Then he ducked back inside the SUV.

"Where are you going?" Russ yelled.

Steve didn't answer. He slid between the front seats into the back. The little girl's large eyes stared at him. She looked to be only about one, and shock seemed to have taken her voice. The water level was already up to her neck, and it was rising rapidly.

Steve took a breath and ducked under the water. He fumbled with the unfamiliar buckle, but managed to undo it. He knew the girl was underwater now. *Does a baby know how to hold her breath?* He tried to pull the baby out before realizing there was another buckle. *Goddamn car seat.*

He released the second buckle and grabbed the girl by the arm. He rose to gasp for air, only to find that that there was no air; the car was now completely full of water. Holding the girl tightly to his chest with one hand, he grabbed the edge of the sunroof with the other and pulled them both out.

He swam upward with only one arm, kicking furiously for the surface, but he felt like he was standing still. Spots began to dance in front of his eyes. He wasn't going to make it. He held the girl tighter, willing himself to find the strength. He kicked harder, stretched farther.

An arm wrapped around his waist from the right, another from the left. Together they pulled, and a few seconds later, he burst through the surface of the water.

He pushed the little girl toward Russ. "Oxygen. She needs oxygen," he panted.

Russ pulled her to his chest, holding her on her back and breathing into her mouth.

Carlos, Steve's sandbag friend, was treading water on Steve's other side, keeping an arm on him. "It'll be okay, man."

Steve nodded, not questioning where the little man had appeared from, just thankful he'd arrived. Right now all his attention was focused on the little girl. She wasn't moving, wasn't breathing.

Come on. Come on, Steve silently begged while treading water.

Finally, the little girl moved her arm, coughed up a lungful of water, and let out a cry.

Steve let out a breath, realizing he'd been holding his own while waiting for the little girl to catch hers.

Russ grinned at him. "She's okay."

Steve smiled. *Thank God.*

CHAPTER TWENTY-SIX

STEVE SAT under the awning of the bait and tackle shop watching the girl and her mother get loaded into a squad car. They couldn't go to the hospital because of the bridge, but an officer was going to take them over to the elementary school to get checked out.

Carlos had already headed home to dry off, but before he left, he'd shaken Steve's hand. "Good thing you were here today. The rest of us weren't close enough. They wouldn't have made it without you."

Steve hadn't known what to say to that.

Now Russ walked over to Steve, holding out a steaming cup. Steve took it and took a sip. He looked up, surprised. "Hot cocoa?"

Russ shrugged. "I'm not a coffee fan."

"Thanks."

Steve took another sip of cocoa. He glanced up at Russ. They had been friends in high school—not best friends, but they'd hung out a lot. It was weird seeing him now: the cop and the ex-con.

But Russ didn't treat him like the ex-con, and Steve appreciated that.

Of course, Russ was the only one who didn't treat him like a murderer. Steve had given his statement to another deputy who'd managed to be as antagonistic as possible. Not that Steve thought he deserved a medal, but would decency have been a stretch? Now he was just waiting for the big man.

As if on cue, Keith's Jeep pulled into the parking lot, its lights swirling. Keith got out of the car, a giant yellow slicker covering him. He spoke with an officer before stomping toward Steve and Russ.

"Why do I think he's not coming over here to say 'good job'?" Steve mumbled.

From the corner of his eye, he saw a small smile cross Russ's face.

Keith came to a stop in front of Steve, rain running in rivulets down his coat. "Kane, what the hell have you been up to?"

Steve wiped his hand over his face before looking up at Keith. "And how exactly do you figure *I'm* to blame for this?"

Keith stared at him. "Just get out of here."

"Yes, sir." He gave a sloppy salute before handing the mug back to Russ. "Thanks."

Russ nodded. Steve wondered why exactly he'd had to wait around for *that*, but he kept his mouth shut in case Keith decided to change his mind. And Steve was not in the mood to deal with that. He got that everybody hated him. But when he actually saved a life, would it kill any of them to not be complete assholes?

He yanked his poncho back over his head. Carlos returned it to him; apparently someone had retrieved it. But he questioned why he was bothering to wear it now; after all, he was already soaked from head to foot.

Just as he stepped out into the rain once again, a groan of

metal, louder than any he'd heard so far, cut through the air. His head whipped back toward the bridge.

The old bridge shuddered. The front dipped with another screech of metal; the middle bowed. A suspension cable snapped. Then another. People ran from the water's edge.

The front of the bridge tore away from its perch, diving into the water below. The rest buckled and then collapsed down on itself. And just like that, the bridge was gone.

With a giant rush, a twenty-foot wave crashed down on the shore and sped toward the gathered bystanders. Steve grabbed on to the light post next to him, climbing up on its base as the water raced toward him. He held on tightly as the water hit the light post, then rushed back toward the ocean.

A gray-haired woman screamed from behind him. The water had knocked her off her feet and was now pulling her forward. Steve crouched low and managed to snag the back of her jacket as she went by. "I've got you. Hold on."

The woman reached up and grabbed Steve's hand. He held on until the pull of the water stopped.

"Try to put your feet down," Steve said.

The woman was shaking, but she did. Steve climbed down and stood next to her, keeping his arm around her waist. She was shaking so hard he didn't think she'd be able to stand on her own.

"Thank you, thank you," she mumbled over and over again.

"It's all right. You're fine," Steve assured her.

She held on to him as if her life depended upon it.

"Mom!" A man with glasses and salt-and-pepper hair ran over and pulled the older woman to his chest. Steve recognized him. It was Mr. Collins—his old math teacher.

"Thank you so much..." Mr. Collins looked up and blanched. "... Steve."

Steve nodded, his mood darkening a little. He released Mr.

Collins's mother and turned away. He didn't want to wait to see if Mr. Collins had anything else to say.

From the corner of his eye, he saw people getting to their feet. As they stood, they stared in shock at the destroyed bridge. But Steve just turned away from it. The bridge was a town problem—and obviously he wasn't a member of this town.

As he walked away, he remembered his plan to get back in people's good graces by saving every member of the town from a tree. Then he shook his head as he pictured Mr. Collins's face after realizing who had saved his mother.

Apparently not even heroic deeds were going to be enough to change some people's minds about him.

CHAPTER TWENTY-SEVEN

IT TOOK Steve double the time it normally took to get home. The wind and rain seemed to conspire to always be pushing against him. When he reached his Gran's porch, he felt exhausted. And he couldn't believe everything that had just happened. It seemed... unreal.

The lights were on inside, and he could picture his grandmother bustling about. At the door, he slipped off his socks, shoes, and poncho. He left them outside on the porch and stepped inside quietly. If all went well, he'd grab a shower before she caught sight of him.

"Steve, is that you?"

He'd forgotten about his grandmother's superpower: enhanced hearing. He debated for a minute whether to just yell that he was heading up for a shower, but he knew she'd worry. So with a resigned sigh, he headed toward the kitchen. "Yeah, it's me."

His grandmother was at the sink, washing dishes, her back to him. "I made meatballs. I thought we could have spaghetti." She turned the water off, grabbing a towel and turning. "How does that—"

She let out a little shriek and ran across the kitchen. "What happened?"

"It's raining, that's all."

His grandmother reached out and held up his arm to examine it. A gash extended from his wrist to his elbow. He'd been so cold, he hadn't even noticed it—hadn't felt it.

"It's nothing, Gran. Just a cut from work."

His grandmother raised one eyebrow.

Steve pulled his arm back. "Really, I'm fine."

Placing one hand on either side of his face, she studied him. When he was little, he'd thought she was psychic whenever she did this. She always knew his mood.

He pictured Mrs. Collins's mother, and he imagined what might have happened if he hadn't been there. She and his grandmother were about the same age.

He placed his hands over his grandmother's cheeks, wondering what he would ever do without her. Tenderness filled him. "I'm okay. Really. Just cold."

She fixed him with her gaze for another moment before letting him go. "All right. There are clean towels in the linen closet. Make sure you clean that cut. Now shoo."

"Yes, ma'am." He turned and headed up the stairs.

The cordless phone rang just as he passed it. *I thought we unplugged that thing*, he thought as he backtracked to answer it.

Steve put a little edge in his voice when he answered. "Hello?"

"Steve. It's Declan. Are you okay?"

Steve glanced toward the kitchen. His grandmother stood in the doorway, her expression concerned. "It's just Declan," he said.

She nodded and headed back in, but Steve hated the worry he was causing her. He jogged up the stairs, taking them two at a time with the phone. "Hey, Declan. Yeah. I'm okay."

Declan let out a laugh. "Russ told me what happened. I'm so damned proud of you."

"It's nothing."

"Hey. The people of this town should know you saved that woman and kid. They seem to think they know who you are. Maybe this will give them pause."

Once again Steve saw Mr. Collins's face. "Yeah. I don't think it's going to be that easy. Everybody else all right?"

"Yes. Luckily no one was pulled out when the bridge collapsed. It's a damned miracle."

"Guess it's a good thing you closed it."

"Guess it is."

"Look, I'm freezing. I've got to go grab a shower."

"Yeah, yeah, of course. I need to go help out, anyway. I just wanted to make sure you were okay."

"I am. And thanks, Declan." Steve disconnected the call and placed the phone on the table in the hall with a smile.

In the bathroom, he stripped off his wet clothes and turned the water as hot as it would go before stepping into the shower. Pinpricks of pain danced along his skin as the scalding water came in contact with his skin. But after a minute, the heat seeped through the cold.

Steve examined the cut on his arm and realized it was a pretty bad one, deeper than he had first thought, but he didn't think it would require stitches. And at least it had stopped bleeding.

Resting his hands against the wall and letting the water roll over him, he mentally replayed the last two hours. He'd saved three people's lives, and someone had even called him a hero.

Wendy the waitress hated him, and Mr. Collins was disgusted by him. But even with the whole town hating him, compared to his usual day in prison, this day was actually turning out pretty good.

CHAPTER TWENTY-EIGHT

HE DROVE THROUGH THE TOWN, watching everyone scurry around in the rain. He'd already driven past where the bridge used to be. Everyone was now stranded here in Millners Kill. *Oh God, this is just too good.*

He stopped at the light. Skip Hughes, a friend from high school, crossed in front of him. Skip waved, recognizing the car. He waved back. Skip's two little girls flitted along next to him in their colorful raincoats.

Skip had been a member of student council and on the football team. They'd spent almost all summer together after both junior and senior year. But it had been harder to stay in touch as time marched on.

He watched the trio cross the street. The girls were six and seven. Skip put a ton of pictures of them on Facebook. *The proud papa.*

Skip let go of the girls' hands as they reached the sidewalk. They skipped ahead of him, laughing, their matching brown curls blown around by the wind.

He imagined walking up behind Skip, slipping his knife

through the vertebrae in his lower back, then shoving his knife into Skip's neck as the girls' smiles turned to screams of horror.

Skip turned and waved once more.

The man smiled, returning the wave. *Good to see you too, Skip.*

He continued through the town. Few people were out, and there was little traffic. Not that in Millners Kill there was ever much traffic.

He passed out of the town proper just a few minutes later. He hummed along with the radio as he wound his way to the far side of the island. He pulled into a parking spot at the deserted beach. The waves crashed with violence on the shore.

He smiled, feeling the excitement in the air.

He got out of the car. He glanced around. Not a soul.

Rain whipped around him. He bent his head back to let it wash over his face. It was invigorating.

He hit the trunk release on his key fob, walked around to the rear of the car, and smiled down into Elise Ingram's pale face. Her empty eyes stared up at him.

"Oh don't be like that," he said, pulling on his plastic gloves. "You should be honored."

Plastic lined the trunk to keep any blood from spilling into the car. He wrapped the plastic around her before pulling her into a sitting position. Her head lolled to the side, and he pushed her blonde hair back and kissed her on the forehead.

"In fact, you should be flattered. You are the first move in my little game."

CHAPTER TWENTY-NINE

JULIE SPENT the morning trying to button up the house as much as she could—and trying not to think about the fact that Steve was just a few houses away. The basement, she knew, was probably going to be a problem. It had always tended to flood, even when there was only a mildly heavy rain. But she'd just have to deal with that when it happened.

By midday, she figured she'd done about all she could. Now she just had to wait and see what damage the storm brought. So after a quick lunch, she sat down in the den with her anatomy textbook. She told herself that if she was going to come home, she would be sure she dazzled Dr. Santorina when she got back. She was going to know general surgery inside and out. Opening her notebook, she set out to do exactly that.

It was much later when a knock at the door finally took Julie's attention away from her textbook. She blinked her eyes, trying to orient herself. Surprise filtered through her as she saw it was already five o'clock. She'd been at it for hours, with only a few breaks for the bathroom and, of course, more coffee.

She glanced out the window and noticed that the rain had stopped. *Well, at least we get a little break from it.*

The knock sounded again, and she hastily got off the couch and marked her page before heading to the front door. She looked through the transom glass next to the door. A Millners Kill police officer stood there. *Oh, no.* Taking a breath, she unlatched the door and pulled it open. "Yes?"

The officer smiled down at her. "Hey, Julie."

It took her a moment, but then she recognized him. "Russ?"

He reached out and hugged her. "I heard you were back in town."

Julie laughed. "I didn't know you *stayed* in town. I thought everyone from our class left."

Russ dropped her back down. "Most did. More jobs on the mainland. But I always wanted to be a cop, and there was an opening when I got out of college, so I took it."

"It suits you." And it did. Russ looked confident and content. Julie envied him that. Russ had always seemed so comfortable in his own skin. She couldn't remember ever seeing him flustered or stressed. It seemed like the right persona for a cop.

Julie stepped back. "You want to come in?"

Russ shook his head. "No, I just wanted to stop by, say hi. Tell you I was around if you need anything." He shifted his feet. "Um, you heard Steve's back in town?"

Julie nodded. "Yeah."

"Okay, good. Just wanted to make sure you knew, especially with the bridge."

"The bridge?"

"It's been all over the news."

Julie had kept the TV and radio off so she could study. "What about the bridge?"

"It, uh, collapsed."

Julie stared at him, waiting for the punch line, but Russ didn't smile. "What do you mean, 'collapsed'?"

"The whole thing's gone, Jules. There's no way on or off the island."

Julie stared in disbelief. "For how long?"

Russ shook his head. "With the storm, no one's really sure. It'll probably be at least a week before even boats can cross."

Dr. Santorina's pinched face popped into Julie's mind—his bushy eyebrows drawn together, his lips pulled down in a frown.

"Julie?"

Julie pulled herself from her thoughts. "Um, I didn't know. My boss is going to kill me."

"Sorry. But hey, at least maybe we'll get a chance to catch up. Actually, that's why I stopped by. A few people from our class are meeting up at Mel's in about an hour. No one had your number, so I offered to drop by and tell you."

"In this?" Julie gestured to the dark clouds above.

"Well, it's supposed to not rain again for three hours or so. We figured we could make some use of the break."

Julie forced a smile to her lips. Russ had been a good friend. She'd felt bad about losing touch, but when she left, she'd needed a clean start. She'd needed to leave everything from Millners Kill in her rearview mirror. Yet now, now that she was back, the idea of reconnecting was nice—kind of like being home was.

"Yeah. That would be great."

"Okay, well, I need to get going. See you in an hour or so?"

Julie nodded, her mind returning to the fact that she was now stranded in Millners Kill. "Yeah, I'll be there."

Russ gave her another smile and headed down the steps. "Great. It'll be fun."

"Yeah," Julie said faintly. She closed the door slowly, feeling numb.

The bridge was out. It could be as long as a week before she got off the island. Dr. Santorina was going to kill her. No, not kill. But he would make sure the rest of the year was miserable.

She quickly made her way into the kitchen and grabbed her cell phone. Before she lost her nerve, she dialed Dr. Santorina's number. He picked up quickly. "Yes?"

"Dr. Santorina, this is Julie Granger."

"Ah, Dr. Granger. I hope you're calling to say you have returned."

Julie cringed. "Uh, no. In fact, I'm calling to let you know I'll be away longer than expected. The bridge is out, and there's no way to get back."

There was a long pause on the other end of the phone, followed by a deep sigh. "Dr. Granger, your lack of dedication to your studies is disheartening. I had thought you had what it took to be a brilliant surgeon. I find myself re-evaluating that belief."

"Sir, I am dedicated. This situation—"

"—was your choice. And there are consequences for choices. You will have to face yours when you return. Good day, Dr. Granger." He disconnected.

Julie held the phone to her ear for another few seconds before finally laying it slowly down on the counter. *I just ruined my career.*

She sank into a chair at the table, her head in her hands. *I never should have come home.*

DAY 3

"*This is Billy the Kid coming to you live from the rowboat I was forced into after my home flooded. Just kidding, but not by much. It really came down last night though, didn't it? The sewers on my street were overflowing when I headed here this morning. Not looking forward to the ride home, either. A lot of people have already lost power, and roads are becoming inaccessible. And today and tomorrow are supposed to be the roughest days.*

But those poor folks in Millners Kill are really feeling it. The bridge connecting them to the rest of us completely washed out yesterday. They are well and truly stranded for the next few days. Keep them in your mind when you're thinking about how tough you have it. And stay tuned to KLNQ throughout the day for all your weather updates."

CHAPTER THIRTY

EARLY THE NEXT MORNING, Declan drove past the bridge. Or what used to be the bridge. His gut tightened as he imagined how bad things would have been if they hadn't gotten the bridge closed.

The rain had come down ferociously last night. It had let up early this morning, but was supposed to start back up in earnest again later this afternoon. The lake was already swollen and encroaching on the sandbags. Declan knew it would flow over by tomorrow, flooding Main Street. Already, there were reports of high water on roadways. A few people had already lost power and Declan was pretty sure it was only a matter of time for the rest of them. It was going to be a rough couple of days.

He blew out a breath. They'd handle it. They'd have to. And everything was as ready as it could be.

The news of the bridge collapse had spread through town quickly, of course, but Declan was pleased to note that the town had remained relatively calm—so far. There'd been a few panic attacks that had brought people to the medical center last night, and then this morning a few fights had broken out. A few acts of vandalism had been reported as well although Declan was pretty sure that was just teenagers. If it stayed along those lines, they'd be okay.

Keith had been unusually smart and put extra deputies on duty. He'd even arranged to have the one bar in town close early. The last thing they needed was a bunch of drunk idiots banding together.

Still, Declan could feel something in the air. The town felt like a pot about to boil. It just needed a little more heat.

He rubbed his eyes and then took a sip of coffee. *I'm just getting worked up because Steve's back—and because I need to sleep more.*

He turned up the volume of his radio as a call came through. But it was just a downed tree. He turned it down again. He'd been listening to it since last night.

Right now, he wanted nothing more than to go crash on his sister's couch, maybe watch a movie with his nephews. Preferably something with lots of explosions and very little thought required. Picturing the boys' faces, he thought he should stop for some donuts. *Right,* his brain mocked him, *donuts for the boys. Not you.*

His police scanner continued to call out reports, but nothing he needed to worry about. *Maybe I'm just being jumpy for no good reason.*

Then Dee's strained voice came across the radio. "Chief, we've got a report of a 10-54 down at Millners Factory."

Declan took his foot off the gas and pulled to the side of the road. He turned up the volume on the radio.

Keith's voice came across the radio. "Say again?"

"There's a report of a 10-54 at Millners Factory."

"On my way."

A 10-54: possible dead body. *Shit.* Declan threw the car into a U-turn.

It took him only ten minutes to reach the factory, but the chief and at least two deputies had beaten him there. He pulled in behind their cars.

A beefy deputy Declan didn't recognize stood with his arms crossed just beyond the cruisers. His nametag read "Califano." He was about five ten with a tan complexion and a nose that had been broken a few times. He scowled when Declan approached.

"You need to get in your car and head back out. This area is closed. Police business."

Declan held up his badge. "State police—the chief's expecting me."

Deputy Califano obviously wasn't sure what to do. He hesitated before waving Declan through.

"Where are they?" Declan asked him.

"Around back. On the edge of the water."

Declan nodded and headed around the side of the factory. It had been a clothing manufacturing plant decades ago, but Declan couldn't remember it ever actually running—which meant it had gone out of business at least thirty, maybe forty years ago. It was three stories high, and most of the windows had been broken—kids had taken care of that. Declan remembered breaking a few himself when he was in high school. In fact, the factory was a regular hangout for the teenage crowds, especially in summer. On the side by the lake, bonfires were pretty commonplace.

Declan stopped as he rounded the back of the building. The beach was about a hundred yards deep, give or take. Keith was squatting low over something wrapped in plastic about halfway between the water and the building. Russ stood another ten feet away from the chief, looking a little green around the gills.

Declan strode forward. "Keith, what have you got?"

Keith looked up. "You're like a friggin' dirty penny. You keep showing up where you're not needed."

"Gee, Keith, you keep talking like that and I'll start thinking you don't like me." Declan glanced at the plastic. He could make out long hair peeking around the edges. "What have you got?"

With a hard look at Russ, Keith turned his attention back to Declan. "It's the Ingram girl."

Oh shit. He remembered Russ telling him about her going missing. *I guess she didn't run away.*

Declan stepped closer and looked down. Elise Ingram's body was wrapped in plastic, but the plastic had been pulled back from her face. He knew the Ingrams only in passing, but he recognized her. Her skin was pale and there was an angry red slash mark around her throat. Through the plastic he could see more blood. She looked no older than sixteen.

"She's eighteen, right?" he asked.

"Just a few months ago. She's a cashier down at Tops."

Declan knelt down. The girl had been wrapped in a plastic drop cloth. Not that that was going to help them find who did this. Everybody and their uncle had purchased drop cloths lately, in preparation for the storm.

"Who found her?" Declan asked.

Keith nodded back toward the factory where an older man stood waiting with his golden lab. "Frank Gerard. He and Shelby were out for a walk when Shelby started going crazy. Dragged Frank over here."

Declan looked around. "They always walk here?"

"Every morning and afternoon. They got here later today because of the weather."

"They walk last night?"

"Afternoon. Around four."

"Which means she was dropped here after the time of their last walk." He looked around and saw the dog's prints, the chief's, his own. He shook his head. Not that it mattered. With all the rain, any other prints would have been washed away already.

Declan looked down at the girl. Damn shame. "Anybody have it out for her?"

Keith fixed him with a look. "I think we both know who did this."

Declan paused for a moment before he realized what Keith meant. "You can't be serious. He just got back in town, for God's sake."

"And we haven't had a murder since the last time he was in town. That's not a coincidence."

"Keith, Steve just saved three people yesterday. And now you think he killed someone?"

"There are killers who would kill their victims and then arrive in the ambulance to pick them up. Who knows how their crazy minds work?"

"So now he's a serial killer?" Declan shook his head. "You have no proof he even knew the girl, never mind that he killed her."

"True. But take a look at her. She remind you of anybody?"

Declan looked at Elise. Simone Granger had had brown hair, this girl had blonde. Elise's eyes were blue while Simone's had been brown. "They're both young women, but that's it. They don't actually look alike."

Keith stepped toward Declan. His paunch bumped against Declan's jacket. "Yeah, but it's a start. And I'll get proof. And when I do, that boy is as good as dead."

Declan have him a hard look. "You mean arrested, don't you, Keith?"

Keith smirked. "Yeah, sure, Declan. That's what I mean."

CHAPTER THIRTY-ONE

EDGAR FUNDLEY of the Fundley Funeral Home wrung his hands in the doorway of the embalming room. "Are you sure this is all right?"

Declan had spent only about an hour at the scene—he was pretty sure Elise hadn't been killed there. Then he and Russ had transported Elise's body to the funeral home. Normally they'd take a body to the mainland and the ME's office, but with the bridge out, the funeral home was the best they could do.

Declan grabbed underneath Elise's shoulders with his gloved hands while Russ grabbed her legs. "It's fine, Mr. Fundley. Russ?"

Russ nodded. They picked Elise up, removed her from the body bag, and placed her on the table.

Edgar let out a strangled cry.

Declan struggled not to roll his eyes. Edgar was awfully squeamish for a funeral director. "I'm guessing you don't do the embalming?"

Edgar pulled a handkerchief out of his pocket and brought it to his mouth. "No. My sister Adelaide is in charge of that. She's out of town. I handle the personal interactions with the families."

If only she were here, Declan thought. Out loud he said, "Mr. Fundley, I think we have it handled here. We're going to store the body in the refrigerator when we're done."

"Yes, yes. All right. I'll be upstairs if you need me." He all but fled down the hall.

He seems to be in the wrong line of work, Declan thought. Then he glanced over at Russ, whose green complexion had gotten only a little better. *And he may not be the only one.*

Russ took a few pictures of Elise. They had taken pictures of Elise at the scene, but Declan wanted to make sure they didn't miss anything. Declan took the opportunity to inspect the plastic that covered Elise's body. There didn't seem to be anything of interest about the plastic, but once they had it off her, he'd bag it for further analysis by the crime lab.

As Declan stared at Elise, he felt both sadness at her passing and frustration that they were cut off from the resources they'd need to do a full autopsy. He had enough training to do a basic examination, but he knew he'd have to send Elise's body to the actual ME to get an official report. And that would not be happening any time soon.

"Okay. Let's pull back the plastic," he said.

Russ nodded and began unrolling the plastic at Elise's feet. They pulled it back slowly until Elise was completely uncovered.

Declan was surprised to see that all her clothes were still on. The blood from the neck wound had spilled onto her top. Other knife wounds had gone right through the clothing, so clearly she had been wearing them at the time of the murder. But there was very little blood from them. *She was already dead when he made most of these.*

Declan looked up as Russ made a gagging sound. "Russ, why don't you go get some air?"

Russ nodded and walked quickly down the hall, just as Edgar had.

Declan shook his head and looked back at the body. *Just you and me now, Elise. What can you tell me?*

She was still in rigor, but it was starting to relax. She's been dead at least twenty-four hours, probably closer to thirty-six. He thought it was probably the latter, as a greenish hue had begun to develop along the girl's chest cavity—the beginning signs of putrefaction. He'd do an internal temp to close that window more, but first he wanted to see if he could see anything that might give them a clue as to who had done this.

He paused. Frank and Shelby always walked out on that beach, twice a day. If his time window was correct, Elise was probably killed right after work and then the killer held onto her body for over twenty-four hours. Why?

Declan examined Elise's hands. They, too, had been wrapped in the plastic, preserving them. He didn't want to disturb them—he'd leave that for the medical examiner—but he wanted to at least do a cursory check. There were no abrasions, no cuts. So, she hadn't tried to defend herself. Had she been drugged or incapacitated? He didn't think so. She had blood on her hands—he imagined Elise grabbing at her throat after it was sliced.

It appeared that the killer had just walked right up to her and sliced. No hesitation. Which meant he was either really, really angry, or really, really practiced. Or both. And he was someone who she knew, or at least recognized. Someone who didn't send up any red flags. Someone who waited to dump the body.

He did a quick check of her forearms and shins. There didn't seem to be any defensive wounds there either. She definitely hadn't put up a fight. And he saw no obvious evidence of sexual assault although further tests would be needed to confirm that. In fact, he got the impression that none of Elise's clothes had even been removed.

"You knew him, didn't you, Elise?" he murmured.

Russ appeared back at the door. "Uh, Declan?"

"Yeah?"

"Chief wants me back at the station."

"I'm good here. Go on."

Russ nodded and left. His relief was obvious.

Declan stepped back, thinking. With the bridge out, getting an autopsy done any time soon was just not going to happen. But Declan knew that Keith would zero in on Steve right away. Keith would get the town worked up—and Declan didn't like to think about what that could mean.

Damn. Declan walked back to his forensics bag and pulled out the plastic evidence bags. *Time to get to work.*

CHAPTER THIRTY-TWO

IT WAS MID-MORNING, and Steve was heading home from his early shift at the diner. The rain was once again coming down in torrents. *I should call Declan and see how that woman and her daughter are doing,* he thought as he turned onto his grandmother's street. He had meant to call last night, but after he'd taken a hot shower and had a hot meal, he'd all but passed out.

Then this morning he'd gone straight back to work at Mel's. They'd had a bit of a crowd, and even from back in the kitchen, Steve could hear everybody talking about the bridge collapse. He'd also heard his name mentioned more than once, in uncertain tones. Apparently the town monster wasn't supposed to sideline as a hero. By around ten, though, the place was dead, so Mel had sent him home.

When Steve reached his grandmother's, he shook out his poncho and left it hanging on the light by the front door. He looked down at himself and shook his head. Despite the poncho, he was soaked again. He was beginning to think there was nothing that was going to keep the rain out. It found every opening and slipped in.

He opened the door, and Bess was waiting for him with a towel.

He smiled. "Thanks."

"How bad is it getting?"

Steve pictured the streets he'd walked through. "Pretty bad. Most of the sewers are filled. The water's got nowhere to go. We should probably stay in until the worst passes."

She nodded. "I made some soup."

"I'd love a bowl as soon as I shower."

"Well, hop to."

He saluted her. "Yes, ma'am."

She swatted him playfully.

He laughed as he headed up the stairs. Fifteen minutes later he was showered, changed, and re-bandaging the cut on his arm.

"Steve, you out?" his grandmother called from downstairs.

"Yeah, Gran." He put the last piece of tape on the fresh gauze covering his cut from yesterday. He was finally feeling warm. He headed out of the bathroom and for the stairs.

"Bring down your laundry," Bess called.

Steve dutifully went back in and collected his clothes. This time when he headed down the stairs, his grandmother was waiting in the kitchen doorway, a basket of laundry in her hands. Steve placed everything in the basket, then reached out to take it from her.

She stepped out of his reach. "Nope, I got this. You should rest that arm. I'm so proud of you, honey."

"I know, Grandma." She had been saying she was proud of him ever since she'd found out about the bridge rescue. "But it was nothing, really."

"You listen to me, Steven Michael Kane: you are a hero. You saved that woman and her baby. People have said enough bad things about you that aren't true. So you take credit for the heroic thing you did that *is* true."

He reached for the basket again.

She moved it out of his way again. "I said I've got this. Besides, I can't have the town hero doing laundry."

Steve groaned, but his grandma just smiled at him. In fact, she'd been smiling nonstop since Jack had called yesterday and told her what had happened. And as much as Steve hated being the center of attention, he had to admit that seeing her smile made it worthwhile.

"Yes, ma'am." He looked out the window. "Looks like the rain stopped."

Bess headed for the basement stairs. "No. This is the small break they said we're getting." She glanced back at him over her shoulder. "I made some muffins. They're on the kitchen table."

"Blueberry?"

"Yes."

Steve spied the covered plate on the countertop. *Ah, there is goodness in this world.*

But just as he reached for the plate, the doorbell rang. *So close.* He could smell the blueberry muffins, and his stomach growled in response.

His grandmother yelled from downstairs. "I'll get it."

Steve turned and headed back for the door. "No, it's good. I got it."

Through the window in the door, he saw the tan and brown uniform of the Millners Kill police department. *Shit.*

He heard his grandmother coming back up the stairs from the basement. He struggled to think of something to say that would make her walk back into the kitchen, but his mind was a blank. So he turned to the door and opened it.

"Um, hey Steve," Russ said.

Steve nodded. "Russ."

Russ looked at his feet. "Um, look, the chief wants you down at the station."

Bess came to stand next to Steve in the doorway. "Russ Nash, how are you? Did you come by to say hi to Steve? Did you hear what he did yesterday?"

Russ smiled. "Hi, Mrs. Davidson. Yes, ma'am, I did. He's a real hero."

Bess beamed and wrapped her arm around Steve's forearm. "That's what I keep telling him."

Steve turned to his grandmother, keeping his voice light. "I'm just going to go for a little ride with Russ. Okay?"

His grandmother looked at Steve, then at Russ. She narrowed her eyes. "Is that right?"

Steve stared at Russ, begging him silently not to worry his grandmother.

Russ nodded. "Yeah. I thought we could go for a ride. Um, and there's some, uh, paperwork stuff we need him to fill out. I didn't get a chance to after the bridge."

Bess nodded with a smile. "Oh, all right. Don't stay out too long." She gave Steve a hug. "Give me a call if you won't be home for dinner."

"Will do," Steve said, returning the hug.

He watched Bess return to her chair before stepping out onto the porch and closing the door behind him. At the top of the stairs, he turned to Russ. "This isn't about the bridge, is it?"

Russ pulled out his handcuffs and shook his head. "Chief wants to ask you some questions."

Steve was honestly at a loss. "About what?"

"There's been a murder."

Steve went cold. He could feel his defenses fall over him like armor. His voice had an edge to it. "And I'm the prime suspect."

Russ hesitated. "Chief wanted me to cuff your arms behind you."

Steve sighed. *Of course.*

Before he could turn around, Russ placed the cuffs on Steve's wrists. "But I think in front will be all right." He looked Steve in the eyes. "I'm sorry about this."

Steve sighed, but said nothing as he followed Russ to the squad car. *You and me both.*

CHAPTER THIRTY-THREE

RUSS DROVE into the parking lot at the back of the police station and pulled right up to the curb. There were only a handful of cars there, most likely belonging to the other officers. Large puddles of water lay stagnant around them.

Steve looked around. There was no one there. "Why are we going in through the back?"

"Fewer people will see you going in," Russ said as he got out of the car and opened the back door for Steve.

Surprised, Steve nodded his thanks.

Russ herded Steve inside the station and down a back hallway. He stopped at an open door on the right and guided Steve through.

A giant mirror hung on one wall in front of a metal table and three chairs. The table was bolted to the floor—Steve knew this from experience. He'd been here before. This was Millners Kill's one and only interrogation room.

Russ gestured to the chairs. "Take a seat."

Steve did, then placed his hands on the table.

Russ took the chain that was anchored to the table and

connected it to Steve's handcuffs, then stepped back. "You need anything?"

Steve shook his head. "No."

"Okay, well the chief should be in soon." Russ closed the door behind him.

Soon. Right. Steve knew the chief wasn't going to be rushing in here. A giant clock across from him told him it was 11:38. He figured the chief would keep him waiting for about two hours.

He was wrong. It was over three. Keith strolled in at 2:42.

Deputy Califano followed him in, pushing a TV and VCR on a rolling cart. He situated them in the corner and plugged in the cords. "You need me to stay, Chief?"

Keith waved him away. "No. I'm good."

With a glare at Steve, the deputy left.

Steve ignored him and looked at the cart, feeling strangely comforted to see a piece of technology he recognized. But what on earth did they have on tape that related to him?

Keith took a seat across from Steve and linked his fingers together on the table. "So, I guess you know why you're here."

"Russ told me there was a murder."

"Oh, he *told* you? Or did you already know?"

Steve stared at him in silence. Apparently Keith's interrogation skills hadn't improved any in the past ten years. He'd always sounded like the bad cop in a cheesy '80s movie.

Keith leaned back in his chair. "So why don't you tell me where you were at the time of the murder?"

"I don't know the time of the murder."

Keith sneered. "Right. You killed that girl."

Steve stared back at him. "No. I did not."

A knock came at the door. Steve turned as his brother walked in.

"Chief. Steve."

Keith stood up. "What are you doing here, Jack?"

"Well, I heard you had my brother in custody. I thought he could use a lawyer."

Keith snorted. "He's not in custody. We're just chatting."

Jack looked pointedly at the cuffs around Steve's wrists. "Oh really?"

"Just a precaution."

Jack's voice turned a shade harder, as if he was trying to keep from yelling. "Keith, this is an illegal arrest. Anything said up until this point is inadmissible. Did you even read him his Miranda rights?"

Keith looked away. "I'm sure somebody did."

Jack glanced over at Steve, who shook his head.

"Right." Jack pulled a chair over next to Steve and sat. "How about we start with you taking the cuffs off of my client?"

"I don't have the key," Keith mumbled.

Jack stared daggers at Keith. "We'll wait."

Keith looked between the two of them for a moment, then stormed out of the room.

Jack turned to Steve and smiled. "Well, that was fun. So do you know why you're here?"

"Russ said there was a murder. But no one's given me any details."

The smile dropped from Jack's face. "It was Elise Ingram."

Steve drew in a sharp breath. He pictured Elise from the supermarket briefly, but the image he had of her as a kid stayed longer. "Oh, man. What happened?"

"She was found down on the beach by the old factory. I don't know the cause of death."

Steve felt a sinking in his gut. "She rang up my groceries when I went shopping for Grandma the day before yesterday, the day I got back."

"That's right." Jack looked a little shaken. "But it'll be all right. Did you talk to her at all?"

Steve shook his head. "Not really. Just a little while she rang everything up."

"And then what?"

"Then I left and ran into you. Haven't seen her since. Or even thought of her."

Jack nodded. "Keith's reaching. He's hoping you'll let something slip."

"There's nothing to slip. I didn't do this."

Jack clapped him on the shoulder. "I know."

Russ walked in with the handcuff keys. He wouldn't look Steve in the eye as he removed the cuffs. "I wanted to tell you I'm sorry for cuffing you, Mr. Kane. I misunderstood the chief's request."

Once the cuffs were off, Steve rubbed his wrists. "It's okay, Russ."

Russ met his eyes with a nod. "Um, and I need to read you your Miranda rights."

Before either Jack or Steve could say anything, Russ rattled them off. "Do you understand these rights as they have been read to you?"

"Yeah. I understand them," Steve said.

Keith walked in, followed by Deputy Califano. The deputy went and stood in the corner next to the TV, and Keith retook his seat. "That will be all, Deputy Nash."

With a glance at Steve, Russ left, his shoulders taut.

"Now that that's sorted out," Keith said, "I have a few questions for your client."

Jack glanced over at Steve. "It's up to you."

Steve wanted to tell the chief to go screw himself, but he knew he'd only be delaying the inevitable. He shrugged. "Sure, whatever."

Keith took his seat. "Do you know Elise Ingram?"

"Yes."

Keith smiled, but it wasn't kind. "So you admit you knew the victim."

Jack interrupted. "Keith, you know damn well the Ingrams lived down the street from us. Of course he knows who Elise Ingram is. There are five thousand people in Millners Kill. Everybody knows who everybody is."

Keith glared at Jack, his jaw tight. "Fine. Have you spoken with Elise Ingram since you were released?"

Steve glanced at Jack, who nodded. "Two days ago at Tops. She was the cashier. She rang up my groceries."

Keith pulled a picture from the folder in front of him and slapped it down on the table. "How about when she looked like this? Do you remember seeing her then?"

Steve blanched. In the photo, Elise was pale, making the angry red mark around her neck even more obvious. Blood had pooled around the cut, and some had splashed on her face. Blue eyes stared straight ahead, seeing nothing.

Steve tightened his jaw. *Bastard.* "I never saw her like that."

Keith leaned forward. "But you admit you had a relationship with the victim?"

"No. I didn't have a relationship with her. I spoke with her for five minutes, if that."

Keith gestured to the deputy. The deputy turned on the TV and hit play on the VCR. It was a surveillance tape from Tops. Elise was at the register in the middle. Steve saw himself in line behind a couple.

"Why'd you get in Elise's line?" Keith asked. "There were two other lines open."

Steve looked dumbfounded. Why? He'd been staring at the ground, trying not to make eye contact with anybody. He'd gotten in the shortest line. He didn't even know the cashier was a girl until he got to the front.

He shrugged. "I don't know, I just did."

Keith nodded like he'd just scored some sort of point.

Steve ignored him and watched the tape. He saw himself reach the front of the line. Elise leaned over the conveyor belt, her smile big. Steve saw himself look anywhere but at her.

"Looks like you're casing the place," Keith said.

Jack interrupted. "Keith, is Steve here for burglary or murder?"

Keith narrowed his eyes. "He's here for whatever I say he's here for." He pointed at the TV. "It looks to me like your brother here was flirting, and it didn't work."

Jack chuckled. "Then you need to have your eyes checked. Elise flirted with him. Not the other way round."

"Well, maybe he didn't like her coming on to him. Maybe he thought he was better than her. And then he *proved* to her he was better than her."

"Maybe you've been watching too many movies of the week," Jack replied, his voice cool. "If you're going to charge my client, then charge him. If you're not, this interview is over."

"I can hold him for twenty-four hours."

Jack nodded. "Yes. You can. But you and I both know you don't have the probable cause to detain him longer than that. You're fishing."

"So maybe I'll hold him for twenty-four hours, just for the hell of it."

Jack held up his phone. "That's an abuse of power, Chief. And I've been recording this whole little interview."

"You can't—" Keith spluttered. "That's not admissible."

"Actually, the courts have held that as long as one person in the conversation knows it's being recorded—and that would be me—then there is no expectation of privacy. Besides, this is an interrogation room. This conversation should be being recorded, anyway. So yes, it will be admissible. And you need to think very carefully as you decide whether you want to risk your career over a lousy, barely circumstantial case."

"You think your brother can beat me in the court of public opinion?" Keith sneered.

"No," Jack said emphatically. "But you wouldn't be going up against *him*. You'd be going up against me. Do you really think you can beat *me* in the court of public opinion?"

Keith stared back at Jack, and Steve could swear steam was about to shoot out of the man's ears. "You'd risk your career for him?"

"He said he didn't do it. I believe him," Jack said.

Steve was floored. His brother was literally risking everything to stand by him.

Jack's phone beeped, indicating he had a text. He glanced down at it and then looked up with a smile. "Besides, Steve has an alibi."

Steve glanced over at Jack in surprise.

"No he doesn't," Keith countered.

"Time of death was Monday between two and three. Steve was down filling sandbags. He's got a beach full of witnesses."

Keith sat back, his arms crossed over his chest. "Well, I'm going to have to verify that."

"Feel free. But Carlos Ramirez just swore out a statement that he was with Steve from one thirty to four thirty."

Surprise flooded Steve. *How the hell—*

A knock on the door grabbed everyone's attention. Russ stuck his head in. "Um, Chief, there's a phone call you need to take."

Keith waved him away. "It can wait."

"Uh, sir, actually, it can't."

Keith growled and pushed away from the table. "Fine." He stormed out without saying anything to Jack or Steve.

Steve opened his mouth to ask Jack a question, but Jack shook his head, flicking his eyes toward the deputy in the corner.

Instead he typed into his phone and then showed the screen to Steve.

That's Declan on the phone telling Keith the time of death. He found Carlos and got him to sign a statement.

Steve looked at Jack, amazed. Down the hall, he could make out Keith's voice, raised in anger, although he couldn't make out any of the words. *Now what?*

A few minutes later, Russ walked back in. "You're free to go. But the chief wanted me to warn you not to leave town."

Steve stood up, raising an eyebrow. "He thinks I'm going to swim to the mainland?"

Russ shrugged, but Steve could see the smile lurking around the corners of his mouth. "Just telling you what he said."

Russ stepped aside to let the two men pass. As they did, Steve opened his mouth to ask Jack a question, but Jack shook his head. "Not until we're outside."

Steve followed Jack out into the hall and through the back entrance. The rain had started again. They walked quickly to Jack's Acura. Steve hopped in the passenger seat and Jack got in the driver's side.

Steve looked over at his brother. "Thanks for that."

Jack grasped his brother's arm. "I'm not letting some two-bit cop push my brother around." He grinned. "That's *my* job. He doesn't have anything. So don't worry, okay?"

Easier said than done, Steve thought, but he nodded anyway, swallowing down the emotion trying to rise in him. He was humbled by his brother's and Declan's faith in him. He promised himself he wouldn't let them down.

CHAPTER THIRTY-FOUR

AS STEVE and Jack pulled away, the chief and Deputy Califano stood outside the doors of the station, their arms crossed over their chests, glaring at them. Steve knew the chief had no intention of looking at anyone other than him for the murder of Elise Ingram. Steve pictured Elise's pale face. Someone had killed her —on the very day he'd come back to town. There was zero chance that was a coincidence.

He swallowed as Jack turned on the radio.

The announcer's voice came over the speakers. "—storm will be increasing in intensity in the next few hours. Residents are advised to stay indoors and away from windows. This storm is going to be a doozy."

Steve and Jack listened to the rest of the weather report, but then the radio switched over to local news. "A body was found in Mill—"

Jack quickly switched it off. "Well, I think that's enough of that."

An uncomfortable silence descended on the car.

It wasn't until they pulled off Main Street that Jack spoke. "I heard Julie Granger was back in town."

"Yeah, I know."

Steve closed his eyes, not wanting to fill the silence with this particular topic. He wasn't surprised that Jack had heard; in Millners Kill, nothing stayed secret for long. *Except Simone's real killer*, a voice whispered in his mind. *And now maybe Elise's as well.*

"Have you talked to her?" Jack asked.

It took Steve a minute to realize who Jack was talking about. Julie. "Um, yeah. My first night back. But only for a few minutes."

Jack glanced over at him, eyebrows raised. "Really?"

Steve shrugged, not wanting to discuss Julie with his brother. Julie was private. She was his friend. Or at least she used to be. And seeing as how last night's conversation was probably the last one he was ever going to have with her, he wasn't about to talk about it to Jack, or to anyone else. Because some wounds cut just a little too deep.

Steve looked up and saw with relief that they had arrived at their grandmother's house. Jack pulled into the drive and put the car in park but left it running.

"I'm going to head back to town and see what I can find out about the Ingram case. Do me a favor? Stay close to home?" Jack said.

Steve sighed as he got out of the car. Free from prison, but still not really free. "Yeah. No problem."

He looked around as Jack drove off. The rain was still coming down, and the wind had picked up. The trees that towered over the street blew from side to side as if they were being shaken by some angry, invisible giant.

When Steve finally turned to the house, he realized he had

an audience sitting on the front porch, holding a soccer ball. "Micah? What are you doing here?"

Micah wiped at his eyes. "Nothing."

Steve didn't have the energy for this right now, and even if he did, befriending Micah was not going to bring the kid anything good. But he still found himself taking a seat next to him on the stoop. "Having a bad day?"

Micah nodded.

Steve sighed. "Me too. You want to tell me why you're having a bad day?"

"Because my brother's a poopyhead."

Steve pictured Micah's brother. "Yeah. I can see him being a poopyhead."

Micah giggled. "You said poopy."

"So I did."

"Why are *you* having a bad day?"

Steve pictured the chief. "Because someone's being a poopy-head to me too."

The two of them sat for a few minutes in silence just watching the trees blow. And somehow, hanging out with a six-year-old who had no business being friends with him provided Steve with some peace.

Steve glanced at Micah out of the corner of his eye. Micah had his chin resting on his hands, his soccer ball between his knees—the picture of glum. "You want to kick the ball around?" Steve asked.

"It's raining."

Steve shrugged. "So we'll get a little wet."

Micah started to smile, but then it dimmed. "My brother said I'm not any good."

"Well maybe you just need some practice. You know, I used to play in high school. Come on. I could use a little exercise."

Micah gave him a little smile, then scrambled down the stairs. "Okay."

Steve followed him down and lined up about ten feet away from him. The boy dropped the ball at his feet, but then had to chase it as it rolled down the lawn. Biting his lip, Micah kicked it. It rolled only six feet, and in the opposite direction of Steve.

Steve tried not to smile. "That was good. Now try kicking with your laces."

CHAPTER THIRTY-FIVE

JULIE SAT IN HER CAR, three houses down on the opposite side of the road from Steve's house. This morning she had tried to focus on her studies, but had been unable to concentrate. The fear that she had ruined her future kept intruding.

So she'd gone to the coffee shop, and there she'd run into another old classmate, Mary, who was out with her four-year-old daughter. They got to talking and time just flew by. When Mary had brought up Steve, Julie had deflected the questions and quickly changed the topic. But the questions had been enough to push Steve back to the forefront of her brain. Truth be told, he'd been a constant presence in her mind ever since her dad had mentioned he was in town.

When she finally said goodbye to Mary, she'd had every intention of going straight home. But then she'd seen Jack's car pull out of the station and she'd found herself following.

Now she slumped down in her seat as Jack pulled his car out of the drive and drove past her. She looked at the ridiculous situation she was in: her head resting below the steering wheel, her legs curled under the dash. *What the hell am I doing?*

Her inner rational person argued for sanity. *You're a second-year resident. You should be getting your parents' house together and getting back to your life. Not hunched down in your seat like some amateur PI.*

She shook her head at her own behavior. Was this really what she'd come to? Hospitals had fought over getting her into their residency programs. She was building a reputation as a highly skilled surgeon. She had her eyes set on a neurosurgery fellowship at Johns Hopkins. And yet here she was, acting like Veronica Mars.

Before she'd slipped below the dashboard, Julie had seen the passenger door of Jack's car open, and she had watched the tall, muscular man who had gotten out. She still couldn't believe that this tall—and let's face it, hot—man was Steve. Whenever she'd thought about seeing him again, part of her had expected him to be the same Steve—short and skinny. But this wasn't the boy she knew. This was a man. A man she didn't know. And yet...

He turned and walked to the porch, and Julie sat up in her seat. Time to go. This had been a stupid idea. She had already placed her hand on the key when she noticed Steve stop and sit on his porch, next to a little boy. She hadn't noticed the boy before.

A few minutes later, Steve was kicking a soccer ball with the kid. And the kid was smiling.

Julie watched for a while, her confusion growing. Who the hell *was* he? Was he Steve Kane, the skinny boy who had killed her sister in cold blood? Or was he this grown man who made a little boy smile by playing soccer with him? Or was he both?

Was it possible for someone to have two sides to them: one light and one dark?

She turned the key in the ignition. Her radio, tuned to a local station, sprang to life. "The body found on the beach at Hamlet Cove has been identified as eighteen-year-old Elise Ingram."

Julie's gaze flew to Steve and her heart began to race. Another teenage girl had been murdered—just after Steve came back to town.

"The police have not arrested anyone for the murder, but an unnamed source at the Millners Kill Police Department has said that Steve Kane is a person of interest. Kane was recently released on parole after serving a ten-year sentence for the murder of Simone Granger."

Julie flicked the radio off. Her hands began to shake. She looked back at Steve's house. Bess had now appeared on the porch with a tray of muffins and drinks. Steve and the boy took a seat on the porch steps with their snack, and Bess walked back inside. It looked like the little boy was chattering away, but Steve just nodded, only occasionally speaking. Nothing about his body language suggested aggression or violence.

Julie felt sick. Was she watching her sister's murderer? *And the murderer of Elise Ingram?*

Was everyone right? Was he the devil they'd made him out to be? Had she just been stupid all these years? And now was this murderer sitting calmly on his grandmother's porch, planning his next kill?

Julie pulled away from the curb slowly, knowing her mind wasn't focused on driving. But she needed to get away.

Clenching the steering wheel, she drove past Steve, not looking over. But she couldn't get away from any of it, could she? With the bridge down, none of them could.

CHAPTER THIRTY-SIX

HE LOCKED his car and stepped out onto the sidewalk. He kept his eyes down, not wanting to make eye contact. *Idiot chief. He almost ruined the game before it could begin.*

He had planned on Elise not being found for a few days. Let the town's concern for the girl grow before he tipped the police to her location. He should have remembered old man Frank and his dog took their walks along the beach.

If Steve had been locked up, all his fun would be over. Thank God for big brother Jack and his fancy lawyering. Although, with the chief, fancy was probably too strong a word.

But no matter, now the game was on. And the pieces were all coming into play. In fact, now that Julie Granger was back in town, the game could *really* get underway.

He'd never imagined she'd return at the same time as Steve. It was like God was blessing him with this opportunity. Julie would be the final move in this game. But first, a few pawns must be sacrificed.

He rubbed his hands together, struggling to hold back his joy. *But who to sacrifice first?*

The pictures of all the people Steve cared about flowed through his mind. *So many lovely options.*

But none of them would do. They'd cause grief and despair. They'd make the town tip a little more toward panic. He needed a victim that would push people's buttons—and make everyone in town turn against Steve.

And with the bridge out, the likelihood of that panic turning homicidal was almost guaranteed. Trapped people always lashed out. It was practically a certainty.

He just had to direct that anger.

He smiled as an image of the perfect person floated into his mind. *And I know just how to do that.* He whistled. *Oh, it's going to be a fun night.*

CHAPTER THIRTY-SEVEN

JULIE PULLED her Kindle onto her lap and opened to the latest mystery she was reading. Five minutes later, she realized she had absolutely no idea what she had just read. She lifted her eyes from the screen and placed the Kindle on the side table next to the couch. *Damn.*

She had been having the same problem with her textbook, which was why she'd decided to take a break. But apparently, in her current mood, reading of any sort wasn't an option.

Her gaze flitted around the living room. Her parents had replaced all the family pictures with neutral landscape scenes—the realtor had strongly encouraged them to stage the house with non-personal items. So all the old familiar pictures, the ones that had been on the walls since Julie was a kid, had disappeared.

Under other circumstances, Julie might have found the seascapes rather nice, peaceful even. But tonight, with the wind howling outside, they just left her feeling alone.

She placed her Kindle on the table and crossed to the large bay window that looked out over the front yard. The blue spruces that lined the yard to the right were blowing in the wind.

Across the street, the Simmons boys, ages eleven, thirteen, and fourteen, were wrestling in their front yard. Julie frowned, not sure if they were playing or serious. As Julie watched, the Simmonses' front door opened and Arianna Simmons yelled for her boys to come in. The three boys kept wrestling, so Arianna yelled again. Finally they detangled themselves and obeyed, all grinning.

Julie shook her head with a smile. Those three boys had always been thick as thieves. Julie had babysat for them when she was younger and she could still picture their cute little baby faces. But when the boys disappeared into the house, the happy memories disappeared with them, and Julie was left with only the empty street which offered no company.

Julie turned from the window. She'd been home for hours and she was beginning to feel trapped. She contemplated calling one of her high school friends. It had actually been fun catching up with them the other night at Mel's.

But with the new murder, she didn't want to see the pity in their eyes or hear it in their voices. So she'd tried calling Leslie, but had gotten voicemail. Now she stared at the blank TV screen. She wished it had something to distract her, but when she'd checked it earlier, it seemed like every channel was now doing non-stop news coverage of two main stories: the storm and Elise's murder.

And more time seemed to be focused on the latter. News reporters were rehashing everything they knew about the Elise Ingram murder—which wasn't much. So they would then spend even more time re-telling the story of Simone's murder and the trial of Steve Kane. One station looked like they had employed a B-movie theater's graphics department to create the logo for their segment—"Killer in a Small Town"—complete with what looked like blood running down the screen. That was what had finally motivated Julie to turn off the TV in disgust. She didn't want to watch the coverage; she didn't want to think about the murder. But she couldn't seem to think about anything else.

She pictured Steve on the porch with the boy. She'd done some asking around and had learned that the boy's name was Micah Donaldson. He was six years old and lived down the street from Steve, with his brother and mom. According to one neighbor, Micah was a little slow but incredibly sweet—which meant incredibly trusting. If Steve was a monster, the boy would never see him coming.

Just like none of the rest of us saw him coming.

Julie walked into the dining room and took a seat at the table. Her parents had left a lot of furniture—more staging. She drummed her hands on the mahogany surface that they had almost never eaten on.

Steve wouldn't hurt a kid, she assured herself.

But do you really know Steve? another part of her brain whispered.

She pictured that little boy's face—that huge smile of his.

"Enough." She stood. Grabbing her jacket off the back of one of the kitchen bar stools, her bag from the counter, and her keys from the hook by the back door, she let herself out.

The wind blew fiercely as she stepped into the carport, and her hair swirled like a tornado around her face. She fought the wind to her car. Rain lashed out at her. The wind slammed the car door shut behind her as she all but fell into the driver's seat.

She sat for a minute, stunned by the assault from Mother Nature. *No one should be out in this.*

She grabbed one of the ponytail holders she always kept in the console between the seats and used it to pull her hair back.

Okay, I'll just go check. Make sure Micah's okay. And that'll be that, she thought as she pulled out into the street.

But she reached down and patted the Glock 9mm tucked into the holster under her jacket. She'd gotten the gun as soon as she'd turned eighteen. In fact, her dad had been the one who'd driven her to the firing range every weekend for six months until she could hit the bull's-eye almost every time. And when Julie had moved away, she'd kept up the practice, getting to the range once or twice a month.

She generally left the weapon at home even though she had a concealed carry permit—but there was no way she was coming to Millners Kill without it. And after she learned that Steve was out, she'd started wearing it everywhere—both around the house and when she was out. Truth was, she all but slept with it.

But she was fine. She was okay. She was driving around in a storm while armed.

All things that perfectly sane people do, she assured herself.

CHAPTER THIRTY-EIGHT

STEVE SAT in the dark in his grandfather's chair trying to make sense of today. It had started off well enough: he'd gone to work at the diner which had been good.

But then he'd been pulled in and questioned for murder—not good. He'd come home and played soccer with Micah—good again. And he'd come inside to listen to more death threats on the phone—more not good.

And then, just after his grandmother had gone to bed, someone had thrown a brick at the house. It was lucky that the windows were boarded-up, so it bounced off harmlessly. But Steve had gone outside and found the brick. It was wrapped in a note with a single word emblazoned on it: *Murderer*.

Steve had gotten rid of the note, but the whole thing had made him even more jumpy.

He closed his eyes. The crime scene photo Keith had shown him reappeared in his mind. Who could have done that? It couldn't be a coincidence that he returned to town, and another teenager was murdered. No way.

But Steve knew he was looking at the problem differently

than almost everybody else in town—because only he knew for sure that he hadn't killed Simone. And he knew that someone else had gotten away with murder.

Was that person still in town? Had they started back up? But why now?

Because you're back, a voice whispered at the back of his mind.

Steve knew that was probably true. Somehow, by coming back, he'd awoken something that had been sleeping for years.

But was that even possible? Could someone kill that brutally and then just stop?

Even as the question flashed through his mind, Steve knew the answer was a big yes. When he was inside, he'd taken a few college courses on criminology. And contrary to popular opinion, serial killers didn't kill victims one right after the next very often. In fact, it was not unusual for killers to go for long stretches of time between murders.

Some even stopped altogether. Look at the BTK killer. Dennis Rader killed ten people between the 1970s and 1990s. Then he seemed to disappear. In reality, he simply went back to his normal life—a life that included a wife, daughters, and being a leader in his church community.

The only reason he was caught was because he began writing to media outlets in 2004. He had done this before, while killing, but this time it led to his arrest in 2005. But for all intents and purposes, the killing had stopped long before that.

Steve knew the Rader case was unusual. It usually wasn't until serial killers started spiraling out of control that they tended to get caught. Rader, though, was a serial killer who had quit.

The thought brought Steve up short. *Were* they dealing with a serial killer? When he'd been inside, he had spent night upon night trying to figure out who had killed Simone, and he had come up empty. He truly believed it would end up being one of those crimes that was never solved. But now, with Elise's death, the picture had changed. If the murders were by the same person, then a whole new set of evidence was available to investigators.

Of course, technically the murderer wasn't a serial killer yet. According to the FBI, three kills were necessary for that designation. *Hopefully this killer will be sated at two*, Steve thought.

Holding on to the bat, Steve walked to one of the front windows. The wind blew hard, and the rain was coming down in a steady stream. The rain was the media's concern, but Steve was more worried about the wind—it felt like it was trying to rip the house from its foundation.

Steve watched the storm playing outside his window, but his mind was still trying to understand this killer. Where had the killer been all this time? Had he really stopped for ten years—only to be brought back to life by Steve's return?

Although, in a way, it *would* make sense for the guy to start back up. After all, Steve had taken the rap for him before; with Steve back, perhaps the killer felt he could kill again with impunity. And from what Steve understood, that impulse to kill never really went away, it just built up in between kills.

And sure enough, right now the police were only interested in Steve. This guy was getting a free ride.

Outside, the moon was full and the trees blew wildly, making the shadows dance. A chill fell over Steve. It was not a comforting night.

A thump sounded at the side of the house. Steve's head whipped toward the sound; his heart raced and his body went still. He strained to hear more. But he couldn't make out anything above the howling wind.

Inside the house everything was silent. Steve wanted nothing more than to sit back in his grandfather's chair and forget the noise, but the thought of his grandmother lying asleep and vulnerable upstairs urged him to check it out.

Nerves taut, he carefully made his way to the back door. Pausing there, he strained to listen again, but he could hear nothing but the wind. He slipped outside, locking the door behind him and pocketing the keys.

With the bat still clasped tightly in his hands, Steve crept along the back of the house. Leaves, branches, and even garbage cans were all being tossed and rattled by the wind. Rain pelted him. When reached the corner, he peered carefully around it.

A giant shadow lay across the drive.

Steve's heart skipped a beat, but then he realized it was just a giant tree branch. The wind must have ripped it off and tossed it against the house. He let out a breath.

A little jumpy tonight.

He walked over to the branch, examined it, then looked up. Sure enough, it had been sheared off from the neighbors' large maple tree that hung partly over his grandmother's drive.

Steve pulled the branch out of the drive and over against the side of the house. There wasn't much he could do about it tonight, but when the storm was over, he'd break it up.

Steve stood there for a minute, watching the trees blow above him. A garbage can rolled down the street. Besides the sounds of the storm, it was quiet. No one was out, with good reason. Steve was getting wet, but it was just a light rain, and he didn't care.

Staying in the shadows, he walked to the curb. By some miracle the streetlights were still on, although with the wind blowing like it was, he knew it was only a matter of time before the power went out.

You'd have to be crazy to—wait a minute. Steve squinted. Someone was sitting in a parked car a few doors down, across the street. Right in front of Micah's house. Steve squinted, wondering if he was seeing things.

The shadow in the car moved. *Shit.* There was someone there.

Steve flashed on the photo of Elise Ingram. Would someone go after Micah or his family? No. There was no reason to think that. If the same guy was responsible for both murders, he seemed to be focused on teenage girls.

But the nervous feeling wouldn't leave him. *I'll just check and make sure.*

Steve carefully made his way down the sidewalk, trying to look casual. *Just a guy going for a stroll in the middle of a rainstorm with no umbrella.* As he passed the car, he glanced over surreptitiously. His heart began to pound. There was definitely someone sitting in there.

He continued on a few houses past Micah's house, then crossed the street, behind the car, and started to make his way back toward the car, staying low and in the shadows. He duck-walked right up to its bumper, then, staying down, he crept around to the passenger side. He peered in through the back door. *What the hell?*

The car was empty. He stared at the interior, stupefied. Had he been mistaken? Was it just the shadows playing tricks?

The barrel of a gun pressed between his shoulder blades.

"Don't move."

Steve debated for only a second. Before the person could even twitch, Steve ducked under their gun arm and slapped the gun hand away. With his left hand, he grabbed the gun arm, keeping it pointed away from him, and his right fist raced toward his assailant's face.

"Steve, no!"

His fist stopped only inches from her face. "Julie?"

CHAPTER THIRTY-NINE

JULIE GULPED IN AIR, her heart trying to gallop out of her chest. She nodded her head furiously.

"Julie," Steve said again, releasing her and stepping back. "I didn't know. I'm sorry."

Julie stared at him and the bat at his feet. She leveled her gun at him again. "What are you doing here, Steve?"

He looked from the gun to her face. "It's not what you think."

She didn't say anything.

"I saw someone just sitting in this car in the dark. Some kids live in this house. I was worried, so I crept up on the car from behind. But it was empty. It must have been a trick of the light."

Julie tried to gauge his sincerity. Fact was, she *had* been sitting in the car, so that part of Steve's story was true. And he sounded like he was telling the truth. But apparently, when it came to Steve, she was a lousy judge of character.

"And you just happened to have a bat handy?" she asked.

He glanced down at the bat. "Um, my grandmother's been getting threatening calls. I've been sleeping part of the night downstairs, keeping it nearby."

"Oh." Compassion for Bess rose up in Julie. She'd always liked Steve's grandmother. She treated Julie like she was one of her own, not just a kid from the neighborhood. The idea of someone threatening that sweet woman did not sit well with her.

Steve looked back at her, obviously waiting for Julie to make the next move. Problem was, she wasn't sure what she was supposed to do here. She had her gun trained on him, but he hadn't actually done anything. Emotions and logic warred inside her. It was make or break time. She either had to trust him or...

She lowered the gun. "I was worried about Micah. I was the one sitting in the car."

"You were worried about him? Why—" He cut himself off. "You heard he was spending time with me."

"Yeah. I just..." She paused. "I wanted to make sure he was okay."

Steve took another step back. "No. I get it. I understand. I'm glad someone else is looking out for him. Well, I guess I'll leave you to it." He turned to go.

Julie felt guilty as she watched him leave. *Shit.* She needed to pick a side and stay there. Either she believed he killed Simone or she didn't. But this waffling was eating her up.

She sighed and walked around to get back in the car. But as she did, a movement near Micah's house caught her attention. She went still.

What was that? She squinted. The dancing shadows made it difficult to see, but it looked like someone was in Micah's back yard—someone carrying something big.

The shape moved again. Fear lanced through Julie.

Heart racing, Julie looked over to where Steve had almost reached his grandmother's house. "Steve!"

CHAPTER FORTY

STEVE'S HEAD jerked around at Julie's yell. She was already running up Micah's drive.

What the hell? Steve sprinted after her. He raced down the street, up the drive, and into the boy's back yard. When he got there, Julie was disappearing into the trees. He ran after her and reached her in seconds. He grabbed her shoulder. She let out a muffled scream.

He put up his hands. "It's just me."

He realized as the words came out of his mouth that they might not be overly reassuring to her. But there was no time to go into that now. "What's going on?"

"I saw someone in the back yard. When I ran back here, they were disappearing into the trees. I think they were carrying someone."

Steve's gut clenched. But he also knew tonight was spooky, and the moving trees made shadows seem to come to life. "Are you sure?"

Even in the dim light, Julie's eyes looked huge as she nodded.

Steve grabbed her hand. "Which way?"

Julie pointed straight ahead.

"Let's go."

Together they raced through the woods. The wet ground sucked at their shoes. Steve's heart pounded, and his mind alternated between two phrases: *Please let Julie be seeing things* and *Please don't let us be too late.*

Thankfully the storm had brought in only sporadic cloud cover so far, so the light of the moon was bright enough to see by. The trees thinned out and Steve could just make out some movement ahead. "There!" he yelled.

He sprinted ahead of Julie. Fifteen feet away from him someone was struggling with a large squirming bundle in his hands.

Relief and terror collided in Steve. *It's Micah. He's alive.*

Steve put on a burst of speed and tackled the man around the knees. Steve's bat went flying. The man let out a grunt. Micah flew out of the man's hands and rolled away.

Steve tried to climb up the man's back, but the man rolled over and swiped at Steve with a knife. The blade caught Steve in the forearm and sliced deep. The man kicked Steve in the chest, throwing him backward.

Steve rolled away from him. The mud sucked at him as he got to his feet. Ahead of him, Steve saw Micah get to his feet. Micah took a step toward Steve.

"No!" Steve yelled. "Run, Micah, run!"

Micah hesitated for only a second before running into the trees, back toward his house.

The man had also gotten to his feet, and now he turned to face Steve. A ski mask covered his face, and gloves covered his hands. Steve couldn't see who the man was.

Steve clenched his fists. But he knew *what* he was. This was the monster who'd killed Simone—the monster who'd set *him* up for the crime.

Steve rose to his knees and lunged toward him, intending to tackle him yet again. But a gun blast sounded from behind him, and Steve instinctively dove for the ground.

The man took off running as Julie continued to fire after him.

Steve got to his feet, ready to follow him, when Micah crashed into him, wrapping his little arms around Steve's legs. "You came. You found me."

Steve looked at the spot where the man had disappeared. It was too late. The trees thickened there, blacking out the moonlight. Steve would never find him in the dark.

He wrapped his arms around Micah. "Are you okay?"

Micah nodded, but he didn't look up.

Steve lifted Micah off the ground, holding him tightly in his arms. Julie took off her jacket and wrapped it around the trembling boy.

"Thanks," Steve said.

Julie gave him a small smile. "You're welcome."

His gaze met hers, and for the briefest of moments, he felt like he had his old friend back.

Then she stepped away and the moment was gone.

But that was okay.

Because it was a start.

CHAPTER FORTY-ONE

THE RAIN HAD GOTTEN MUCH WORSE; it was now coming down in sheets. As Steve carried Micah back through the trees toward his house, water dripped down his face. Micah kept a death lock on Steve's neck.

"It's okay, Micah. You're safe," Steve said over and over again. But Micah never loosened his grip.

Julie ran ahead to wake Micah's family. By the time Steve stepped out of the woods with Micah, all the lights were on in the little house. A woman wearing a raincoat over pink pajamas rushed over to them.

"Micah, baby!" She hovered next to them, running her hands through Micah's hair, patting him on the back.

Micah clung to Steve even tighter.

"I'll carry him back to the house," Steve said.

Micah's mother looked up at him for the first time. Shock splashed across her face. "You're—you're Steve Kane."

Steve nodded, adjusting Micah in his arms. "Yes, ma'am, I am."

"I'll take him," the woman said quickly. She tried to pull

Micah out of Steve's arms, but Micah just tightened his hold on Steve's neck.

"Ma'am," Steve said gently but firmly, "he's really scared, and I think it would be better if I just carried him to the house."

Steve could tell she didn't trust him with her son. But with a sigh, he started walking toward the house. Micah's mom stayed right beside him the whole way, her hand resting on Micah's back. Steve climbed the back steps and took a seat on the wicker couch, Micah cradled in his lap.

Micah's mom hovered by his elbow, trying to get Micah to go with her. But Micah either couldn't hear her or was still too scared to let go.

Julie appeared at the back door, carrying some towels. She wrapped one around Micah and another around Steve before looking back at Micah's mom. "I called the police. They'll be here in a few minutes. Your other son is up. I put a show on for him."

"I need to call my brother," Micah's mom said. She glanced at Julie.

Julie nodded. "I'll stay with them."

Micah's mother looked reluctant to go. She glanced once more at Steve and then back at Julie. "Thank you for bringing him back." Steve didn't fail to notice that she addressed her gratitude to Julie, not him. "I'm Michone. Michone Donaldson."

Julie smiled. "I'm Julie." *No last name*, Steve noted. Not for the first time, it occurred to him that Julie was probably almost as famous in Millners Kill as he was. *The sister of the dead girl. Friends with her sister's killer.* Both of their identities were inextricably tied to that tragic event. And the town of Millners Kill would never be able to see them any other way.

Michone rose to go, giving Micah one more stroke on the head and Steve one more suspicious glance. Steve ignored her. Obviously she didn't trust him. But Micah trusted him. And the boy was safe. That was all that mattered right now.

Julie sat down next to him. "How is he?"

Steve turned his head sideways to peer at the boy's head on his shoulder. Micah's eyes were closed. "Believe it or not, I think he may have fallen asleep."

Julie smiled. "Well, he knows he's safe. And don't take Michone's reaction personally. She's terrified."

Steve doubted she realized how telling that statement was. Ten minutes ago she had been holding a gun on him, and now she was telling him not to take it personally if Michone didn't trust him.

A squad car rolled to a stop in the drive, its lights flashing but the siren off. Micah stirred and Steve hugged him a little tighter. "It's okay. You're safe. It's the police," he whispered.

Russ jumped from the driver's seat and Steve said a silent thank-you. Russ would be easier to deal with than any other member of the Millners Kill Police Department.

Julie walked over to the side of the porch. "Back here."

Russ stopped and changed direction, dodging the puddles in the drive as he made his way over to them.

Steve sighed as Russ reached the bottom of the porch steps. "All right. Let's get this over with."

CHAPTER FORTY-TWO

JULIE SPOKE WITH RUSS FIRST, leading him off the porch and over to the covering over the garage. He saw Russ taking notes as Julie pointed to the trees. Steve appreciated her taking the lead. He wanted to get Micah settled before he spoke with Russ.

Micah's mother reappeared and walked over to Steve. Steve stood. "He's asleep. I think you can take him now."

She nodded and reached for him. Carefully, Steve placed Micah in her arms. She cradled him to her, a tear rolling down her cheek. "I don't know what I would have done if something had happened to him." She looked up at Steve. "Thank you. I'm —I'm sorry for before."

Steve shook his head. "It's okay. I understand."

She nodded and carried Micah into the house. Steve closed the door after them and then stepped to the edge of the porch, looking at Julie and Russ, who'd taken shelter now under a maple tree on the other side of the drive. Julie's hands were actively conveying something and Russ was still taking notes.

Steve blew out a breath and walked down the steps toward

them. He had just joined them when a pair of headlight beams washed over them. Steve turned to the drive to see a Hummer pulling up behind Russ's car. A giant of a man jumped out and rushed into the house.

Steve looked back at Russ.

"Michone's brother," Russ replied to the unasked question. "You ready to give your version of events?"

"Sure."

"I'll wait over—" Julie stopped herself and grabbed Steve's arm. Blood dripped from the wound. "You're hurt."

Steve tried to pull his arm away. "It's nothing."

"Really? And where did you get your medical degree? Because *my* medical training tells me that needs to be bandaged up before it gets infected. I'll grab my bag." She headed for her car.

Russ watched her go. "I don't remember her being so tough."

"I do," Steve said.

While Julie was getting her bag, Steve quickly recounted everything that had happened from the time he'd seen Julie in the car.

"And you didn't get a look at him?" Russ asked.

"No. He was completely covered head to toe. I think he was a little shorter than me, but honestly, I couldn't swear to it. I couldn't even tell you what race he was."

Julie appeared next to them. "Come on. Let's get that wrapped."

Russ nodded. "I'm going inside. You guys hang around, okay?"

They both nodded as Russ dashed through the rain and headed for the door. Julie led Steve back onto the porch. "Take a seat."

Steve did. "So, a medical degree, huh?"

"I'm a second-year resident." Julie kneeled down in front of him and poured water from a bottle over his arm. She mopped it up gently with some small pads and peered at it. She pulled out a bottle of peroxide. "I'm afraid this is going to sting a little. But I can't really tell if everything's out."

Steve tensed. "Okay."

He gasped when the medicine hit the wound. His arm felt like it was on fire.

Julie smiled. "Warned you."

She blew on the wound to cool the sting.

Steve looked at her and felt himself stir. He looked away, thanking God it was dark.

Julie grabbed a tube from her bag.

Trying to distract himself from her closeness, Steve asked, "What's that?"

"Dermabond. You need this stitched, but I don't have anything to do that with. So this will basically glue your skin together."

She held the wound together and applied the bond. After waiting a minute, she wrapped it with a bandage. Steve realized he now had matching wounds, one on each forearm.

"There. That should do it. Try and keep it clean and dry, okay?" She looked up at him. Their faces were only inches apart.

Steve held his breath, not wanting to move and scare her away.

Michone's brother walked out the back door, followed by Russ. Julie jumped back from Steve, putting her supplies back in the bag. "Hey, Reggie."

Steve stood up just as quickly, almost guiltily.

Without a word, Reggie pulled Julie into a hug that had her yelping. The guy was seriously huge. "Thank you," he said.

Reggie let Julie go and then turned to Steve. Steve forced himself not to take a step back. Reggie thrust out a hand the size of a baseball mitt. "Thank you. Micah told me about you. I wasn't happy about him hanging around with you, but right now, I am damn thankful he did. He means everything to my sister. To me."

Steve shook the big man's hand. "You're welcome. And I think he's a pretty amazing kid too."

Reggie nodded before turning back to Russ. "I'm going to take Michone and the boys over to my house. They'll be staying with me until this guy is caught."

Russ nodded. "That's a good idea. If you want, you can take them now. After we're done here, I'll come by and get Michone's official statement."

"Good." Reggie looked back at Steve and Julie. "And I mean it—thank you." He turned and went back into the house.

"Um, I'll go help them get the boys in the car," Julie said, following him.

Alone, Russ and Steve walked to the edge of the porch, watching Michone carry a bag to the car. Russ looked over at Steve. "Micah will be okay. Reggie was a UFC fighter after he left the marines. I'd like to see someone try and get to that kid now. It was a good thing you were here."

For a while they stood in silence while Michone loaded up a couple of suitcases in Reggie's car. Then she and her older son climbed in. Steve watched Julie help Reggie get Micah settled in the backseat of the Hummer.

"You know," Russ said, "you're making a habit of this hero thing. It's a good thing you were here."

Julie paused at the open door of the Hummer, and her eyes met Steve's.

"No," Steve said. "It's a good thing Julie's lousy at stakeouts."

Russ gave a little laugh. He looked at Steve out of the corner of his eye. "Did Reggie and I intrude on a little moment back here?"

Steve jerked his gaze from Julie to Russ.

Russ looked back at him, eyebrows raised.

Steve opened his mouth and shut it before turning to watch Reggie back the Hummer out to the street. "No. She was just bandaging up my arm."

"Uh-huh."

Steve shook his head, but he liked that Russ thought he'd seen something. Who knew? Maybe he had.

He turned back to Russ. "Anything else you need?"

Russ shook his head. "No. I think—"

The sound of a siren cut off his reply. Both men turned to watch the chief's Jeep Cherokee pull into the driveway. He cut the siren off but left the lights shining out into the night.

Julie quickly walked up onto the porch and stood next to Steve. He was surprised. It felt like a show of support.

Hiking himself out of the car, Keith made his way toward them, a determined look on his face. He eyed Steve before turning to Russ. "Why isn't the suspect in handcuffs?"

Russ took a step forward. "Chief, Steve didn't—"

The chief pointed at Steve while keeping his eyes on Russ. "He's a murderer, and he was here at the time the kid was taken. Do I need to spell it out for you?"

Julie stepped forward. "Steve didn't try to hurt Micah. He was the one who saved Micah."

Keith looked her over, and Steve could feel Julie's anger rise. "Ms. Granger, this has been a very emotional night. Perhaps when you've had a chance to step back, you'll see the situation more clearly."

Julie gasped. "Did you actually just suggest that I'm too *emotional* to understand what's going on?"

Keith didn't even reply. "Russ, arrest Kane and bring him down to the station."

Julie moved a little in front of Steve. "You can't. He didn't do anything wrong."

Steve stepped around her, worried now that the chief would

arrest Julie just to spite him. "It's okay. Until he rules me out, he won't focus on anyone else." He held his hands together in front of him. "Let's just get this over with."

Russ didn't look happy about it, but he stepped forward and clapped the cuffs on Steve's wrists "Sorry about this," he whispered.

"I'll call Jack," Julie said.

Steve shook his head. "No. Let him sleep. I didn't do this. It won't stick."

"Fine, but I'm following you to the station," she replied.

Touched, Steve nodded.

DAY 4

"Billy the Kid here. So I don't know about you, but I'm about done with this storm. It starts. It stops. It starts again even harder. Enough already! Power is out all over upstate New York and cell towers are down as well. How will we ever survive without our phones!

And have you heard what's happening over at Millners Kill? First their bridge went out. Then people started getting murdered. There have been two deaths reported so far. And someone tried to grab a kid from his house last night. Man! What is wrong with people?

And in the middle of all this is Steve Kane. You guys remember him, right? The guy who killed Simone Granger ten years ago? Well, he showed up back in town just before all this began. I don't know about you, but that seems way too big a coincidence to be believed. So keep the good folks in Millners Kill in your thoughts. And for those of you listening from Millners Kill, keep your shotgun handy."

CHAPTER FORTY-THREE

STEVE SPENT the night enjoying the Spartan accommodations of the Millners Kill Police Department. Keith had interrogated him when they'd arrived but he hadn't learned anything—unsurprisingly, seeing as there was nothing to learn.

For a while, Steve was surprised to find that he was able to take the interrogation in stride. Knowing Micah was safe was all he cared about. But his anger started to boil when he realized Keith wasn't going to look for the actual assailant. As far as Keith was concerned, he already had his man.

He'd spent the rest of the night on a hard bench in a jail cell that reeked of body odor. It was just before five a.m. when Russ arrived to unlock Steve's cell door. "You're free to go."

Steve passed right by him without a word.

Russ put out a hand to stop him. "I'm real sorry about this."

Steve looked at him. Russ's eyes were filled with remorse.

Steve sighed, knowing there was nothing else Russ could have done—short of quitting the force, anyway. And then the chief would have just had one of his other deputies arrest him instead. "Not your fault, man."

A hint of anger crept into Russ's voice. "They should be thanking you, not locking you up."

Steve clapped him on the shoulder. "Don't worry about it. Keith's never going to change. Did you look in the woods? Find any sign of the guy who grabbed Micah?"

Russ looked dejected. "I tried to follow his trail, but with the weather..." He shrugged. "The chief won't like it, but I'll canvass the neighborhood and see if there were any witnesses. I don't want to get your hopes up, though. There's just not much to go on."

Steve knew Russ was right. "Well, I've got to go. I'm due at Mel's in a few minutes."

"Need a lift?"

Steve shook his head. "Thanks, but after last night, I think I want to stretch my legs. But could you call Jack? Have him run over and check on Gran?"

"I'll run by. I'll tell her I picked you up early this morning."

"Thanks."

They crossed through the doors leading into the front foyer. The rain was slamming against the front windows as the wind added gusto to the downpour. Russ looked over at Steve, his eyebrows raised. "You *sure* you don't want a ride?"

Steve had no doubts. He needed to walk. He needed the reminder that he was still a free man, even if it meant walking through a monsoon.

He pulled the hood up on his jacket. "Yeah. I'm sure."

CHAPTER FORTY-FOUR

AH, Steve, Always the good kid, doing the right thing. Saved two lives yesterday and another last night. His face darkened when he thought of Steve tackling him in the woods.

His anger afterward had been unrelenting. But then he'd found an outlet for all that anger. He hadn't planned on moving on this one so quickly, but Steve had forced his hand. Why hadn't he just let him take Micah?

Oh well. It was not what he had wanted, but it should do the trick—especially coming on the heels of the attack on Micah.

He pulled up his hood and quickly got out of the car. Ducking into the coffee shop, he pulled back his hood and shook himself out. He smiled at the barista behind the counter. "I'm glad you guys are still open."

The young man smiled back at him. "Well, with the bridge, boss thought people might need a little something. Your usual?"

He smiled. "Yes, please."

CHAPTER FORTY-FIVE

STEVE DUCKED his chin and squinted against the pelting rain. He was only a block from the police station and already soaked through. His hair was plastered to his face. He'd stopped fighting the wind over his hood only a few feet from the police station. It was just a measure in futility.

Maybe I was a bit hasty turning down Russ's offer.

Mel's Diner was just up ahead. Mel had called Steve last night before everything and asked if Steve would mind coming in to help out—said he'd decided to open for those who needed to get out of the house. Steve had been happy to take the shift though he was doubtful Mel was going to get any customers. Sure, people were stuck in town now, but with this weather, only the idiots would leave their houses. Which apparently meant him and Mel.

And once word spreads about the attack on Micah, everyone will be staying close to home.

A heavy wind gusted across the parking lot—so strong it pushed Steve backward. He pressed through it to the diner's front door. The "open" sign wasn't on yet, but the door was thankfully unlocked, and Steve stumbled through. Shaking out his hair, he wiped at his eyes. "Hey, Mel. It's me. It's really getting crazy out there."

He walked around the counter. "Don't think we're going to get many—"

His foot bumped against something. He looked down.

He went still as his breath left him. For a few precious seconds, his mind couldn't process what he was seeing. Then the horror of it slammed into him, and he stumbled back against the counter.

Mel lay face down on the floor in a pool of blood. A knife stuck out of his back, and his shirt was shredded and soaked in blood. His head was turned to the side, and a line of dried blood ran down from his mouth. His unblinking eyes were large, staring, lifeless. A larger pool of blood spread from around him, already beginning to dry.

Steve was frozen in place by disbelief. "Mel?"

It was the knife that pulled him back to reality. It was one of the diner's thick steak knives. Even the handle was covered in blood.

Steve had seen stabbings before. Prison hadn't exactly been a pleasure cruise. But this was different. This wasn't the result of a gang fight or a territory dispute; this was senseless. Cruel.

Steve's mind was suddenly filled with memories of Mel teaching him to cook, coming to his soccer games, and a thousand other moments. Until Mel, no one had even begun to fill the void left after his dad had disappeared. When Steve's mom had died, Mel had been the one who had stepped up, looked after him, and helped his grandmother out. How could someone do this to him?

Tears threatened to spill, but Steve choked them down. There'd be time for that later.

He went down to the opposite end of the counter and pulled

out the old phone. He hit the number nine and then stopped. *Wait a minute.* There was no way Keith was going to believe this wasn't him. Look at how the chief had reacted last night after he'd saved Micah.

Automatically he felt guilty at the thought. He should be focused on Mel now. But the reality was, Keith would never really investigate this murder. He'd never follow up on any leads that didn't point directly to Steve. And the killer would go free.

Steve scrambled to form a plan. He was no PI, but the least he could do was examine the scene. Maybe if he identified something useful, he could pass that info to Russ or Declan.

Slipping out of his shoes, he walked back to the other end of the counter.

Mel's hands were splayed out. Coffee cups and a sugar holder were smashed to the floor in front of him. Steve didn't move Mel, but he was pretty sure if he did there'd be more shards.

On the counter beside him, the sugar container was tipped over, along with the pepper. The salt shaker had rolled farther down the counter. So, Mel had been taken by surprise. He'd grabbed the counter, knocking stuff off as he fell.

Steve crouched down as close to the body as he could get, careful to stay clear of the pooled blood. There were no bruises on Mel's hands, no cuts on his forearms. The poor man hadn't seen the attack coming, hadn't had a chance to defend himself.

Sick bastard. Anger and nausea warred inside Steve. Whoever had done this had come up from behind, stabbed Mel in the back, and then kept stabbing. There were at least two dozen stab wounds.

Steve paused. *Wait a minute.* He looked around. Blood was splashed along the cups and saucers stored under the counter and along the back shelves. Whoever did this had been in a mad frenzy. They would have been covered in blood.

Steve looked back to the door and then toward the kitchen. So why was there no blood trail? Did the killer just stop and clean up after himself? People didn't do that.

Steve felt cold. *But this guy did.*

Steve had seen a guy in prison like that. He'd walked calmly up to this neo-Nazi that had been saying some not so nice things about him, and with a smile on his face, he'd plunged a shank into the guy's neck, again and again. He'd been dripping in the guy's blood.

Then he'd stopped, wiped his knife off on the guy's shirt, and strolled away with that same calm smile on his face. He'd even whistled as the blood dripped off him, leaving a trail in his wake. Steve had recognized the tune—the theme song from *Gilligan's Island*.

The guy had been put in the hole for thirty days. And when he got out, everyone gave him a wide berth. No one wanted to mess with that kind of crazy.

Was that the kind of guy he was dealing with here?

Another thought hit Steve like a punch to the stomach. Mel was always cautious. He wouldn't turn his back to a stranger, and he would never let a stranger in after closing. Which meant that whoever Mel had let in, it was someone he knew. Someone he trusted.

And that person had literally stabbed him in the back.

Steve blew out a breath. He needed to call someone. People would learn he was on schedule to come in this morning. If he didn't call, it would look suspicious. And if he did, he would have to be the one that discovered the body.

The thought brought him up short. Was that part of the plan? To make sure that *he* was the one who found Mel? After all, it's not like Keith was going to look any further once Steve Kane was involved.

Steve debated in his mind for a minute, looking for any other possible course of action. "Shit."

He walked back to the phone and picked it up. At least there was one small way he could make it easier. He dialed.

"Declan? It's Steve. I need you to come to Mel's Diner. Mel's been killed."

CHAPTER FORTY-SIX

DECLAN DROVE DOWN THE ROAD, struggling to keep from pressing the gas pedal to the floor. Tension made his shoulders and hands ache as he held the steering wheel in a death grip. The windshield wipers beat furiously at the driving rain, but to little effect.

Steve hadn't gone into detail, but his words had chilled Declan to the bone: *Mel's been killed.*

Declan had thrown on his clothes and sprinted out of the house, scrawling a hasty note to his sister and father. He'd turned off the scanner last night, needing to get a good night's sleep. When he checked his cell, he saw he'd missed a bunch of messages from Russ. Not much detail, but someone had tried to grab Micah Donaldson last night. And apparently Steve and Julie Granger had saved him.

And now Mel was dead. What the hell was going on? Declan knew how much Steve cared about Mel. He couldn't have done something to him, could he?

Automatically, he felt guilty at the thought.

Declan pushed the pedal a little more and the back of his car hydroplaned. He slowed down. *Damn it. Damn it. Damn it.* He needed to get to the diner before Keith. He needed to take control of the scene.

Turning onto Main Street, he saw the diner's sign up ahead, although it was still off and the diner itself was dark. He let out a breath at the empty parking lot. Well, at least he had that working for him.

He pulled to a stop in front of the diner. He reached over and grabbed his plastic booties and gloves from the glove box. Throwing open the door, he dashed for the door of the diner. Steve held it open for him.

Although it was only a short distance from his car to the door of the diner, Declan was still soaked when he stepped inside. He stood dripping on the welcome mat and looked at Steve. "Steve? Are you all right?"

Steve gave him a jerky nod. "Mel's this way."

Declan put out a hand to stop him. "I'll go. You stay here."

Steve nodded, looking around, clenching his hands. He didn't have any blood on him or any other signs of violence. Declan felt a small measure of relief at that.

Declan shrugged off his coat and hung it up on the coat rack by the door. He'd prefer to do all this outside, but the weather was making that impossible. He flipped on the switch by the door, bathing the room in light. "Did you touch the body?"

Steve blinked a few times and shook his head. "No. I found him and then used the phone under the counter to call you."

Declan looked at the footprints leading around the counter. He couldn't see any sign of Mel. He nodded to the footprints: "Those yours?"

Steve nodded. "I didn't realize—I took my shoes off after. I didn't want to mess up anything left behind."

Declan noted Steve's stocking feet, and that Steve seemed to be slipping into shock. He pulled his keys out of his pocket. "I want you to go sit in my car. Put the heat on."

Steve shook his head. "I don't want to leave Mel."

Declan looked him in the eyes. "I'll take care of Mel for now. Okay? Go ahead. You can leave him with me."

Steve's chin trembled. "I didn't know... I just walked in... I didn't know."

Declan pressed his keys into Steve's hands. "Go wait in my car."

Steve nodded, all expression slipping from his face. He retrieved his shoes, put them on, and walked out. Declan watched him go with a heavy heart. *The kid doesn't need this now.*

Letting out a breath, Declan turned around, put his booties on over his shoes, and pulled on his gloves with a snap. Then he headed toward the counter, walking slowly, checking the ground to make sure he didn't step on any blood splatter or other evidence. He saw his first spot of blood at the edge of the counter, only two inches from it. He'd let the forensics team sort that out.

He groaned when he realized he probably *was* the forensics team. What Keith knew about crime scene investigation could fit in a thimble with room to spare.

Then he moved around the side of the counter and saw Mel. The man's back had been ripped to shreds by the stab wounds. The murder weapon was still there, plunged into the center of Mel's back up to the hilt. Declan closed his eyes for a moment, letting the grief and shock roll over him. *I'm sorry, Mel. You didn't deserve this.*

Taking a breath, he shoved his feelings aside. They'd only get in the way.

He focused on the wounds on Mel's back. They looked deep. *Someone with some muscle*, Declan thought. He pictured Steve's arms and then blocked out the image.

He noted the shards and the pool of blood. From where he was standing, it didn't look like Mel had put up much of a fight. *Just like Elise. And Simone.* In all three cases, the victims had known their attacker. Which meant the murderer—if these crimes were all committed by the same person—most likely lived in Millners Kill. The thought did not sit well with him.

While his mind whirled through possible suspects and tried to stay away from placing Steve on that list, he pulled out his phone and snapped pictures of the counter, Mel's back and face, and the knife. He had a better camera in the trunk of his car, but he didn't know how much time he'd have before the scene was pulled away from him, so he wanted to capture as much as he could as quickly as he could.

He crouched down, careful not to disturb anything. "You didn't see it coming, did you?" he whispered.

He noted the dried blood. He took more shots of the wounds and Mel's hands. This wasn't recent. He'd need to check to confirm, but he was guessing at least six or seven hours. Mel wasn't in full rigor yet, which meant he'd been dead less than eight hours.

If Steve had just gotten here, he couldn't have done it—unless he was here earlier, too. Declan let out a breath. *But I never really believed he could have done it*, he told himself. Although he wasn't sure if he was confirming something in his mind or just reassuring himself.

Standing, he walked carefully around Mel and into the kitchen. The blood splatter ended at the door. The kitchen itself looked undisturbed. Declan walked through the kitchen and to the back door. He pushed on it. Locked. And it could only be locked from the inside.

Killer must have gone out the front. He'd have to ask Steve if the door had been locked or unlocked.

Sirens sounded from the front of the diner, startling him. *Son of a bitch*. Declan made his way back to the front, careful once again not to disturb the scene. He could already hear yelling from the parking lot.

He'd just reached the counter when the front door blew in. A deputy held the door open while Keith made his way in. Leaves and rain blew through and into the diner. Keith stomped in, soaking the floor and tromping across it in his big boots.

"Stop!" Declan yelled.

Keith hesitated.

Declan stared at him. "Now back up, stepping in your same footprints. You are contaminating the scene." He glared at the deputy. "And close the damn door."

The deputy stepped inside and let the door fall shut behind him. But before it closed, Declan saw Steve being dragged from his car and manhandled to the ground. Steve didn't appear to be resisting.

Keith sneered but stayed where he was. "This is *my* crime scene, not the state's. And seeing as we already caught the perpetrator red-handed outside, I don't think it'll be much of a trial."

Declan ground his teeth. "So your theory is Steve killed Mel, called me, and then calmly sat outside waiting to be arrested?"

"Never said he was bright."

Declan stared at him in disbelief. *What an—*

"Wait a minute," he said. "How did you know about Mel's death?"

"Got a 911 call."

"From who?"

Keith shrugged. "Didn't leave his name."

"What exactly did he say?"

"That Mel was dead."

Declan looked around the diner. None of the windows offered a view behind the counter. "How did the caller know that?"

"I don't know. They probably walked in, saw him, and left to call."

"When did this call come in?"

"Five minutes ago."

Declan supposed it was possible that someone had come in before Steve. But why? Everyone knew Mel's didn't open until six. And it's not like there were a lot of people out this morning. "You have that call taped?"

"Of course."

"Good. We'll need it."

Keith took a step toward Declan. "Maybe you didn't hear me before. This is my crime scene."

Through the window, Declan saw Steve being shoved into the back of a squad car, none too gently. Declan was torn. He wanted to go with Steve, but he knew the real answers were here. He put up his hands.

"Okay—your crime scene. But I have more experience with them. How about you leave me a deputy and I'll process the scene for you?"

Keith shook his head, but before he could speak Declan plowed on. "After all, it always looks good when you take advantage of the resources at hand. Constituents really love that. Besides, you have Steve to interrogate."

Keith seemed to consider Declan's words. "I still need to see the crime scene."

Declan held up his phone. "I've already taken pictures. I can send them to you. We can button this up nice and quick. I'm sure you have a lot of other important duties to see to today with the storm coming in."

"Damn right I do." He grunted. "All right, you do the scut work and I'll interview Kane. Send me those pictures." He turned on his heel and headed for the door. The deputy jumped to attention, pulling open the door for him.

Declan quickly pulled out his phone and dialed. "Pick up. Come on, pick up," he murmured.

"Hello?" came the sleepy reply.

"Jack. You need to get down to the police station. Steve's in trouble."

CHAPTER FORTY-SEVEN

DECLAN TURNED BACK to Mel's body. There had to be something here that could help Steve.

Wrong focus, Declan. There must be something here that can tell you who killed Mel. You don't know for sure it wasn't Steve.

He nodded to himself. He needed to be objective. Anything other than that and he was no better than Keith.

The door behind him opened. Declan glanced over as Russ stepped in. "Chief said you needed some help processing the scene."

"You know anything about forensics?"

"I took a couple of classes at the community college and down at the academy."

"Good enough. Go to the trunk of my car and pull out the black duffel bag. It's got my gear." Declan patted his pockets. "Shit. I gave Steve my keys."

Russ pulled a set of keys out of his pocket. "I grabbed them."

Declan smiled. Apparently not everybody at the Millners Kill Police Department was a complete idiot. "Great."

Russ disappeared outside and returned in a few minutes.

Declan noticed that when he left and when he returned, he was careful to open the door only enough to let himself through, letting very little of the storm in. The kid had the makings of a decent cop.

Russ held up the bag. "What's first?"

"There are some extra booties and gloves in there. Once you have them on, grab my camera and start taking pictures. I already took some with my phone but I want better shots. Careful you don't step in any of the blood."

Russ nodded and got to work. Declan pulled out the evidence cards, then placed them near anything he wanted extra attention paid to.

An intake of breath had him looking over at Russ, who was now standing above Mel, looking a little paler than he had five minutes ago.

"You okay?" Declan asked.

Russ nodded, but his breathing was a little labored. "I really liked Mel."

"I know. He was a good man. But the way we honor him right now is by doing the best job we can, okay?"

Russ swallowed. "Yeah, okay."

Declan raised an eyebrow.

Russ shrugged self-consciously. "I'm just not real good with blood."

"That's not a bad thing to be."

"Yeah, maybe for someone who's *not* a cop," Russ muttered.

Declan and Russ spent the next hour processing the scene. When Declan was sure they'd gotten as much as they could, he walked over to the bag and put his gear away. "All right, Russ. Tell me what we know."

Russ followed him. "Mel was taken by surprise. He didn't have a chance to defend himself. The doer stabbed him thirty times by my count."

Declan noted that Russ seemed less nauseated now, more confident. "Notice anything about the stab wounds?"

"It's hard to tell with the shirt, but they all look deep. No hesitation."

Declan nodded. "What does that tell you?"

"Our guy was committed."

"Yes." Declan pulled a bottle of Luminol out of the bag. "What else did you notice about the blood?"

Russ paused. "I mean, there's a lot, which means our guy would have been covered in it. But there's no blood leading to the door."

"Which tells you?"

"He wasn't panicked. He was in control. He cleaned up."

Declan nodded, handing Russ the bottle. "Spray this over the path from the door to Mel and then through the kitchen."

Russ started to spray while Declan pulled down all the blinds.

"Hey, Declan?" Russ called.

Declan looked over.

"Should I spray the counter? I'm just thinking maybe when the killer stood up, he might have grabbed on to it for support."

"Good thinking."

Russ smiled and sprayed the counter on both sides of Mel's body. He went back and did the kitchen area, then returned to Declan. "Done."

"All right. Let's douse the lights."

Russ reached over next to the door and flipped the switch. "Oh my God."

Glowing splotches of blue-green showed up all over the place. Blood was splattered along the counter and across the kitchen window. The floor was a mass of color just on this side of Mel's feet. The killer must have literally been standing in a puddle of blood. Even Declan was shaken by the amount of it. It was odd though: Why would the killer bother cleaning all that up? It was as if the doer wanted to be sure that whoever found Mel didn't know his body was there until they were almost of top of it.

Declan headed back to the counter. "He cleaned up there," he said, pointing at the sink.

Russ pointed to a bright circular spot on the floor next to the sink. "Would that be where he dumped his bloody clothes?"

"Probably. So he got changed, which means he brought a change of clothes with him. He planned this."

"You think this was Steve?"

Declan looked over at Russ. Declan's gut told him no. But the evidence? It didn't really tell him anything. "We need to figure out what time he died. That'll give us the window."

"Can you tell that yet?"

"Not for certain. But it was hours ago, at least six or seven. We can do a liver temp, that'll let us know."

"If it was hours ago, that means it can't be Steve. He was locked up in our jail last night."

Declan jerked his head up. "What? Why?"

"I left you a message. The chief arrested him after Micah was grabbed."

"I thought he saved Micah."

Russ shrugged, looking away. "The chief took a while to be convinced of that."

Declan shook his head, but he realized that Keith's stubbornness was actually a good thing. Because if the times of death lined up, it meant Steve had an alibi—a very good one.

"But that means someone else did this," Russ said. "Do you think they're the same person who killed Elise Ingram?"

Declan paused for a minute, considering what they knew about Elise's death. "Both were killed by knives and without any witnesses. The likelihood is that, yeah, it was the same doer."

Declan looked over to the circle of blood on the floor next to the sink. "And our boy's a planner. I'm betting he dumped all his clothes into a garbage bag and took it with him. But we'll check to be sure."

"I can't believe someone would plan something like this," Russ whispered.

"Yeah. But he must have. He covered his bases pretty well."

Russ walked over to Mel's body and pointed at the edge of the counter. "Maybe not *all* his bases."

Declan walked over and looked down with a smile. He looked back up at Russ. "Well, I do believe we have some fingerprints."

"Could they be Mel's?"

Declan shook his head. "Doubtful. When he went down, he stayed down. These fingerprints were made in blood. Mel's wouldn't have been."

A smile began to break over Russ's face. "So we've got him?"

"We just might."

CHAPTER FORTY-EIGHT

THE SQUAD CAR pulled out of the parking lot with its sirens blaring. Steve had to brace his legs to keep from sliding across the plastic back seat. He was soaked to the bone.

When the police had arrived, Steve hadn't even noticed. It wasn't until after he'd been yanked out of Declan's car and thrown face down in a puddle that he'd shaken off the shock that had come over him in the diner.

They'd left him like that, face down in the pouring rain, for several minutes. The rain had soaked through every piece of clothing he had, right down to his underwear. Even now, water dripped from his hair into his eyes, and with his hands cuffed behind his back, there was nothing he could do about it.

He scooted over so he could lean his head against the window. *Mel's dead.*

He shut his eyes tight as if he that would help him block it out. No such luck. If anything, it was worse with his eyes closed. The image of Mel lying on the floor, his eyes staring at nothing, was imprinted in his mind.

Steve shifted and opened his eyes as the car turned. They

pulled up in front of the police station, and the deputy slammed on the brakes. Unprepared, Steve fell forward, his face crashing into the glass divider.

The deputy grinned at him from the rearview mirror.

Steve pushed himself back using his shoulders. *Asshole.*

He had just gotten himself upright when the door next to him was yanked open. Hands reached in and dragged him out. Steve tried to duck his head, but the hands holding him wouldn't let him, and he slammed into the top of the door frame. He hadn't even felt the pain yet before he was shoved to the ground and his forehead met the sidewalk with a loud crack. Then the pain exploded.

"Sorry about that," the deputy said coldly, pulling him up with a grim smile. But then the smile dropped from his face.

Blood dripped down Steve's forehead and onto his shirt. The deputy pulled him close. "You did that to yourself, you hear?"

Steve was feeling lightheaded and could only nod. He blinked hard. His vision was getting a little fuzzy around the edges.

The deputy shoved him toward the stairs, his grip tight. Steve tried to clear his vision, but he couldn't seem to manage it. And his feet were moving slowly as if he were walking through water. He almost laughed. *Maybe it rained more than I thought.* He tried to look down to see if he was walking through water, but it only made him stumble.

The deputy decided to take him up the wheelchair ramp, which was good, because Steve didn't think his legs would be able to manage the stairs.

The deputy pulled Steve into the foyer and leaned him against the desk. Steve looked at the woman behind the desk. Bee? Lee? What was her name?

The woman pursed her lips and glared at the deputy. When

she spoke, there was a hard edge to her words. "What happened?"

"He hit his head."

"Right. All by himself, I'm sure."

"Just tell me where I'm taking him," the deputy growled.

"Holding one. And make sure someone sees to his head."

The deputy just grunted in response.

Steve was hauled through the main room and down a hallway to the holding cells. The deputy unlocked one of the cell doors and shoved Steve inside—hard.

Lightheaded and still cuffed, Steve couldn't stop himself from crashing into the back wall. A new pain, this time in his cheekbone, exploded outward. Steve leaned against the back wall, taking deep breaths. Behind him he heard the door slam shut—a noise he was all too familiar with.

Finally, he slid down the wall and turned around. He leaned his head back against the wall, letting the dizziness wash over him, and then the darkness.

CHAPTER FORTY-NINE

FROM SOMEWHERE IN the police station, Steve could hear yelling, but he couldn't make out the words. He blinked his eyes open and realized he'd blacked out a little. He wasn't sure for how long.

The yelling came closer. "I demand to see him. I'm his lawyer! Where is he? Back here?"

Steve almost smiled—Jack. He looked up just as Jack came into view.

Jack looked into the cell and went still. Then his face twisted in rage. "Who the *hell* is responsible for this? Somebody is losing his job. And god damn it, you better open this cell *right now*."

Keith spoke, still out of view. "Counselor, your brother put up a fight when one of my officers went to cuff him. Any injuries that resulted from that incident are solely the fault—"

Keith cut himself off as he came closer and got his first glimpse of Steve. Even through Steve's blurry vision, he could see Keith's jaw tighten, and he clearly heard the muttered curse. Keith pulled his keys off his belt and unlocked the cell.

Jack rushed in, knelt next to Steve, and gently pulled his head into his lap. Steve winced as he lay on his bound hands.

"Sorry, sorry," Jack said, helping him sit back up, but he kept a supportive arm around his shoulder. "Someone get these cuffs off him and get me a first aid kit."

Steve smiled—or at least he thought he did. He wasn't sure because Jack was fading in and out. "Thanks, big brother."

And then the darkness took him again.

CHAPTER FIFTY

JULIE DROVE SLOWLY TOWARD TOWN, looking for a store with its lights on. She had stayed at the station until late last night, but it had been a futile gesture. The chief hadn't listened to anything she'd had to say.

She'd finally gotten home a little after three. She'd been exhausted. But here she was awake only a few hours later. Unfortunately, her sleep had been accompanied by the nightmare of a masked man chasing her. And when she woke, she hadn't been able to stay in the house alone, even with the storm raging outside.

So she'd headed to town, hoping there was somewhere to go, anywhere. She told herself she wasn't checking on Steve even though he stayed at the back of her thoughts. Who was he? The good guy or the bad one? Everyone kept telling her he was a murderer, but every memory she had of him told her the opposite.

Up ahead, she saw that the coffee shop was open. *Oh, yes please,* she thought, and she pulled into a spot. A nice hot cup of gourmet coffee was just what she needed.

Despite the torrent of rain outside, the place was surprisingly busy. It was also loud, with everyone talking animatedly. But storms would do that. Warmth was already beginning to spread through Julie as she got in line.

She didn't intend to eavesdrop on the conversation of the two women in workout clothes in front of her, but she couldn't help overhearing. The brunette was nodding her head, her eyes wide. "Found his body first thing. He was literally standing over it, the gun in his hand."

"Oh my God," the blonde gasped, her hand to her throat. "Did the police get him?"

"Yes, thank goodness. But still, it's terrifying to think they let that monster out."

Julie went still.

"He's the one who killed that girl ten years ago, right?" the blonde asked. "What was her name? Shelly?"

"Simone."

"What is the world coming to?"

Julie reached up with a shaking hand and tapped the brunette on the shoulder. She tried to keep her voice even. "Excuse me, did you just say someone was murdered?"

Both women turned to her, obviously delighted to share the latest gossip with someone new. The blonde nodded. "Yes—it happened just a little while ago. You know Mel, from the diner? He was killed."

Julie's stomach bottomed out. *Mel?* She pictured Mel from two nights before when she'd caught up with friends. He'd hugged her and then dragged her to a booth to hear all about her new life. And he'd made her promise she'd stop in again before she left town.

"And it was that man who killed the Granger girl way back," the brunette chirped in. "That Steve Kane. They found him right over the body."

The blonde shook her head. "We were just saying it was incredible they let him out."

"It's amazing two brothers can be so different. Jack has done so much for this town, and that other one—well, it must be something in his head. There's just something wrong with him. They should lock him up and throw away the key."

Julie nodded absently, her mind overwhelmed. Steve had killed Mel? Why? When? "Do they know when Mel was killed?"

"It must have been this morning, because that's when they found him at the diner."

The brunette nodded. "That's two murders now. Elise Ingram and Mel. I swear, someone should just take that boy out back of the police station and shoot him."

The line moved, and the women stepped up to the counter and ordered their coffees. Julie stood behind them, shocked. He'd been out of prison for only a few days, and already two people were dead. A chill crept through her. What was going on?

The women stepped aside and Julie moved forward, her mind spinning.

"Can I help you?" asked the young man behind the counter.

Julie stared at him blankly.

"Ma'am? Can I help you?"

Julie gave herself a mental shake. "Um, a soy latte, please."

The boy nodded and turned to make her coffee.

A few minutes later, Julie was back in her car, although she couldn't remember exactly how she'd gotten there. Her latte was in her hand, which meant she must have paid for it. She took a sip. Yup, she'd added sugar, too. She must have been on automatic pilot.

She knew she should head home. Already she was beginning to shake. Her eyes flooded with tears. *Mel*. She leaned her head back, memories of Mel looping through her mind. And in each memory Steve was right next to her.

She swatted the tears away. *I need to go home.*

But the moment with Steve on the back porch of Micah's house came back to her.

She turned on the ignition. *I just need to make one quick stop first.*

CHAPTER FIFTY-ONE

JULIE PULLED her hood tighter around her although there was apparently no way to keep the rain out. Water seemed to be spraying in every direction. She could feel the beads of moisture slipping down her neck, under her jacket.

She jumped over a puddle and jogged up the steps of the police station, then took shelter at the side of the doors. *What exactly is my plan here?*

With a shaking hand she took a sip of her coffee, which by some miracle she hadn't dropped.

Just then two men dashed up the steps. "Julie?"

Russ pulled back his hood as he stepped into the covered area.

"Hey, Russ."

Russ glanced at the man next to him. Declan Reed, Julie realized with a shock. She'd heard he'd gotten stationed back here when Steve had gotten arrested. But she hadn't seen him in years.

He nodded at her. "Ms. Granger," he said, then turned back to Russ. "I'll see you inside." He disappeared through the doors.

Russ stood awkwardly next to her. "Um, are you all right?"

"Yeah. I'm fine." She nodded.

Russ leaned down. "I guess you heard about Mel?"

She saw the concern on his face. He'd always been a good friend. Fact was, she'd had a lot of good friends here. She'd made friends since she left, too, of course, but there was something about the people you grew up with. They knew you from mud pies to prom dates. And no one had been a better friend growing up than she had. Steve. She looked away, blinking back the tears. "Yeah. I heard. I can't believe it."

"Me neither." Russ's normally calm face was troubled.

With a shock, Julie realized he'd probably seen Mel, been at the crime scene. "Are *you* okay?" she asked.

"I'm supposed to be. But that..." He shook his head. "I wasn't prepared for that."

She placed her hand on his arm. "I'm sorry."

Russ's chin trembled and he let out a breath. "What are you doing here, anyway?

Julie shrugged. "I don't know. When I heard about Mel, and that Steve had been arrested, I just kind of came here. Can you tell me anything?"

Russ glanced through the glass doors of the station. No one was paying them any attention. "It looks like it happened last night."

"But I thought they arrested Steve this morning."

"They did."

"Wasn't he locked up all last night?"

"Yup."

"I don't understand."

Russ opened his mouth and then shut it, shaking his head. "The chief has a bit of a blind spot when it comes to Steve."

"What about Declan? What's he doing here?"

"Steve called him after he found Mel."

"And Declan called you?"

"No, actually—" Russ broke off. "I really shouldn't be telling you any of this."

Julie raised her hands. "Who am I going to tell? Besides, who has a more vested interest than me?"

"Julie, I know that. But don't you think it would be better if you just put this all behind you? You don't need to concern yourself with this now."

She pictured how Steve had looked at her last night. She had thought seeing him would bring resolution—confirm everything she'd been told for the last ten years—but it had only made everything more confusing. Yet at the same time, she knew in her bones that he couldn't kill Mel. Even if she could believe he killed Simone or Elise, she'd seen him with Mel. She knew how much Mel meant to him. There was no way.

But Russ was right—she should put it all behind her. Whatever Steve did now had nothing to do with her. The damage to her and her family was done.

She nodded with a sigh. "You're right. I'll see you later." She started to head back for her car, but then turned. "Just let me know if anything happens, okay?"

"Julie..." Russ said, drawing out her name.

She shrugged. "I just want to be kept in the loop. That's all."

"That's all?"

She nodded. "What else would it be?"

Russ gave her a pointed look—one of those looks that only old friends could give one another and convey a world of meaning.

She put up her hands and turned to the car. "Don't answer that."

CHAPTER FIFTY-TWO

DECLAN NODDED at Dee as he crossed through the doors leading into the squad room. He was still a little surprised at seeing Julie Granger. What was she doing here?

He shook off his curiosity. That would have to wait. He needed to see about Steve first.

"Where's Steve?" he asked Dee.

She gestured toward the cells. "Cell one."

Declan could feel the eyes of the officers in the squad room on him as he headed to the cellblock. As a state policeman, he already wasn't popular. But now that he was viewed as helping Steve, he was downright unwelcome.

Declan was surprised to find an officer stationed by the holding cells. That was odd.

Only one of the four cells was occupied. Declan looked in and blanched. "Jesus."

Steve's face was a mess. There was a laceration on the side of his head, and both his cheekbone and eye were bruised.

Jack looked up from his chair next to Steve's cot. He rose,

walked over to the cell door, pushed it open, and stepped out. Now Declan understood why the officer was stationed there.

Jack motioned for Declan to follow him a little distance away, out of earshot of the officer.

Declan gestured to the cell. "What the hell happened?"

"According to Keith, Steve fell."

"Yeah, I'm guessing with a little help. He okay?"

Jack shrugged, but his eyes looked worried. "I don't know. I think he might have a concussion. I'd get him released to a hospital, but of course with the bridge out, that's not an option. So I'm staying with him. I don't feel safe leaving him here alone. What about the crime scene? Did you learn anything?"

"Single killer. Almost three dozen stab wounds." Declan paused. "I think he wanted us to think it was a crazed, angry attack."

"You don't think so?"

"No. Actually I think it was pretty unemotional, despite all the wounds. The guy took the time to clean up after himself. And it was done way before Steve showed up. Sometime between midnight and three."

A smile slowly broke across Jack's face. "Which means..."

Declan nodded. "I'm heading to Keith now." He clapped Jack on the shoulder.

Before he walked away, he went back and glanced once more into Steve's cell. Bad idea. It just made his anger boil. He turned away, his fists clenched.

When he got to Keith's office, he stopped outside to take a couple of deep breaths and count to ten. But it didn't work. He was still ready to rip someone apart.

Calm down. You can't help Steve if you're all worked up.

He stepped into Keith's doorway.

Keith looked up with a growl. "I don't have time for you right now."

Declan stepped in and closed the door behind him. "Make time."

Keith glared at him and pointed toward the cellblock. "Kane is staying in that cell."

"He didn't kill Mel. Mel died between midnight and three a.m."

"How the hell could you know that?"

"I did an internal temperature on Mel, and the rigor mortis confirms it."

Keith smirked. "So, what, you're a medical examiner now?"

Declan clenched his fist, warning himself not to take the bait. "No. But I'm trained in forensics."

Keith crossed his arms over his chest. "I still have plenty of cause to keep—"

Declan lashed out. "So what is it you're suggesting? That while Steve was in your jail cell, he escaped, slipped past every officer on duty, ran down the road, committed a very bloody murder, cleaned himself and the murder scene up, and then slipped back into his cell? Is that your theory?"

Keith's eyes narrowed to slits.

"Don't you get it?" Declan said. "The Millners Kill Police Department *is* his alibi. Steve didn't do it. And the longer you focus on him, the longer the *actual* murderer has to get away."

"I can hold him for twenty-four hours."

"To what end?" Declan said, and he knew he sounded exasperated. "It wasn't him. So during this storm, when you're stretched for manpower as it is, you're going to leave an officer here to guard a man you *know* didn't commit the crime. And a man who needs medical attention at that! Any chance the deputy who drove Steve here can explain that?"

Keith ignored the question. "Kane needs to be watched."

Declan threw up his hands. "Where do you think he's going to go? We're cut off here. And if something happens to Steve while he's in police custody, I will make it my life's work to see that *you* are held responsible." He clamped his mouth shut even though he wanted to keep ranting. He was afraid that if he didn't stop now, he wouldn't be able to keep himself from leaping over Keith's desk and making Keith's face look ten times worse than Steve's.

Keith gritted his teeth and tried to stare Declan down.

Declan met his glare, unflinching.

Keith looked away with a growl. "Fine. He can be released. But if anyone else gets hurt, it's on your head."

CHAPTER FIFTY-THREE

STEVE OPENED his eyes and stared at the bright fluorescent lighting. He blinked, and his head pounded. He held a hand over his eyes and groaned.

"He lives."

Steve squinted over at Jack. "Not so sure yet." He sat up and slowly swung his legs over the edge of the bed.

Jack held out a bottle of water and two aspirin. Steve took them, swallowed the aspirin, and took a long swig of water. He leaned back against the cement wall. "So, are you locked up in here as well, or just visiting?"

Jack smiled. "Just visiting. But I don't plan on letting you be locked up here for very long."

Steve started to laugh, but it made his head pound, making him groan instead. "Pretty sure good old Keith is going to keep me in here for a while. How long have I been here?"

Jack glanced at his watch. "Going on four hours now."

Steve's stomach growled, but he didn't want to eat. The idea of food made him think of Mel, and that chased away his appetite. "You know about Mel?"

Jack's voice softened. "Yeah. Declan took care of him. Mel's at the funeral home now."

Steve's head jerked up. He took in a couple of deep breaths, waiting for the pain to pass. "The funeral home? What about an autopsy?"

"They'll do one, but not until the bridge is back up."

The bridge. Right. He'd forgotten about that little tidbit. "Does Grandma know?"

Jack nodded. "I called her."

Steve closed his eyes. "Damn. I really wish she didn't have to know."

"Well, better from me than someone else."

That was true enough. "Why are you still here?"

Jack gave him a long look. "I know you didn't kill Mel. Same way I know you didn't kill Elise Ingram or Simone Granger. And I don't trust these deputies. I figure I'll just hang around and make sure you're safe."

Steve stared at him in surprise. He wasn't used to someone looking out for him. It felt... well, nice. "Thanks."

"Besides, I don't think you'll be here much longer."

"You always were an optimist."

Russ appeared at the cell door with Declan beside him. "You're free to go," Russ said.

Steve stared. "What?"

Declan pulled the cell door open. "You're free to go. Although the chief cautions you to stay in the area." Declan smiled. "So no swimming in raging flood waters trying to escape."

Jack pulled Steve to his feet. "Come on. Let's get moving before Keith changes his mind."

Jack helped Steve into the hall, and Declan helped support him on the other side.

"How?" Steve asked as they walked.

"Seems you have an alibi," Declan said.

"I do?"

Declan nodded. "The Millners Kill Police Department. Mel was killed while you were locked up."

Ten minutes later, Steve rested his head on the window of his brother's car. Jack drove slowly. In part because of the weather, and in part because of him. Steve appreciated it. His head pounded with every turn, and his cheekbones felt like they were swollen to twice their normal size.

"We're home," Jack said quietly. Steve opened his eyes. He must have dozed off.

He looked outside. The rain was lashing down. Little rivers of water were flowing down either side of the street. And the porch seemed awfully far away.

"You all right?" Jack asked.

"Yeah. Let's go." Steve opened the door and stepped out into the rain. He didn't even try running to avoid getting wet. Honestly, he wasn't sure his legs were going to stay under him as it was. He shuffled up the front steps. Jack stood on the porch, patiently waiting for Steve to catch up before opening the front door.

As soon as they entered, Bess came bustling in from the kitchen. "Thank God, I was getting—" She let out a shriek and ran over to Steve.

"Oh, Steve. What did they do to you?" She gently cupped his face. There was a tremble in her hands and she looked pale.

Steve placed his hands over hers. "I'm okay. It's nothing."

Tears crested in her eyes. "They can't do this to you."

Steve pulled her into his chest. Her shoulders heaved. Damn. Seeing her hurt was worse than actually getting hurt. He pulled her away. "Why don't you go get a cup of tea? I'm going to get cleaned up."

"No. I should help you—"

Steve looked over at his brother. "Jack."

Jack nodded and put his arm around their grandmother. "Come on, Grandma. I'll get you a cup of tea, and then maybe you can make Steve and me something to eat."

Steve's heart broke at the anguish on her face. "But I need—"

Jack began to lead her away. "It'll be all right."

She looked up at him. "It's not fair what they did to him. It's not right."

"I know, I know," he soothed. "I'll take care of it."

Steve watched them go, his heart heavy. He leaned back against the wall. Maybe he needed to move out of town and take Grandma with him. *Maybe we could live over on the mainland, and I could just come back for work at the diner.*

The thought brought him up short. He no longer had a job. Who knew what would happen to the diner with Mel gone. Maybe Shawn would take over after a while. Maybe it would close for good. It was hard to imagine anyone would ever want to eat there now, knowing what had happened in that room.

I'm unemployed. The thought struck fear in him. *They'll send me back to prison.* He felt horrible worrying about that with everything going on, but he couldn't help it. He'd focused on his release date for years. Now after being out for only four days, he might already be going back.

He closed his eyes. *Mel's dead, and I'm heading back to prison. How the hell did all of this happen?* Then again, maybe things would be better with him back inside. His release only seemed to bring disaster.

A soft knock sounded at the front door. Steve sighed. *No more bad news*, he prayed.

He debated for a second just ignoring whoever it was, but then he crossed to the door and glanced through the transom glass. Julie.

He opened it. "Hey."

"Oh my God."

Steve groaned. He hadn't actually looked in a mirror yet, but the reaction of his grandmother, and now Julie, told him all he needed to know about his appearance. "It's nothing. It looks worse than it is."

"I doubt that." She swung a backpack off her shoulder. "I brought medical supplies."

"How did you know?"

"Russ. As soon as you left the station, he called me. Come on. Let's get you looked at."

Julie walked past him and headed up the stairs. As Steve followed, memories of the thousands of times they'd pounded up these same stairs to wash their hands before dinner flashed through Steve's mind.

But he said nothing, just followed her to the bathroom. Right now he was beyond exhausted. It was an effort just to make his feet move.

Julie turned on the shower. "Hop in and warm up. I'll go grab you some clothes."

He stripped out of his soaked clothes as soon as she closed the door. He stepped into the shower and felt the relief as the heat from the shower soaked into his bones. He stayed in the hot shower for a long time, his hands leaning against the wall. It was an effort just to stay upright. His eyes had begun to close when he heard the door open. He jerked his head up and winced as pain slashed through it.

"Here are your clothes. Give me a yell when you're decent," Julie said before closing the door again.

He closed his eyes again, letting the warmth flow through him. After a while, another knock sounded. "Steve? You all right?" Julie asked.

Steve jerked his eyes open. If he stayed in here any longer he was going to fall asleep. "Yeah. Be out in a minute."

He turned off the water, toweled off, and pulled on the

clothes Julie had left for him. Then he opened the door. "All good."

Julie stepped into the bathroom and closed the lid on the toilet. "Sit."

He did as he was ordered. She examined his face with a tsk. "Look up," she said. He did. "I'm going to need to sew that."

"Okay," he said, feeling weariness fall over him.

She cleaned his face with a warm, damp towel, then placed something cold on his cut. "This will numb up the area." She waited a few seconds. "Can you feel that?"

"No."

"Good."

She stood between his legs and began to sew. Steve tried not to focus on the fact that her breasts were right at his eye level. He closed his eyes. She smelled like lavender.

He must have dozed off again because she patted him on the shoulder. "Steve," she whispered softly. He looked up into her face. Her hair fell over her shoulder, gently brushing his chin. "You're all done."

He nodded.

"Come on." She put an arm around his shoulders, pulling him up. "You look exhausted."

She helped him to his room and lay him down on the bed. To Steve, nothing had ever felt so good as that bed. He was so tired, he wanted to weep with joy.

Julie pulled a blanket over him. "I'm sorry about this, but I'm going to have to have someone wake you every hour, to make sure you don't have a concussion. But for now, get some sleep."

"Mm-kay. Thanks, Jules," Steve said, losing the battle to stay awake.

And maybe he imagined it, but he could have sworn she ran her hand through his hair as she whispered, "You're welcome, Steve."

CHAPTER FIFTY-FOUR

IT WAS dark by the time Julie dashed out to her car and jumped into the driver's seat. She'd now learned to keep a towel in the passenger seat, and she used it to wipe down her arms and wring her hair. As she did, she looked at Bess's house in the fading light.

When Russ had asked her to tend to Steve, she had planned on just stitching him up and then heading out. But Bess had been so distraught, and Jack had wanted to go into town to see what was going on, so she'd ended up staying.

She was fairly certain Steve didn't have a concussion. She'd woken him up every hour, although she was late once because she fell asleep in the chair next to his bed. She shook her head. A week ago she never would have been predicted she'd be taking care of Steve Kane. It was surreal. Everything about being back in Millners Kill was surreal.

And yet, at the same time, it was like no time had passed.

A figure moved in one of the upstairs rooms—Steve's room. Julie watched his shadow cross from one window to the next. It was good to see that he was awake and able to move around. But her stomach clenched when she pictured his battered face. He didn't kill Mel. The police knew that. They'd had him in custody at the time of Mel's death. Yet they'd still done that to him.

Steve's light turned out, but she knew he wasn't going to bed. A few more crank calls had come in while she was there. Steve was heading downstairs to sleep in his grandfather's old chair, with a bat next to him. In case someone tried to hurt his grandmother.

Julie placed the key in the ignition and turned it on, but she didn't make a move to leave. Since Steve had gotten back in town, he'd saved three lives. And each time, his own life had been at risk. Were those the actions of a murderer? Was he just trying to make up for past actions? And what about the new murders? Who was responsible for those? It couldn't be Steve.

Was it possible there were two murderers at large? Had Steve murdered her sister, and someone else murdered Elise and Mel?

In medical school, her professors had hammered home Occam's razor when diagnosing patients: that the explanation requiring the fewest assumptions was the most likely. So what was more likely: that there were currently two murderers in town, one current and one from the past? Or that there was only one murderer, both then and now?

She pictured Steve's eyes, felt the heat of his hand as she'd held it when she checked his pulse. Butterflies raced through her stomach. She leaned forward and rested her chin on the steering wheel. *God damn it.*

CHAPTER FIFTY-FIVE

DECLAN SAT at one of the back tables in the faculty lounge of the elementary school and rubbed his hands over his face. Two bodies and one kidnapping attempt in as many days, plus the bridge had been completely washed out. And just before it all began, Steve returned to town.

Declan had listened to the 911 tape about the diner, but the voice was muffled, and he was pretty sure whoever it was had tried to disguise his voice. All he could say for certain was that the caller was male. So there was no help there.

He'd been going over and over the two murders and the attempted kidnapping. He knew in his gut they were all connected. It was too big a stretch to believe that a town as small as this one could have multiple murderers at work at the same time.

But he couldn't find anything concrete that actually linked them. The three victims were all different ages and ethnicities. They lived in different parts of town. They were grabbed differently as well. Elise had apparently been grabbed on the way home from work. Mel was attacked in his diner. And Micah was taken from his bed.

And these murders all started when Steve came back to town. That was a coincidence that couldn't be overlooked. Somehow, this all had to tie to Steve. But how?

The front door banged outside the office. Declan looked up as Russ, water running off his poncho, appeared in the doorway, two large boxes in his arms.

Declan smiled. "Any problems?"

Russ placed the boxes on the table closest to the door. "No. Luckily, the town going crazy distracted Dee long enough for me to slip these out of the station. Although I did have to swing by the station three times until I had those conditions."

Declan walked over and read the label on one of the boxes. *Case File 12098: Simone Granger (Box 1 of 2)*. He glanced at Russ. "You sure you're okay with this? You could get in a lot of trouble if anyone realizes you've grabbed them."

Russ pulled off his poncho, shook it, and hung it on the rack by the door. "I'm sure. You think these latest murders are related to Simone's, and so do I. So hopefully these files will tell us something."

Declan flipped the lid off the first box. "Did you get a chance to send out those fingerprints?"

Russ shook his head. "No. We're still on snail mail, remember?"

Declan groaned. He'd forgotten about that. The state had automatic fingerprint machines, but in a place like Millners Kill, that kind of equipment was viewed as an extravagance. Small departments like this had to make a card and send it to the state via the United States Post Office. The state would then scan it into SAFIS and see if they got a hit. But there was no mail service with the bridge out, and even if there were, there was no guarantee they'd get a hit back quickly.

"But I marked it priority," Russ said. "As soon as we can get mail out the door, it'll be on its way."

Declan reached into the first box and pulled out a stack of papers with a sigh—tonight's reading. "All right then. Let's get to work."

CHAPTER FIFTY-SIX

JULIE LET herself through the front door and dropped her backpack on the table by the door. Behind her, the storm blew the door wide, ushering leaves and rain into the front foyer. She wrestled it closed and turned the deadbolt, then leaned against it, a puddle of water developing under her feet.

After leaving Steve's, she'd been too restless to head straight home, so she'd driven around the island. Millners Kill was a disaster. A few roads had full-fledged rivers running through them, others had giant puddles, and electric lines were down all over the place. It didn't take Julie long to realize she needed to get inside. Being out was pure suicide tonight. But even once she'd decided to head straight home, it still took her over an hour to get here. She'd had to backtrack at least five times due to road blockages, and she couldn't chance driving any faster than ten miles per hour.

She stripped off all of her clothes—just the short walk from the car had soaked them—and dropped them next to the door. Wearing just her bra and underwear, she walked to the laundry room just off the kitchen, flipping on the lights as she went. The house felt less empty with the lights on.

She got out her sweatpants, an old t-shirt, and some socks from the dryer—like a college student, she'd brought her dirty laundry with her on this trip—and pulled them on. Luckily, she had done her laundry as soon as she'd arrived, before the power went out.

She headed into the kitchen and pulled a coffee mug from the almost empty cabinets. Her parents had cleaned out most things, but she guessed they'd left a few things behind for "staging"—buyers supposedly didn't like to visit a completely empty house.

She hit the button of the Keurig for a large mug of coffee. *Thank God they didn't take you, my little friend.* She poured in a little sugar and took a sip. She nearly swooned with happiness.

But as much as the coffee warmed her, it couldn't distract from her worries. She'd tried to call her parents on the drive over, but she hadn't been able to get a signal. She knew they'd be worried not being able to reach her. She sighed. *Well, at least the power's still on.*

Two people had been murdered since Steve had come back to town. And she knew Steve hadn't killed Mel; she was sure of that. If, that is, the time of death was right. Which meant, by Occam's razor, he didn't kill Elise either. And then there was Micah. Why would someone grab him?

Julie walked into the den and turned on the light next to the couch. It gave the room a soft warm glow. She walked to the window and watched the storm rage outside. It made the empty house feel even emptier. She wrapped her hands around the mug, wishing the warmth would seep into the rest of her body.

She winced as she pictured Steve's face. She knew she should feel vindication. But she didn't.

Dark clouds whirled by outside. Julie went to the couch in

the den and placed her mug on the side table. She pulled the blanket off the back of the couch and wrapped it around her, then grabbed the remote and turned on the TV. She needed noise. She needed to feel like she wasn't alone in this big old house.

For a while she watched an old sitcom, but her eyes kept drifting to the large bay window. She could feel eyes on her. The hair on the back of her neck began to stand up.

"Oh, enough," she said after a few minutes. She strode over to the window and looked out. The streetlights and the moon were bright enough to illuminate the yard. And it was still empty. The only things moving were the tall evergreens blowing in the wind. *No one's there. You're working yourself up over nothing.*

Nevertheless, she pulled down the blinds. Then she walked the house, making sure all the doors and windows were shut and locked.

She stopped at her backpack by the front door and pulled out her Glock. She'd had it with her all day; she felt safer knowing it was nearby.

Back in the den, she placed the gun on the side table next to the couch, then curled up again. This time she really forced herself to focus on the show. She needed to stop creating fears where there was nothing.

CHAPTER FIFTY-SEVEN

HIDDEN among the spruces in Julie's yard, he watched Julie settle in on the couch. How many times had he stood out here and watched her when he was younger?

And tonight the show had been especially good: he had watched her pad through the house in just her black bra and panties. She still looked good.

Rain ran down his face. He didn't care. The rain was irrelevant. Julie was the reason the game could continue. He'd worried after Steve's arrest that it would be all over. Killing Mel could have turned into a mistake. He was too close. The connection too easily made. But the opportunity had presented itself and he just couldn't resist. He should have been smarter, though, held back.

He frowned. He didn't like thinking he wasn't in control. Control was everything. *A momentary glitch—that was all.*

He'd been away from the blood for too long. And after Elise, and then Micah—well, it was understandable that he had wanted more than a taste. So he had plunged the knife into Mel—again, and again, and again. The rage had poured out of him. God, the release.

Psychologists would say that he got some sort of sexual release from the deaths. But they understood so little. Sex was physical and done. Blood, death... it was so much more. Dripping in it, bringing it to the surface, having that power over life and dead—it was beyond anything this life could offer. It was the fulfillment of a life's purpose. He was at his best in that moment. He was perfection.

A shadow passed the den window again, drawing his attention. *Ah, back in the den.* Julie had wandered the house for a bit, but now she was back. He wanted to move closer, peer in the window. But that would unwise. He couldn't risk being spotted.

He blew a kiss to the window as Julie closed the blinds. His angel. Because of her, the game would be his best yet. *Until we meet again, my Julie.*

CHAPTER FIFTY-EIGHT

DECLAN SAT in the faculty lounge of the elementary school, pushing through the Granger file. He'd run over to his sister's house to check on his sister and dad, but he'd been too antsy to stay, so he'd headed back to the school again.

He was missing something. He knew it. He pushed back from the desk and rubbed his eyes. The power had shut off an hour ago, so he was forced to use a lantern, and it was straining his eyes. And despite all the time he was putting in, none of it seemed to be helping. So far he hadn't figured out much of anything.

He kept coming back to the one detail about the case that had been bothering him for over ten years: the bloody clothes found in Steve's closet. They were a big part of the reason why Steve was pursued as a suspect to begin with. But before Steve's trial began, those clothes disappeared from lockup. They had never been recovered.

Declan was sure that someone had long since turned them to ash. But who had taken them? And why? It couldn't have been

Steve because he was in custody when the items disappeared. So who else?

Keith, of course, had dismissed the disappearance as a mix-up —the clothes had been misplaced, or maybe taken by some crazy stalker obsessed with the case—but Declan had never bought that. That evidence could have nailed the coffin shut on Steve— or it could have set him free.

Declan pushed the papers away. There were no answers here. He stood up and walked to the window. Large ponds seemed to have popped up all over the island. Main Street was now a river. In the middle of it all was a killer. And Declan had no idea who it was.

Steve was alibied for both the attempted abduction of Micah and the death of Mel. For Elise's as well, although he was wasn't as confident on the time of death for that one. But he still didn't think it was Steve. And the likelihood that there were two murderers in such a tiny town was so low it was laughable—which meant Steve wasn't responsible for *any* of the recent killings. *So who, then?*

A squad car pulled into the lot. Declan watched Russ get out and duck into the front entrance. Good. Declan had appreciated the young cop's help earlier, but then Russ had had to go back on duty, leaving Declan to stare at the files alone. And to be honest, Declan could use the company right now.

Russ walked into the lounge looking a little worse for wear. He unzipped his raincoat to reveal a shirt that was splattered with mud.

"What happened?" Declan asked.

Russ pulled out a chair and slumped into it. "Flood waters are all over town. Giant puddles, too. People aren't realizing how deep the water is, and they're driving in and getting stuck. I've pulled people out of at least five cars now." He gestured to his shirt. "I'm out of clean shirts."

Declan poured him a cup out of a silver thermos on the table.

Russ nodded his thanks and took a sip. He looked back at Declan, a smile on his face. "Hot cocoa?"

"I made some at my sister's. I remembered you saying you didn't like coffee."

Russ took a big drink and then sighed. "Oh, this so hits the spot."

"Did you get a chance to check on the fingerprint?"

They had decided to scan the fingerprint and send it over by email. The folks at the state didn't like deviations from procedure, but under the circumstances, Declan figured they could make an exception.

Russ shook his head. "By the time I got back to the station, the power was out. We'll have to wait until it comes back up."

"Damn. That's our best lead."

Silence fell over the two men. Declan knew Russ was on the edge of exhaustion, and he wasn't doing much better himself. But he had to keep trying. He needed to feel like he was making headway—or that he at least had a plan.

"You know," Russ said slowly. "They still have the old finger-print cards in the basement of the station."

Declan looked over and raised his eyebrows. "You want to manually compare the print to every fingerprint in those files?"

Russ shuddered. "God, no. But we still have Steve's from back then. We could at least compare his and rule him out." The words Russ didn't say hung in the air between them: *Or prove it was actually him.*

Declan knew matching fingerprints wasn't as easy as most people thought. It took an expert or a computer program to discern the differences between the loops, whorls, and arches on a finger. Even then there was debate as to how many similarities were needed although most experts agreed you needed at least twelve to declare a match.

Declan shrugged. "It's worth a shot. We could try, but unless there's something that really stands out in the fingerprint, I don't see how that will..."

Russ's head had fallen to his chest. He jerked his head back up and blinked his eyes repeatedly. *He's literally asleep on his feet,* Declan thought.

"How about we check that out first thing in the morning?" Declan said.

Russ blinked his eyes a few more times. "I can get to it tonight."

Declan shook his head. "No. I think you need some sleep, and I know I do. We'll get to it first thing in the morning."

Russ stood up. "Okay. You going back to your sister's?"

Declan glanced outside, imagining the flood-covered streets. "No. I'll just bunk down in the med center."

"Okay. I'm going to head back to the station, bunk there. Just in case." Russ headed out. Declan walked to the window, taking a sip of cocoa as he watched Russ's squad car pull slowly out of the parking lot.

With a sigh, Declan headed back to the table. He looked over the boxes. Each one had the case identifying information printed neatly on it. The handwriting was neat—obviously a woman's. *Must be Dee. Nothing happens in that station without her.*

He went still. *Nothing in that station happens without her. I am so stupid.*

She'd been questioned at the time about the missing evidence, but had said no one had been in the station. But now that years had passed, maybe she had a different story to tell. *And maybe this one has more characters.*

He grabbed his jacket and headed for the door. Apparently he'd lied to Russ. Because there *was* someplace he needed to go.

CHAPTER FIFTY-NINE

STEVE SAT in his grandfather's chair, every bone in his body aching. He was glad Jack was here to help with his grandmother. He hated seeing her face when she caught sight of him. It was like she aged a little more each time.

The picture of Mel lying on the diner floor flashed through his mind. He gripped the arms of the chair, the grief and anger pouring through him. Mel hadn't deserved that. He was a good man. And as of right now, there were no leads. Jack had said that Declan didn't have any evidence besides the time of death. And Keith, of course, was next to useless.

Steve shifted in his chair and forced himself to think of something else. Julie's face floated through his mind. He felt the ghost of Julie's hand on his skin. Her touch had been feather light, and more sensual than anything he'd ever felt. At one point during the afternoon, he'd woken up to find her sleeping in the chair next to him. He'd stayed quiet and just watched her. She'd looked so peaceful, so young. Her skin was flawless. She was stunning. And for some reason, she had stayed to make sure he was okay.

Stupid. She was just helping you out. There was nothing more to it than her being a good person. He knew that was true, but a part of him couldn't help but wish there had been a little more to it.

She had left only after Jack had returned. The house felt a little emptier without her presence.

Steve's gaze drifted to the stairs. Jack had looked so tired, so worn down when he'd come in. Steve might have been the one locked up, but each of the people touched by Simone's death had done their own time in their own way, even Jack. Always having to be the good brother, always having people whisper about who Steve was and what he had done. Even though it wasn't fair and there was nothing Steve could have done to prevent it, he still couldn't help but feel guilty.

Steve let out a yawn and rubbed his eyes. *I can't believe I'm still tired.* He knew he'd been asleep for hours, but apparently his body still wanted more. He'd slept most of the day.

Steve closed his eyes and let sleep take him. He worried that the image of Mel would haunt his dreams. But he shouldn't have. He dreamed of Julie.

CHAPTER SIXTY

DECLAN LEANED FORWARD, his chest all but pressed up against the steering wheel. The windshield wipers beat furiously but still he could barely make out the road.

"This is stupid," he muttered.

He had barely gone faster than fifteen miles per hour the whole ride. Two of the roads he'd planned on taking were completely washed out. He'd had to backtrack, making his way through the rain-filled streets. A couple of times he'd held his breath going through a puddle the depth of which he wasn't sure about.

Finally, though, he was heading uphill on Franklin Street. He spotted Dee's small brick ranch on the right. Dee and her husband, Bud, had lived there for thirty years and raised three girls together. But Dee lived alone now; Bud had passed away just last fall from lung cancer after being on disability for years, and all the girls were grown and had moved away for better opportunities. Declan wondered why Dee stayed on. She didn't have many friends. In fact, he couldn't think of one. Her life had been Bud and her girls. Now she kept to herself, only socializing at church.

Declan pulled into the drive and turned off the headlights. The lights were on in the front living room. Declan knew Dee had a generator—most people on the island did. The clock on the dash read 9:18. He listened to the rain pound on his roof. He wanted to wait until the rain eased a little bit, but as that didn't seem likely to happen anytime soon, and he hadn't brought a sleeping bag or food, he probably should just suck it up.

Steeling himself, he pushed open the door.

The wind pushed back. He wrestled his way out of the car, wondering yet again why the hell he was doing this, tonight of all nights. Simone Granger had been gone for ten years. Steve was finally out of prison. Certainly this could wait a few more days, at least until the storm blew over. But something inside was pushing him to find the answers as soon as possible. With the recent murders, the town had turned into a powder keg. And Declan couldn't help but feel that these new murders were tied to Simone's.

Running as fast as the weather would allow, he ducked into the carport next to Dee's house. Shaking himself like a dog, he blew out a breath.

The light next to the carport entrance came on and the door opened. "Declan Reed, what the hell are you doing?"

A bead of water rolled from his hair, down the middle of his forehead, and off the end of his nose. "Hey, Dee. Uh, I just had a couple of questions for you."

Dee looked pointedly outside. "And you thought tonight was the best night to ask them?"

He shrugged. "I'm like a dog with a bone."

She held open the door. "Well, leave your jacket out there and come on in."

Declan shrugged off his jacket and hung it on an exposed nail next to the door. He slipped off his shoes in the small mud room and then followed Dee into the kitchen. The kitchen was circa 1960, with a white-gray linoleum floor, dark wood cabinets, and a Corian countertop. It might not be fancy, but it was neat.

Dee gestured to the old wooden table tucked under the windows in the corner. "I just made some tea. Take a seat."

Declan did and watched while Dee poured from a teapot into two mugs. She placed one in front of Declan before sitting across from him. He reached down and took a sip. "Chamomile?" he asked, surprised.

Dee nodded. "My daughter Lorraine got it for me and Bud. It helped him sleep. Helps me sleep too."

"I'm sorry about his passing."

She waved away his words. "It was his time. He was on borrowed time ever since the mill."

Declan nodded, knowing what she meant. Bud had been in an accident at the lumber mill about twelve years ago. A stack of logs had come loose from their holdings, and Bud had been crushed. The bones in his legs were broken, but more critically, his spine had been damaged. He'd been confined to a wheelchair from that point on.

"So, Declan, what can I do for you?" Dee asked.

"I wanted to talk to you about the Granger case. About the evidence that went missing."

Dee raised her eyebrows. "Why on earth do you want to ask about that now?"

"The night the clothes went missing, you were on the desk. And there was only one deputy on duty."

Dee kept her eyes focused on her tea. "Yes. That's right."

"Did anyone else stop by the station that night? Anyone have access to the evidence room?"

Dee shifted her eyes away to the window. "It's all in the report."

Declan clenched his hands around his mug and studied her. "Dee, a kid went to prison. If someone took those clothes, we need to know."

Dee shook her head, but she wouldn't meet Declan's gaze. "Why would someone take evidence? And even if they had, how would that help anyone now? Steve's out. It's over. Just let it go."

"Dee, those clothes were supposed to have been sent out for DNA testing the next day. They might have proven Steve didn't do it."

"You can't know that."

"No—I can't. And neither can you, or anyone else, because someone took that evidence. Someone stole our best chance of either proving or disproving Steve's innocence. So I'm asking you again: Did anyone else visit the station that night?"

Dee looked away. Declan didn't say anything, letting the quiet and Dee's conscience put the pressure on her to respond.

Finally Dee spoke. Her voice was quiet. "You have to understand—Bud had just gotten hurt. The mill refused Bud's workman's comp claim. They said it was his fault. I was the only source of income and the one with the insurance. I needed to keep my job."

A tingle of excitement ran across Declan's skin. He knew there was more. He struggled to keep his tone even. "I understand."

Dee nodded. "He never threatened me or my job directly. But the next morning, when the chief announced the evidence was gone, he had this hard look in his eyes. I swear he stared right through me. And I knew the threat was there."

Declan stilled. "Dee, what are you saying? Who else was at the station that night?"

Dee looked up, her eyes filled with guilt. "Keith. Keith was there."

DAY 5

"Well, it's over, folks. The meteorologists have officially declared the storm done. But now we've got the cleanup. The towns closer to Lake Ontario got the worst of it, but pretty much every town north of Poughkeepsie has been hit hard. Flooding is rampant. So for those of you stuck, I hope you have the board games and puzzles ready, because it's going to be a long haul.

And if you're wondering what's happening over in Millners Kill, well, so are the rest of us. With the cell towers down and many of the landlines, there's been no information coming out of there. So let's just hope they're all keeping safe and that the authorities can get over there sooner rather than later."

CHAPTER SIXTY-ONE

THE STORM HAD FINALLY PASSED. It was drizzling, but at least the torrential downpour had ended. Trees were down all over the place, and Bess's house had lost power sometime during the night. Without the bridge to the mainland, Steve wasn't sure when the repair guys would get the power up and running again, but he had stocked up enough wood to keep the stove going, and that would keep the house warm at least for a few days.

Luckily, Steve's grandmother still had a landline. It was an old rotary phone that had been in the house as long as he could remember, but beggars couldn't be choosers. Although, seeing as how everyone now relied almost entirely on digital phones and cell phones, Steve wasn't sure there was anyone they could call.

He grabbed his jacket after breakfast and headed for the back door.

"Where are you going, honey?" his grandmother asked.

He kissed her cheek. "Just going to see if the storm did any damage."

He let himself out the back. A few more branches were down, and a tree had come down across part of the driveway. It had just missed his brother's car. But all in all, it could have been far worse. He made his way around the side of the house, his spirits lifting. *Looks like we escaped the worst of it.*

But when he turned the corner at the front of the house, he went still. *Oh my God.* He couldn't believe what he was seeing.

He forced himself to walk up the front steps, his emotions warring between anger and fear. He let himself in the front door just as his brother was coming down the stairs. Jack had stayed the night and was planning on staying until the power was restored.

"Hey, is that bacon I smell?" Jack called out.

"You know it is," Bess called back from the kitchen.

Jack smiled and looked at Steve. "That woman is trying to make me fat."

"Yeah. You seem to really resent the cooking," Steve said, trying to keep his tone light.

Jack rubbed his stomach. "Hey, I don't want to hurt her feelings."

Keeping his voice down, Steve said, "Before you eat... I want to show you something outside."

Jack raised his eyebrows. "Now?"

Steve nodded, and something in his expression must have gotten through to Jack.

"Gran, keep that breakfast warm," Jack called. "I'll be right in." He grabbed his jacket and followed Steve out the front door.

"What's going on?" he asked.

"Turn around," Steve said, his voice heavy.

Jack did—and went still. "Jesus."

The word "MURDERER" had been sprayed across the boarded up windows in black paint.

Steve turned to Jack. "Help me take these boards down before Gran sees them?"

It only took about ten minutes to get the boards off and into the garage. But even then, Steve couldn't get them out of his mind. His chest tightened at the thought of someone being out here while they'd all slept. Was it the same person who'd thrown the brick the other day? What if they came back when his grandmother was home alone? He couldn't let that happen.

He grabbed Jack's arm before they went in through the back door. "We don't tell her, right?"

Jack nodded, his face grim. "Right."

Taking a breath, Steve opened the door.

Their grandmother looked up from the kitchen table. "Everything all right?"

"Yeah. Just a few trees came down. But we'll take care of it," Jack said.

"It's going to be one hell of a cleanup," Steve added quickly, not giving his grandmother a chance to ask more questions. "Any idea when they'll get the bridge up and running?"

Jack grabbed his covered plate off the stove and took a seat across from their grandmother. "I managed to get through to the state last night," he said. "They think a couple of days at least, and more likely two weeks. But they'll be able to air drop necessary supplies in. And there's a medevac available, although it's busy running rescue missions all over the county. We're not the only ones hit hard. People are missing, and there've been reports of mudslides. It's a disaster pretty much everywhere."

"How about Millners?" Steve asked.

Jack shook his head. "Nothing that bad—besides the bridge of course. The flooding was bad, but nothing we can't handle. Keith is going to hold a meeting at noon today at the elementary school. In fact, I need to get moving. I want to touch base with some people beforehand."

Their grandmother stood up, picking up her plate. Steve took it from her. She looked a little pale this morning. Steve worried for a moment that she'd seen the graffiti, but he discarded that thought as soon as he had it. If she'd seen it, she would have tried to remove the boards to keep *him* from seeing it.

"Why don't you go relax?" Steve said. "You still have that scarf to finish for Jack."

Gran smiled, but her eyes looked tired. "Maybe I will. Thank you, honey." She walked slowly out of the room.

Steve took the plate to the sink and washed it. He glanced out the window above the sink before taking a seat at the table.

"You looking for something in particular out there?"

"Just making sure no one's looking at us."

Jack frowned. "It'll blow over."

Steve gave a bitter laugh. "Someone vandalized our home last night. And two people have been murdered. Most people are going to think it's me."

"But you're alibied for both killings. And the abduction."

"Don't think too many people are going to be looking closely at the details. Besides, everyone still thinks I killed Simone."

"So I take it you're not going to be coming to the town meeting?"

"Well, I'm guessing one goal of the meeting is to calm the town down, so... no, I don't think my presence is going to help with that."

Jack clapped Steve on the shoulder on his way out of the room. "You're probably right. But when all this craziness is past us, we'll make sure that changes."

"Seriously, you are *way* too much of an optimist to be a politician." Steve called out to him. "Hey, Jack."

Jack glanced over his shoulder.

"Be careful when you go into town."

Jack grinned. "You got it, little brother."

CHAPTER SIXTY-TWO

DECLAN WOKE up on the couch in the principal's office around nine. He hadn't gotten to sleep until nearly four. It had taken a while to get back here from Dee's last night, and then he'd spent time looking over the files again, this time with the knowledge that Keith had been the one who had taken the evidence that most damned Steve. He just couldn't figure out why Keith would do that.

He sat up and yawned, his back protesting his uncomfortable sleeping position. He had a few hours before the town meeting. He wanted to look at everything they had on the recent murders. There had to be a connection. There just had to be.

He stood up, grabbed his jacket, and headed for the door. He was hoping maybe Dee had remembered something else that might help. His mind turned over what Dee had told him over and over again, trying to make some sense of it. It made no more sense now than it had last night.

Unless, of course, Keith was afraid the DNA evidence would come back and *clear* Steve. If Steve was proven innocent, then Keith wouldn't be the cop who had solved the biggest crime in

Millners Kill's history; he'd be the cop who'd botched the investigation.

That last thought kept rolling through Declan's mind as he made his way to the police station. Was Keith small-minded enough to railroad a kid for his own political gain? Declan didn't have an answer for that questions. But he intended to get one.

When Declan jogged up the stairs of the station and pulled open the door, he was surprised to see Dee wasn't at her desk. He couldn't ever remember walking in and not seeing her. It was jarring. He looked around just as Russ came out from the back.

"Morning, Russ."

"Hey, Declan. I was just running out for coffee. Want some?"

"That would be great." He nodded toward Dee's empty desk. "Where's Dee?"

Russ shrugged. "I don't know. I haven't seen her yet. I called her house but didn't get any answer. Power is out all over the island. I was going to run out there and check on her, but the chief wants coffee."

Declan nodded, but a twinge of concern was beginning to build. After their conversation last night, Dee had seemed fine. In fact, she'd seemed relieved to finally have unburdened herself. She'd even agreed to write out a statement. Declan had it carefully tucked away in the trunk of his car. He glanced at the desk. Had she felt too guilty or worried to come in?

"You know," Declan said, "I've got some time now. Why don't I run over and check on her?"

Russ's relief was palpable. "That'd be great. You know where she lives?"

Declan pictured the little house. "Yeah." He turned and followed Russ out. "You guys getting a lot of calls?"

"I've been running around all night. A couple more people drove into water, not realizing how deep it was. We had two house fires, one heart attack, but no fatalities. I even had to disarm a group of guys over at Mel's last night."

"What?"

"They got it in their heads that vigilante justice was the way to go."

"They were going after Steve?"

Russ put up his hands. "Don't worry. I talked them down and got their weapons."

"How'd you do that?"

"I told them they had a choice—hand over their weapons, or go to jail and *then* hand over their weapons."

Declan smiled. "Nice job."

Russ shrugged. "But it's getting ugly out there. People are scared. And some of that fear has turned to anger."

Declan sighed. "Yeah, I know."

"I got to tell you—I can't wait for that bridge to be back. I feel like we're stranded here."

"Well, that's because we are."

Russ gave a laugh. "Guess so. And it's really beginning to work people up. I better get back out there. See you later." With a wave, Russ headed across the parking lot.

Declan keyed open his car. As he climbed in, he wondered about Dee. *She's fine. The roads around her house are probably flooded. That's all.*

"Declan!" Russ's yell came through the car window loud and clear—as did the urgency in his voice.

Declan jumped out of his car. Russ was at the other end of the lot, standing next to an old white Toyota Corolla. Declan's heart began to pound. He knew that car. He'd seen it in Dee's carport last night.

And there was someone sitting behind the wheel.

Declan ran across the parking lot as Russ opened the door.

Dee fell from the car, and Russ reached out to catch her before she hit the pavement.

But it wouldn't have mattered if she'd hit. From the blood soaking her shirt and the deep slash across her neck, it was apparent that Dee was well beyond caring about a little fall.

CHAPTER SIXTY-THREE

STEVE SPENT most of the morning clearing the yard of debris, and he grew more tense with every car that passed. Thankfully his grandmother was still blissfully ignorant of their late-night visitors.

Steve had cleared the small branches out of the yard, but now he needed to tackle the big job: the tree that had toppled over, roots and all, into the driveway. He'd have to break out the old chainsaw to take care of that.

He picked up the chainsaw and headed for the tree. He chuckled. If the phones were working, the whole block would probably soon be calling the police station with the news that a murderer was wielding a chainsaw in the suburbs.

He glanced over at Micah's house. *I'll check there when I finish up here.*

His grandma stuck her head out the door. "Steve, honey, could you clear the Griffiths' next door? Their kids are out of town."

"Okay. After I finish this up."

She smiled and ducked back in the house.

The Griffiths were a little older than his grandmother, and he'd known them most of his life. He'd also seen them turn their back on his grandmother when he was arrested. But good Christian woman that she was, his grandmother had never turned her back on them.

It took Steve another hour before he had cut down the tree and stacked the wood next to the back door. He leaned against the stack and took a swig of water as he looked over at the Griffiths' yard. He could tell it had been neglected even before the storm had come along. Now tree branches were strewn across it, and they, too, had had a tree come down. It looked like it had missed their garage by only a few inches.

Putting the cap back on his bottle, Steve grabbed his gloves and headed over to the Griffiths'. He started in the front yard because there weren't as many branches down there. He piled them all at the curb although who knew how long it would be before the town picked them up.

Then he headed down the driveway toward the back yard. He hadn't seen any movement inside the house. Maybe the Griffiths were out of town. He put them out of his mind as he started piling up the debris from the back yard.

But on his fifth trip from the back yard to the curb, Steve heard the unmistakable sound of a round entering a shotgun. He went still.

"Just what the hell do you think you're doing?"

Steve looked over his shoulder. Mr. Griffith stood there in his bathrobe. His white hair sprang out from his head. His hands shook, and Steve worried the shaking might set off the gun. He knew it wasn't all from fear. His grandmother had told him that Mr. Griffith had been diagnosed with Parkinson's a few years back.

"Mr. Griffith, it's me. It's Steve."

Mr. Griffith held the gun higher. "I know who you are. I asked what you're doing in my yard."

"My grandmother asked me to clear the yard of debris. See?" He gestured with his head toward the end of the drive. "I've already cleared your front yard."

"We don't need no help from the likes of you."

"Harold, put that gun down this instant!"

Mrs. Griffith came barreling down the back stairs. Where Mr. Griffith was skinny as a pole, Mrs. Griffith was large as a bus. Steve and Jack had often joked when they were kids that she must be eating all of his food.

"This murderer's—"

"I know, Harold." She reached her husband's side, placed a hand on the barrel, and slowly lowered it until it pointed at the ground. "It's all right. I'll take care of it."

"It's not right what he—"

"No, but we talked about this. Now you go on inside. I made some snickerdoodles."

"Fine." He gave Steve a hard look. "But you remember I have this." He held the gun by the barrel.

"Yes, sir," Steve said, feeling relief as he watched Mr. Griffith walk into the house. He turned back to Mrs. Griffith. "Thank you."

"Well, as a Christian I couldn't in good conscience let him shoot you." She looked down her nose at him. "Some of us take the Bible seriously."

"Yes ma'am. Uh, do you want me to finish?"

She looked around, her face tight. "Yes, thank you."

Steve could tell it pained her to be kind to him. "Sure, no problem."

He adjusted the burden in his arms and headed toward the curb. *Made it through ten years locked up to be nearly taken out by a born-again geriatric.*

Steve dumped the pile of branches by the edge of the road and headed to the Griffiths' back yard. It was time to tackle the tree that had come down near their garage, and that meant he'd need the chainsaw. Hopefully the sound of it wouldn't send Harold into a shooting spree.

As he headed back to his grandmother's porch to fetch the chainsaw, he saw an old, dark green Ford F150 drive slowly by. The same truck had driven by at least twice before. There were three guys in the front seat, all with ball caps and scruff. Steve didn't need to be psychic to know they were watching him.

But he'd had enough of pretending he didn't see them. He stepped to the edge of his gran's porch, crossed his arms, and stared at the truck as it passed.

The window rolled down. "Murderer!" one of the men yelled before peeling down the street. Steve watched them go, not bothering to try and get the license plate. He knew no one would go out of their way to track those guys down.

As he headed back to the Griffiths' yard, he thought about Jack's comment from earlier about winning the town over.

Yup—Jack is definitely too optimistic to be a politician.

CHAPTER SIXTY-FOUR

DECLAN NODDED at Edgar Fundley as Russ pushed the stretcher into the funeral home. "Mr. Fundley."

Edgar looked at the body bag on the stretcher and pressed a handkerchief to his mouth. "Oh my."

After discovering Dee's body, Declan had processed the scene as quickly as possible. The last thing they needed was the town learning there was another murder—especially right before the whole town was gathered together. Crowds tended to whip emotions up, not calm them down.

So he and Russ had loaded Dee into a body bag as quickly and quietly as possible outside the police department. Luckily, no one had been seen them. Then they'd loaded the bag into Russ's cruiser and headed straight to the funeral home. By some miracle, no one had seen them. Thank God for the town meeting.

"Russ," Declan said, "can you push that down to the end of the hall?"

"Sure thing." Russ headed down the hallway with the stretcher.

Declan turned to Edgar. "Mr. Fundley, I cannot stress enough how important it is that you stay quiet about this."

"But someone's been murdered—"

Declan cut him off. "Yes. And we *will* find that someone. But right now we need to keep the town calm. Announcing another death will only make people panic."

Edgar nodded, but his eyes were following Russ and the body bag.

"Mr. Fundley," Declan said.

Edgar jerked his eyes to Declan. "Yes, yes, I understand."

Declan studied the funeral director for a minute. The man looked paler than normal—as if he might pass out if someone breathed heavily near him.

Declan sighed. He would have to trust the man to stay quiet. He had no choice. With a nod at Edgar, he headed down the hall to Russ.

"We sure this is the right course of action?" Russ asked, not looking at Declan.

Declan jabbed the elevator button. "Russ, you had to disarm a lynch mob last night. Announcing Dee's death is not going to do anything but work the town up. We need to keep this quiet until the bridge is open."

"But why kill Dee? Why now?" Russ asked.

Declan thought back to his conversation with Dee last night. As far as Declan could tell, the only people who knew that Keith had taken the evidence were Dee and Keith, and now him.

And what about Keith? Declan thought. It was Keith who had found the bloody clothes in the first place—after two other searches of Steve's house hadn't turned up anything. Had there even been an anonymous report, as Keith had claimed, or had Keith *put* the clothes there? And if he'd put them there, where the hell had he gotten them from?

Did that have anything to do with Dee's death? He didn't see how. No one could have known about it. "I don't know."

"She was killed the same way as Elise," Russ said.

"I know," Declan said as the doors opened. "Listen, why don't you head back? I'll take Dee. You're going to be missed soon, and it's getting close to the meeting time."

Russ nodded. "Okay." He started to head away, then turned back. "What do I say about Dee if anyone asks?"

Declan pushed the stretcher into the elevator. "Tell them you haven't spoken with her."

Russ clamped his jaw shut and nodded before striding back toward the entrance.

When the elevator doors opened onto the basement, Declan wheeled Dee down to the embalming room and shifted the body bag from the stretcher to the table. He paused for a moment, then unzipped the body bag.

Dee's pale face stared back at him, her eyes and mouth open in horror.

She'd had such a tough life. And just like Elise and Mel, she deserved so much better than this.

"I'm so sorry, Dee."

CHAPTER SIXTY-FIVE

NINETY MINUTES LATER, Declan pulled into the parking lot of the elementary school. It was packed. He had to circle a few times before finally giving up and parking on the cement playground. He hopped out of the car, jumping over puddles as he made his way to the entrance.

He'd gotten Dee situated. He'd only had time for a cursory examination. He'd bagged her hands, but he wasn't hopeful about getting anything from them. Dee only had one wound—at the neck. She'd bled out within seconds. Most of the blood was on her clothes and her car.

And she had only been dead for a little while when they found her—her body wasn't even cold yet. He figured her time of death was sometime between seven and eight. Dee had been scheduled to start at eight, so she was probably killed as soon as she arrived. And the lack of defensive wounds meant she knew her killer. She hadn't seen it coming—just like Mel and Elise.

That fact kept repeating in his brain. This killer was someone who raised no red flags—who all three victims knew. Which meant it was probably someone that Declan knew, too. And Declan had no idea who it was.

Declan pulled open the school's main doors and hurried down the hall. He was running late. The meeting had begun a half hour ago.

It looked like everyone from town was here. Even before he reached the gymnasium, he could hear the crowd.

And they weren't happy.

Declan ducked in the back door of the gymnasium and stopped just inside the entrance. Tall windows lined each side of the room, providing light. Folding chairs had been lined up into rows. All the seats were taken, and more people were lined up along the sides and in the aisles.

Keith stood on the stage, a few deputies lined up behind him. Russ stood at the end of the deputies, his eyes downcast.

Declan searched the crowd and found Jack standing against the wall on the left. His arms were crossed over his chest, a frown on his face. He spotted Julie as well. She didn't look any happier.

He recognized another dozen people from town who seemed to be experiencing a range of emotions—confusion, anger, fear, annoyance, and a host of others, none of them good.

Up on the stage, Keith waved for people to quiet down. He spoke through a bullhorn. "I realize people are upset, but things are under control."

"Under control?" a man in the front row yelled back. "Two people have been killed. And Micah Donaldson was almost killed."

"When are you going to arrest Steve Kane?" another man yelled.

"As I've said, we know who the perpetrator is," Keith said. "It's just a matter of time until we find him. If you see Steve Kane, do not approach him. Call us and protect yourself however you deem necessary."

tion. He bent at the waist with a yell, trying to relieve the
ure on his arm.

Not much of a height issue now, Declan thought. He leaned
n so Andy could hear him clearly. "What you just did is
d assaulting a police officer. Now, I'm willing to forgive and
t, but only if you take yourself home right now. Do we have
al?"

'I'm not going to—"

Declan twisted Andy's hand in one direction and pulled
tly on his elbow in the other—as if he were wringing a towel.

Andy winced, his face growing redder. "Okay, okay."

Declan released him and stepped back.

Andy stood. "Screw you, Declan."

"Go home, Andy, before I have you arrested."

Andy's wife put her hand on his arm and pulled him down
aisle.

Declan shook his head and turned back for Keith. *All the
ots are out today.* Ahead, the chief was still surrounded by
vnspeople peppering him with questions.

Declan pushed through them and stood right in front of
ith. "I need to speak with you."

The man Keith had been speaking with turned to Declan.
ley, I was—"

Declan glared at the man, who wisely shut up. In fact, most
the townspeople took a step back.

Keith smirked. "I'm a little busy right now. It'll have to wait."

Declan grabbed Keith's arm and pulled him to the side.
Right now."

"Get your hands off me," Keith said.

One of Keith's deputies stepped forward. Declan didn't
link. He was about done with the Millners Kill police force. He
urned to the deputies. "Unless you want to be arrested for inter-

However you deem necessary? Keith ha⌐   dire
given the town a shoot-on-sight proclamation. I⌐   pres
growing disbelief. His mouth hung open and hi⌐
every word Keith uttered.   dow

"Chief, have you questioned Steve Kane?"   call

"Yes, we've questioned him."   for⌐

"Why isn't he locked up?"   a d⌐

"State authorities intervened to prevent it⌐
locked up," Keith said.

Son of a bitch, Declan thought.   lig⌐

As the questions continued, Keith did absolu⌐
suggest that anyone other than Steve was resp⌐
murders and attempted abduction. By the time K⌐
Declan was seething.

Finally Keith called an end to the questio⌐
meeting was over. Keith handed the bullhorn to   th⌐
stepped off the stage, surrounded by his deputies⌐
people started to make their way out of the gymnasi⌐   *id*
of them stayed in their seats, talking with each othe⌐   to⌐
questions at the chief.

Declan made his way down the main aisle, n⌐   K⌐
than one glare as he passed.

One man stepped in his way. "Why the h⌐   "
defending that murderer?"

Declan glanced up at the man. It was Andy Han⌐   (
Keith's buddies from high school. The man easily ⌐
Declan by fifty pounds, and he had a good few incl⌐
as well.

Declan began to step around him. "Excuse me."

Andy grabbed Declan's sleeve. "I'm talking to you."

Declan grabbed Andy's hand and twisted it to⌐
degree angle. Andy's arm contorted, his elbow facing t⌐

tering with police business, you'll back the hell off. This is state business. *All* of you need to leave."

The deputies looked at Keith, whose face was turning a bright shade of red.

"Now," Declan barked.

The townspeople backed off first. The deputies took a little longer to move away as if to make sure Declan knew he wasn't the boss of them.

Keith shook Declan free. "How dare you. You just—"

Declan gritted his teeth and stepped toward Keith, his anger barely contained. "Shut up."

Keith took a quick step back.

Declan kept walking and Keith kept backpedaling until Keith bumped up against a wall. "You just put a shoot-to-kill order out on Steve," Declan growled.

"He's killed two people."

"You have no proof of that. In fact, you have proof of the exact opposite. He has alibis for both killings. You've done zero investigating. You have two bodies, and you've just assumed it's Steve."

Keith smirked, some of his attitude returning. "He's the only murderer we have in town. Anyone with a half a brain—"

"Well, that rules you out." Declan took a breath, but it didn't reduce his anger. "What happened to the clothes from the Granger case? You took them, didn't you?"

Keith's jaw dropped. His lips moved but no sound coming out. "What? No, I—"

Keith shifted his eyes away. And the truth hit Declan like a ton of bricks.

"You weren't sure it was Steve," Declan said, pointing. "You took the evidence to make sure that even if he was innocent, he still went to prison."

Keith paled and shook his head. "I don't know what you're talking about."

"You made sure he went away because Steve's case made your career. And you weren't going to let a little thing like his innocence get in the way of that."

"Even if that were true, it wouldn't matter. The courts found him guilty, even without the clothes."

Disgust rose up in Declan. He stepped forward. "At a minimum, you obstructed justice. And when we establish communication with the mainland, I'm bringing you up on charges."

Keith seemed to be regaining his confidence. He smirked. "You have no proof."

"I have an affidavit sworn out by a witness. It says you were in the police station the night the evidence disappeared."

Keith narrowed his eyes. "Who?"

"Guess you'll find out when I file charges."

Keith pulled up his belt and hitched it over his stomach. "You mean after I bring in Steve Kane for the second time? It'll be a shame if something happens to him before he can be brought to trial."

Declan tried to calm himself down, but he was still envisioning beating Keith bloody when he counted to ten, and he didn't have time to count to a million. "I swear, Keith, if anything happens to him, I'm coming for you."

"Ooh, I'm shaking. Little Declan Reed's coming after me."

Declan had to keep himself from punching the smug bastard through to the next room. He moved even closer to Keith and dropped his voice. "You forget, Keith. I'm not that little kid you pushed around in high school. And remember, Steve isn't the only one in town who's killed people. Don't forget that."

He shoved Keith back against the wall and then forced himself to walk away. Because if he was in the man's sight for even one more minute, he wasn't sure he would be able to control himself.

But he was sure he'd enjoy it.

CHAPTER SIXTY-SIX

HE LOOKED AROUND THE GYMNASIUM. People were agitated. Then Declan walked in. The state policeman looked upset.

He struggled to keep the smile off his face, waiting. He listened as Keith finished up the question-and-answer session. He forced himself to frown, but it was so hard, when all he wanted to do was laugh. Keith had just declared Steve enemy number one. No mention was made of anyone else possibly being the murderer. *Oh, sometimes it's just too easy.*

But his frown turned real when Keith ended the meeting. Where was the announcement of Dee's death?

Disappointment and annoyance washed over him. Here he was, carefully making all of these plans, and no one was following them. He knew Dee's death was discovered. He'd driven past the parking lot and seen her car; she was no longer in it. So what had happened?

He scanned the room. It appeared that no one was in a hurry to leave. His gaze skimmed past the groups of people until it came back to the only person who could have messed up all his perfectly laid plans: Declan. He was the only one in this town who would be able to hide Dee's death. And the only one who would even consider doing so. *Damn it.*

He scanned the room again. *There must be a way...*

He spotted a woman in her sixties, sitting in an aisle seat, her hair a shade of yellow not found in nature. He watched her for a moment as she spoke with someone behind her, her red lipstick standing out even in the dim light. *Yes, she'll do.*

A disturbance at the front of the hall pulled his attention. Declan had a man in an arm lock. He had to keep from laughing. *Declan Reed pushed to violence. Things are definitely heading in the right direction.*

He pulled a notebook from his jacket pocket and jotted something down, careful to write only in block print. He ripped the paper from the pad and folded it carefully.

His target was involved in an animated conversation with the couple seated behind her. He walked toward her, keeping a pensive look on his face. When he reached his target, he pretended to check his watch while he surreptitiously dropped the note in her lap. She never turned. Never even saw him.

Then he made his way back to his spot. He stood there, watching her, with his arms crossed. After a moment the woman turned around and picked up the note from her lap with a frown. She opened it—and her mouth dropped open. She looked around frantically and then nudged the person next to her, gesturing to the note. Her neighbor shook her head and looked around as well.

He bit back his smile and watched an angry Declan back Keith up against the wall. A minute later, Declan marched away from Keith.

He swallowed his grin. *Who knew Declan was such a badass?*

The woman was now striding toward Keith. He settled back. *Showtime.*

CHAPTER SIXTY-SEVEN

DECLAN STORMED down the side of the gymnasium, his blood boiling. People quickly got out of his way. It took him a moment to realize people had stopped chatting among themselves and were turning back toward the front of the room.

"Chief? Chief?" A voice rose above the din. Everyone turned as Sheila Tidley marched toward Keith.

Declan turned too, dread coursing through him. Sheila was the owner and operator of the *Millners Kill Gazette*. Normally, the most exciting thing they had to report on was the annual spelling bee. But Sheila was obsessed with the murders; she had been updating her website almost hourly before the power went off.

Keith turned. "Yes, Ms. Tidley?"

Sheila held up a piece of paper. "I just received an anonymous report that Dee Pearson was killed in front of the police department this morning. Do you have any comment?"

Keith's mouth dropped open. He looked like a fish dropped onto dry land.

The room erupted. Keith tried to say something, but the crowd drowned him out.

Oh, shit. Declan looked around frantically for Jack. He spotted him in the same position against the wall, near the flag-pole on the other side of the gym. Declan hastened toward him, but the crowd seemed to swell. He started pushing people out of his way.

A deputy grabbed a bullhorn and handed it to Keith, who climbed back onto the stage. "Calm down!" Keith shouted. "Everyone calm down."

Sheila shook off the deputy who tried to grab her arm. She strode up to the edge of the stage. "Chief? Comment?"

"We have no report of any additional murders. We will investigate and release a report shortly."

The room erupted in shouts again.

Declan finally reached Jack's side. Jack stared at the stage, his eyes large. Declan grabbed Jack by the arm, pulled him out the door, and into the hallway.

Jack turned to him. "Is it true?"

Declan looked around—they were alone for now. He nodded wearily. "Yes. Russ and I found her this morning. We were trying to keep it quiet to avoid just this reaction."

"Oh my God."

Declan gave Jack's arm a little shake. "Jack, I need you to call Steve. Get him and your grandmother out of their house."

"The cell phone towers are down."

God damn it. Frustration rolled through him. "Your grand-mother has an old rotary, doesn't she?"

Jack nodded.

"Good. Try the office. They have a landline."

Jack stared at him for a moment before giving himself a shake. "But where can I send them? My apartment's the only other place I can think of, and I don't know how much safer that'll be—people will know to look for them there."

Declan paused for a moment, trying to come up with some place for them to hide. He thought about bringing Steve to the jail for safekeeping but he didn't trust anyone in Millners Kill's police force except for Russ. "Send your grandmother to my sister's," he said.

He wanted to send Steve there too, but his sister would lose it —she would surely balk at housing Millners Kill's most famous murderer, especially now that she believed he was killing again. And Declan was pretty sure Steve wouldn't want his grandmother to be anywhere near him anyway, not if there was a chance of any violence. Declan wouldn't place his sister and her family in that position either.

"And tell Steve to go to my dad's place," he added. "There's no one there now. The key is under the frog in the back garden."

Jack ran his hands through his hair, scanning the hall. "Okay, good. That's good. What are you going to do?"

Declan glanced back at the gymnasium. The crowd could be easily heard through the doors. "See if I can calm any of this down."

CHAPTER SIXTY-EIGHT

STEVE STRETCHED TRYING to relieve the ache in his shoulders and back. He'd showered after coming in, and now he could smell the meatloaf his grandmother had put in the oven. He smiled as he made his way back downstairs. Apart from the guys driving by in the car and the Parkinson's patient with a shotgun, it had been a quiet day. He'd actually expected it to be much worse.

The phone rang when he reached the bottom step.

"I'll get it," Bess yelled from the kitchen.

"No you won't," Steve called back. He and his grandmother had been having races to see who could get the phone. Neither of them wanted the other to hear the venom in some of the callers' voices.

"Hello," Steve said, his voice hard.

"Steve, it's Jack." Jack sounded breathless and more than a little scared.

Steve saw his grandmother watching him. "It's Jack."

She nodded and disappeared back into the kitchen.

He waited until she was out of earshot. "What's going on?"

"There's been another murder."

"What? Who?"

"Dee Pearson."

"From the police station?"

"Yeah. And she was murdered right in front of the station. But there's more. I just came from the meeting. Keith made it pretty clear he thinks you're responsible for the murders. And he basically just told everyone that they can do whatever they feel is necessary to protect themselves from you."

Steve closed his eyes. *That man is going to get me killed.*

"You need to get out of there," Jack said.

Steve's gaze flew to the kitchen door. "I can't leave Grandma."

Jack's words rushed out. "I know. I'm leaving now. When I get there, I'll take Grandma over to Declan's sister's house. She's only a few blocks away. And she could probably use help with the kids. I'm sure they're bouncing off the walls. You can go to Declan's dad's. There's no one there now."

Steve knew that was Declan's idea. "Okay. Now I just need to figure out how to convince her."

"Well, do it fast. The mood of the people at the meeting was ugly. And it's going to get uglier."

Steve pictured Dee. He didn't know her well, but he was sure she didn't deserve this. "How was Dee killed?"

"I don't know. I've got to get moving to beat the crowd out of the parking lot."

"Okay. And Jack? Take care of yourself."

"I will. I'll be home as soon as I can. Be careful, Steve."

"Yeah."

Steve hung up the phone and headed to the living room. His grandmother was heading up the stairs. Steve opened his mouth to call to her and then stopped himself. He needed a minute.

Pictures of his mom's high school graduation still hung on the wall, along with Jack's. Steve's wasn't there, of course. He'd graduated in prison. But other mementos around the room spoke to him. His grandfather's baseball from when Mickey Mantle hit a home run. Pictures of him from baby to fifteen. Jack's many awards.

And now all this was in danger because of him.

He shook his head. No—it wasn't because of him. It was because whoever had killed Simone had never been caught. That monster was the one to blame.

Steve squared his shoulders and headed for the kitchen. *And now because of that monster, I have to convince Grandma to leave the house she was born in for her own safety.*

CHAPTER SIXTY-NINE

STEVE WAS PRACTICALLY CLIMBING the walls by the time Jack burst in the door a half hour later. "Sorry. Roads are a mess and the parking lot was a huge traffic jam."

Steve swallowed down the urge to yell at Jack. He knew his brother had gotten here as fast as he could. But he had already seen a few cars drive by the house. None had stopped or even really slowed down too much. But he'd also seen that same pickup he'd seen drive by a few times before.

Bess placed her knitting down next to her chair. "Jack, honey, do you want some tea?"

Steve grabbed her coat. "No time, Grandma. Declan's sister is expecting you."

"I'm sure she wouldn't—"

Jack shook his head. "I think Sylvia is really looking for a break from the kids."

Bess let out a sigh and let Steve help her with her coat. "Okay, but I don't understand why you can't come, Steve."

"I'll be by later," Steve said, not looking at her.

His grandmother nodded. "Well, I suppose it'll be all right."

She turned for the door and then back. "Oh, I forgot the cookies. Let me go—"

Steve wanted to scream. He needed her away from here. He needed her safe.

"I'll grab them." He nodded at Jack, who ushered their grandmother out of the house.

Steve sprinted for the kitchen. He spied the red cookie tin next to the stove, grabbed it, and hurried back to the door. Jack was standing there, shifting from foot to foot. "Everything okay?"

Steve nodded and handed Jack the tin. "Yup. You two should get going."

"I'll be back for you in—"

"No. I'm going to walk over to Declan's dad's place. It's not that far, and with the way the roads are, it'll probably be faster."

"You sure?"

Steve looked into his brother's eyes and imagined Jack getting caught between Steve and the guys in the pickup. He struggled to shut out the violent image. "Yeah. I'll be fine."

"Okay," Jack said. "I'll check on you later."

"That won't be necessary. Just take care of Grandma."

"Yeah, we'll see about that," Jack said before turning and heading down the porch stairs.

Steve watched Jack get into the car and pull out of the drive. Then he grabbed his jacket and the backpack he had filled with some clothes.

As he headed for the door, he stared for a moment at the baseball bat lying against the stairs. He wanted to bring it, but he decided he'd better not: carrying around a bat wouldn't exactly encourage people to believe he wasn't up to anything.

Although the time to convince anyone he was innocent was probably long gone.

He left through the front door and locked it behind him, slipping the keys into his pocket. He pulled up his hood and glanced around. Jack's car was just disappearing around the corner.

He tightened the backpack on his shoulders and headed down the porch steps. Another car drove by slowly, and Steve could feel their eyes on him. And he thought, for just a moment, that maybe he should go back for the bat.

CHAPTER SEVENTY

DECLAN HAD SPENT the last hour trying to get people from the meeting calmed down and back home. He'd assured person after person that everything was being done in the investigation and that the safest action for everyone was to stay off the streets.

Now he pushed through the doors of the gymnasium and out into the hall. With a sigh he saw that a group of about a dozen people was gathered near the front entrance.

Wendy Mayes, the waitress from Mel's diner, was holding center court. Dark lines of mascara ran down her face as she wrung her hands. As Declan got closer, her words carried. "He could have killed us all. I told Mel to fire him."

A friend rubbed her shoulders, nodding. "I bet that's what happened. Mel told him he was fired, and he killed him."

Declan narrowed his eyes as he drew nearer.

"Oh my God, this is all my fault!" Wendy said. "Why did Mel hire him? I warned him. I told him that man killed once, he'd kill again."

The crowd around Wendy nodded in agreement, and a few men whispered to each other in a way Declan didn't like. He struggled to hide his disgust. He knew he should feel compassion, but he'd just about had it with everyone telling him what a monster Steve was.

He walked up to the group. "Everybody, we're going to need you to head home. We need everyone off the streets so that if there's an emergency, critical vehicles can get through."

"But what about Steve Kane? What if he's at my home?" Wendy squealed.

Declan forced himself not to roll his eyes at her theatrics. "Then go stay with a friend."

"What if he's at her house?"

Declan struggled not to yell at the woman. "Well, pick whichever friend's home you feel a murderer will be least likely to go to, and head there. Now let's go."

He started waving his hands toward the exits, and the group reluctantly broke up. Declan followed them out and stood at the top of the steps until the last of the cars had disappeared from the lot.

He wished he felt better now that the meeting had broken up, but he didn't. If Keith's intent had been to calm down the town with this meeting, he had failed horribly. In fact, he'd done just the opposite. People had been scared to death. A few fights had even broken out in the parking lot when people were leaving. People's nerves were stretched thin.

Declan rubbed a hand over his face. He hoped that with everyone off the streets things would calm down.

But he had a sinking feeling that it was only going to get worse.

CHAPTER SEVENTY-ONE

STEVE MADE his way past the elementary school. Declan's dad's place was only a few more blocks away.

A couple of cars had passed him on his walk over, but none of them had taken much of an interest in him. With his hood up and his head down, Steve hoped none of them even recognized him.

The pressure that had begun to build in him since Jack's call now began to lessen. Gran was safe; that was the main thing. And he was going to be all right, too. He let out a shaky breath. *A couple more blocks—no problem.*

He turned past the high school and glanced up as a pickup turned onto the road in front of him. He ducked his head down quickly, but he'd gotten enough of a look to know it was the same F150 he'd seen driving in front of his grandmother's.

He kept his pace unhurried, hoping they hadn't really gotten a good look at him. The muffler rattled as it made its way slowly past. From the corner of his eye, Steve watched the truck's progress. He felt the eyes of the cab's occupants on him.

Don't go borrowing trouble, he warned himself, trying to keep his shoulders relaxed.

The truck passed, and Steve let out a shaky breath. *Okay. All I have to do—*

The trucks tires squealed as the driver made a sharp turn behind Steve. Steve glanced over his shoulder in time to see the truck hopping the curb behind him.

Heart in his chest, Steve sprinted down the sidewalk.

The truck barreled along behind him, sending garbage cans flying. Steve ducked down a driveway and vaulted over the home's back fence. He heard the truck brake to a stop, then the slam of car doors.

Shit. He didn't stop to look back. He could hear at least two sets of footfalls behind him. He sprinted across the yard and jumped over the fence at the back. He burst across that lawn, down the driveway, across the next street, and into another yard.

But the yard was encased by a six-foot-tall privacy fence. He ran for it, leaped, and scrambled up. He had just gotten one leg over when a hundred-pound Rottweiler charged at him from the other side of the fence, barking madly. With a yell, Steve slipped and fell backward, landing on the ground hard. But he didn't have time to catch his breath; his pursuers were practically on top of him.

He got to his feet just before the first man caught up to him. Steve spun out of the way, swiping the guy's legs with his foot as he did. The man fell hard.

But the second guy wrapped his arms around Steve from behind. Steve threw his head back, catching the guy in the nose, but the guy didn't let go.

The first guy was back on his feet now. He punched Steve repeatedly in the stomach as the pickup screeched to a stop in the drive. The third guy stepped out with a smirk and ran over. He kicked Steve in the groin.

Then Steve lost count of the kicks and the punches as he was tossed to the ground. He put his hands over his head and just prayed it would end soon.

CHAPTER SEVENTY-TWO

JULIE DROVE SLOWLY through the streets. She hadn't liked the tone of the town meeting—at all—so she had driven past Steve's house just to check that everything was okay there. All was quiet. Now she was driving around the neighborhood, looking for what, she didn't know—until she saw it.

Down a side street she saw a man streak across the road; two other men appeared a second later, apparently giving chase. A pickup roared down the street, pulling into the same driveway. She couldn't tell from that distance who they were, but she had a pretty good idea.

She turned the wheel, sped down the street, and slammed on the brakes when she reached the spot where the men had crossed. In the driveway, three men were kicking and stomping on the fourth man. A dog barked non-stop from behind the fence.

Julie grabbed her gun and stepped out of the car. "Get away from him!" she yelled.

The men either didn't hear her or didn't think she was a threat because they continued their assault.

She took a step forward and fired a shot at the lawn a few feet to their left.

The three men leaped back. "What the hell?"

Julie got her first good look at them: Hank Meyers, Andy Hanover, and Sean Tibbets. They were all way too old for this. She looked at the person on the ground and was not at all surprised to see that it was Steve.

She tightened her grip on the gun. "Get away from him," she ordered again.

Steve rolled to his side, and Julie struggled not blanch at the sight of his bloodied face.

"Do you know who he is?" Andy said.

"I know *exactly* who he is," Julie answered. Her gaze flicked between Steve and the men. Steve had gotten to his knees.

"You should be thanking us," Hank sneered.

Thanking them. Her anger boiled. As if somehow beating up Steve, or even killing him, would balance the scales. As if these ignorant idiots weren't just getting some fun out of teaming up against one man.

Julie took a step forward. "Get. Away. From. Him."

Andy nudged Hank. "She's not going to shoot us."

Julie narrowed her eyes. With a grunt she aimed for two inches in front of his shoe.

Hank shrieked as the bullet landed right where she intended.

"Steve, get over here," Julie ordered, not taking her eyes from the men.

Steve got from his knees to his feet, holding his side. His face was bloodied and his clothes were wet and muddy. The telltale red of new bruises was along his cheekbone, mixing in with the older bruises, and she was pretty sure the same sight was now along his rib cage. With a little wobble, he took a step toward her.

Julie didn't question the jolt of concern that flashed through her at Steve's condition or the increase in anger that accompanied it.

"Get in the car," she ordered. "You drive." She stood with her legs braced and both hands on the gun, her gaze not leaving the men.

Steve staggered toward the street where Julie's car was. Julie prayed he could make it that far. Because there was zero chance she could hold these guys back while also helping Steve walk.

Steve made it to the car, but he hesitated at the driver's door. And then Julie realized why: he'd never driven a car. He'd been locked up before he'd ever had a chance.

"Get in the car, Steve," she said again.

"She's not going to shoot us." Hank stepped forward.

Julie glared at him. "Hank, don't tempt me."

He stopped. "You've always been a bitch."

"And you've always been a Neanderthal. Now toss your keys into the bushes."

Hank spluttered. "I'm not—"

Julie turned away from the men and aimed for the pickup truck.

"Okay, okay! They're going." Hank rummaged in his pockets and then tossed the keys.

Steve gunned the engine and rolled down the window. "Julie, let's go."

Julie walked backward toward the car. "You guys just stay there until we're gone. Then you can go look for your keys."

Steve opened the door from inside. Julie backed in, feeling the men's hate. "Go."

Steve peeled out before she had the door closed. She fell against him with a grunt and struggled to right herself. She looked through the rear window and saw the men looking for their keys.

"Turn right on Tulip," she said.

Steve nodded, making the turn. He glanced over at Julie. "Thanks."

She met his gaze and gave him an abrupt nod. Then, staring out the window, she pictured her parents and Simone. *What am I doing?*

CHAPTER SEVENTY-THREE

DECLAN HELD the card with the fingerprint from the diner. He had it right here in his hands—the identity of the killer—but with the internet and power out, he couldn't access any of the programs that could identify it. *Damn it.* And with the meeting and Dee this morning, Russ hadn't had a chance to check for the fingerprint card yet.

Russ slumped into the seat across from him. He'd stepped outside to take a call on the radio. Now he didn't look happy.

Declan raised an eyebrow.

Russ shook his head. "A couple of yahoos attacked Steve a couple of blocks from his grandmother's house."

Declan straightened. "He okay?"

Russ nodded, and a smile crept across his face. "Yeah. Julie Granger showed up. Held the guys at gunpoint until she and Steve could escape."

Declan sank back into his seat. "Huh. Never would have called that."

Russ stayed silent.

Declan glanced over. "I'm guessing you're not as surprised."

He shrugged.

"Come on. Spill."

"Back when we were kids, Steve and Julie were always together. I mean, always. I figured they'd be one of those couples who could say at their sixtieth wedding anniversary that they met when they were five and just knew."

And it hit Declan just how much had been taken from Steve. He wanted that future for Steve—a wife, kids, grandkids. His voice was quiet when he spoke. "Yeah, but with Simone..."

Russ was silent for a moment. "I don't know that Julie ever really believed Steve killed her sister. I mean, her parents did, but... I don't know. And you should see them together. It's electric. I'm just saying... I'm not surprised she was around."

They both fell silent then. Declan felt a sense of contentment at the thought of Steve having someone in his corner.

"What's that?" Russ asked, looking at the evidence card in Declan's hand.

"Fingerprint from the scene."

Russ winced. "Damn, sorry. With everything happening I forgot about that. I'll go dig up Steve's card."

Russ's radio squawked. He grimaced and answered. "Nash here."

"Nash, where the hell are you?" Keith bellowed.

"Over at the school. The last people just pulled out a little bit ago."

"Well then you should be gone too. People are getting into accidents all over the place. You need to be out in the streets, not playing baby detective with Reed."

Declan raised an eyebrow, and Russ shook his head. "Will do, Chief."

Russ placed his radio back on his belt, and for the first time, Declan saw a look of annoyance on the young officer's face. Russ seemed to be one of those guys who let everything roll off their back, but apparently, the chief was pushing even him just a little too far.

"Russ, what do you think of the chief?"

Russ shrugged. "I think he's my boss."

Declan debated for a minute, then told him about the missing clothes and the statement from Dee.

Russ stared at him. "You think the chief manufactured the evidence? And then killed Dee to keep his secret?"

"I don't know what to think," Declan said. "I mean, the Granger case has kept him in office. But those clothes going missing... I can't see why he'd take them unless he'd planted them."

"Or he thought they'd exonerate Steve," Russ said.

"Yeah, that too." Declan fell silent. "But I can't see why else to kill Dee. Other than that she was the only one who could point the finger at him."

"Maybe. But I think you might be trying to link the cases too hard. Maybe Dee was just a crime of opportunity."

Declan nodded, knowing Russ was probably right. Dee's death had served a purpose—it had focused everyone on Steve. The real killer could now walk around scot-free and no one would pay any attention.

Declan sighed, rubbing his hands over his face. "Well, I think the priority needs to be getting the fingerprint card. Then we'll have some proof to defend Steve. And maybe if we're lucky it will help us figure something else out."

Russ heaved himself out of his chair. "Okay. I'll see if I can get into the station and grab it without anyone noticing."

"See if you can hurry it up."

"You're worried things are going to boil over?"

Declan shook his head, thinking about the graffiti on Bess's house and the attack on Steve. "I'm worried they already have."

CHAPTER SEVENTY-FOUR

DECLAN PACED BACK and forth in the school's office. Russ had just called on the radio; he was on his way over with Steve's old fingerprint card. Declan had pinched two magnifying glasses from one of the science classes to help them.

He had never studied fingerprints. He knew you needed about twelve points to line up for something to be considered a match, but he wasn't sure he'd be able to do that. Fingerprints looked so much alike, at least to him. He doubted he'd be capable of identifying a match. But he didn't need to prove a match; he just needed to identify that the fingerprint *wasn't* a match to Steve.

He looked at the ridges and swirls from the prints at the diner. Doubt and uncertainty crept through him. It looked like a thousand other prints he'd seen. He closed his eyes. He was going to fail Steve again.

Taking a breath, he released his doubts. No. If this didn't pan out, he'd find another way to prove Steve was innocent. He crossed the room to the desk and turned on the lamp. Taking out the magnifying glass, he looked over every inch of the card. At what he thought was the pointer finger, he stopped and peered closer. *What is that?*

There was a thin line running through the print. It wasn't perfectly straight, but it was close. An old injury, maybe?

This could be useful, he thought. A clear identifying mark like that would make it easier to prove that Steve's fingerprint wasn't a match.

The door to the office burst open and Russ bustled in. He was out of breath as he pulled a book from his coat, wrapped in plastic. "Here you go."

Declan took the book from Russ and flipped through the pages until he found the print card for Steve. Russ took off his coat, then pulled a chair up to the desk and slumped into it. "Well?"

"Give me a minute." Declan gripped the card and let out a breath. He decided to go straight to the index finger where he'd found the thin line. That would be the easiest place to start. He held the card under the lamp and peered at it through the magnifying glass.

He went still, the hairs on the back of his neck standing up.

Russ leaned forward. "Declan?"

Declan grabbed the print from Mel's diner and examined it again, then shifted back to Steve's fingerprint card. His heart began to pound. *No, it's not possible.*

He stared at the two fingerprint cards, looking back and forth between them. His mind refused to believe what was right in front of him. *All this time. How could I have been wrong?*

Russ grabbed his shoulder. "Declan, what's going on?"

Declan looked up at him, feeling a complete sense of disconnect. "The cards—they match." He swallowed. "Steve killed Mel."

CHAPTER SEVENTY-FIVE

STEVE PULLED CAREFULLY into the driveway of Declan's dad's house. He put the car in park and let out a breath. "That was my first time driving."

"You did pretty good," Julie said with a smile.

Steve's heart fluttered a little. "Thanks for saving me."

Julie shrugged as she got out of the car. "No big deal."

Steve got out and looked at her over the roof of the car. "I don't know about that."

Julie gestured toward the house. "Do you have a key?"

"No, but Declan's dad leaves one under a frog in the back." He headed to the back of the house.

"A frog?" Julie asked, following him.

The little frog sat in the garden behind the house, on a lily pad, grinning up at them. Steve tilted the frog back and swiped the key hidden there. "Got it."

They headed to the back door. Steve unlocked it and held it open for Julie.

"Thanks," she said as she passed.

Steve caught the scent of lavender. He walked in behind her and immediately locked the door behind him.

Declan's dad's kitchen hadn't changed much from when Steve was younger. Declan's parents had gotten divorced before Steve was born, but both lived nearby. Declan had lived with his mom, but he'd brought Steve here a bunch of times when he was younger.

Now that Steve was older, he saw the differences between Declan's mom's house and his dad's. There were no soft touches here—just strong colors, wood paneling, and functional furniture. And if he remembered correctly, there was a wood stove in the living room. "Um, I'll go see about getting a fire started."

"Okay," Julie said. She followed Steve into the living room. She roamed around the room, looking at pictures on the wall, while Steve placed some kindling and firewood into the stove.

"Is this Declan?" Julie asked.

Steve looked over his shoulder and grinned. Steve knew the picture. Declan was dressed as a lion for Halloween. "Yeah. He was six."

Lighting a match from the box on top of the stove, Steve got the fire started. It caught quickly.

"He was cute." Julie continued her inspection as the fire began to glow. "Hey, is that you?"

Steve stood up and walked over. He studied the photo. A twenty-year-old Declan stood leaning on a rake while a seven-year-old Steve sat in a giant pile of leaves. Steve laughed. "I remember that day. Declan made this giant pile of leaves and we took turns jumping in it."

Steve suddenly realized that Julie was really close. He took a step back even though he really didn't want to. Even though the fire was just getting started, he suddenly felt warm. He slid off his jacket and went to place it on the back of the couch. As he did, something silver fell from his jacket pocket.

"What's that?" Julie asked.

Steve knelt down and picked it up with a frown. "It's... Mel's St. Christopher's medal." He stared at it. There was a fleck of blood on it. Mel never took this off. What was it doing in his pocket?

Julie took a step back. "Steve... why do you have that?"

"Huh?" He looked up at her.

Julie's hands were in front of her, her eyes wide. "*Why* do you have that?" she repeated. Her voice was shaking.

He looked from the medal to Julie and realized what she was thinking. He stood up. "Jules, it's not what you—"

Moving faster than Steve would have thought possible, Julie grabbed a lamp off the table next to her and swung it—hard.

It collided with Steve's temple. A starburst of pain exploded across his head. He pitched forward. The carpet rushed toward him. *It wasn't me*, he thought. And then he slipped into darkness.

CHAPTER SEVENTY-SIX

RUSS GRABBED the cards from Declan's hands. "What do you mean, they match?"

Declan pushed back from the desk while Russ pulled the light and the magnifying glass over to him. Declan felt numb. "The pointer on the right hand."

Russ studied one card and then the other. "I don't see—the imperfection?"

Declan nodded. "It's on both cards, in the same exact position. It must be an old scar."

Russ's mouth fell open. "So it *was* Steve?"

Declan nodded slowly.

"But how did he kill Mel? He was locked up."

Declan shrugged. "I don't know. Maybe he messed around with the temperature in the diner, heating it up to keep Mel's body from cooling at a normal rate. Or more likely I messed up. I was foolish to believe I could do the job of an actual medical examiner. The time has to be off."

"But Steve saved Micah. He saved that woman and her child. Is there any chance Steve left this when he found the body?"

Declan shook his head. "No. Steve never touched the counter, at least not when he discovered Mel. And this was a light blood trace, not obvious. He must have overlooked it when he wiped everything else down."

"Are you sure?"

Declan felt numb. "Yeah. I don't know how, but Steve killed Mel."

Declan stared around the office as if answers were going to appear miraculously from the office supplies. He knew he should be moving. He should be finding Steve and bringing him in. But he couldn't get his body to move—or his mind, for that matter. Shock was taking hold. No, not just shock. Sadness. All these years, he'd had faith in Steve. And he'd been wrong. Dead wrong.

A shudder ran through him. *Steve killed Mel. He killed them all. He's not the poor innocent boy who was wrongly convicted. He's a stone cold killer.*

Russ stood up, his eyes wide. "Julie. Steve's with Julie."

Declan felt his breath catch in his throat. *Oh my God.* He jumped to his feet and grabbed his jacket from the rack as he sprinted for the door. "They're at my father's house."

CHAPTER SEVENTY-SEVEN

JULIE'S HEART pounded as she stared down at Steve's unconscious form. *He had Mel's necklace. Mel never took that off.* She
began to shake. She had a vision of Steve stabbing Mel, angrily,
viciously. Followed by an image of Steve covered in Simone's
blood.

It was him. All this time, it was him.

She made a wide arc around Steve as she ran to the kitchen
and scooped her car keys off the counter. Then she sprinted out
the back door, stumbled down the steps and around the house.

Stupid. I am so stupid. She was weaving like a drunk, but she
couldn't walk straight—she couldn't think straight. *He did it. He
killed them all.*

She yanked the car door open, and all but fell into her seat.
Her hands were shaking so hard, it took her three tries to get the
key in the ignition. She felt hot and a bead of sweat rolled down
her back. She kept glancing up at the house, expecting Steve to
vault out the door at any moment. Finally, the engine flared to
life. She slammed the car into reverse, peeled out of the driveway,
then shifted into drive and slammed on the gas.

Oh my God. Oh my God. Julie took a corner too fast and her heart leaped into her throat as she barely missed a Honda parked on the street.

Calm down. You need to calm down, she warned herself. But she couldn't stop the tremors that wracked her body. She also couldn't seem to slow down. She'd been wrong. All these years, everyone had been right. It had been Steve all along.

Tears clouded her vision. She swiped them away, picturing Simone. Seeing her parents crouched over her sister's lifeless body.

"I'm so sorry, Simone," she whispered.

Oh, God. She felt nauseous as she thought about how tenderly she'd bandaged him up after the police had brutalized him. And then she had saved him when those men had tried to hurt him. *I should have let them kill him.*

But I helped him go free. Her stomach rolled. *Whoever he kills next, that's on me.*

In ten years, she'd been unable to accept the truth. But there was no hiding from it now. She raced through the streets, not paying any attention to where she was going. She was in shock, just driving without thinking. When she finally blinked and got her bearings, she realized that she had driven all the way to the far side of the island. And she was driving way too fast.

She tapped the brakes, knowing she needed to turn around. She hydroplaned a little, and the back of her car swung out. Heart racing, she jerked the steering wheel to the right. But she jerked too hard. The car began to spin.

"Oh, no, no, no," Julie mumbled, trying to bring the car under control. A wave of water flew up as she careened into a deep pool of standing water. The water stopped her spin with a jerk, but it also doused the engine.

Julie turned the ignition off. She said a little prayer and then turned the key. Nothing. "Oh, come on," she pleaded.

She pumped the gas and tried again. Still nothing.

She looked out her window; the water reached halfway up her door. *The engine is literally flooded.* The car was never going to start.

Should she stay here and wait for someone to find her? But there was no one around, and it was getting dark. To make matters worse, the skies chose that moment to open up, and rain thundered down on the roof of the car. *Great.*

She imagined the water level rising until it covered her car. Unrealistic or not, she still felt a panicked need to get out of the car. Besides, Steve could be up, could be looking for her. And no way in hell was she going to sit here and wait for him.

She rolled down her window, thankful that at least that worked. Raindrops stung her face as she pulled herself out through the window. She balanced on the door for a minute before lowering herself into the water below.

"God damn it." The water reached her upper thighs, and it was freezing. She waded through it as quick as she could, but she was still damn near frozen by the time she got out of it.

She jogged in place at the side of the road, trying to stay warm as she looked around. There were no houses in sight. She wasn't sure, but she thought she might be at the edge of the protected land, which meant that the nearest buildings would be the rental cabins about a mile down the road. Mostly they were used by vacationers, so there might not be anyone around, but at this point she'd be willing to break in if that's what it took to get warm. She'd pay for the damages later.

A shiver tore through her, and she knew she needed to get moving. She was already beginning to feel sluggish from the cold. She started to jog down the street, waving her arms to try to increase her temperature.

She'd find a phone, call for help, and warm up. Steve would

never look to find her way out here. And as long as Steve couldn't find her, she'd be safe.

CHAPTER SEVENTY-EIGHT

THE PAIN in his head was his first sensation. It passed through in waves. When it finally stopped, he opened his eyes. He was on the floor. He stared at the carpet and frowned. That wasn't his grandmother's carpet. He pushed himself up, and his stomach rolled with the pain in his head.

He pulled himself up to the couch, closed his eyes again, and leaned his head back. What the hell? His mind was foggy. He couldn't remember how he'd ended up on the ground. He looked around.

"Julie?"

No answer. He saw the smashed lamp next to the chair. And the memories returned. *She thinks it's me.*

Because I had Mel's St. Christopher necklace.

Mel never took it off. Never. When Steve had found Mel, he hadn't even noticed it was missing. But everyone knew he wore it. How the hell had it gotten in his pocket?

Steve struggled to think. Had he picked it up the morning he'd found Mel? Although he'd been in shock, he didn't think so.

After he called Declan, he'd stayed by the door, not going back to the body. Besides, he didn't even have this jacket then.

So he hadn't put the medal in his pocket.

Then who had?

The only people who'd had access to the jacket were his grandmother and Jack. He discounted Bess right away. Besides the fact that she didn't have it in her, there's no way she would physically be able to move Elise's body or have the strength to plunge that knife into Mel.

That left Jack. Steve's mind rebelled at the thought. Jack had been his strongest supporter all his life. It couldn't be him.

Not all your life, a voice whispered in his mind. *Only since your father died.*

Grudgingly, he had to acknowledge that that was true. When he was kid, Jack had actually been horrible to him. His dad had even tried to keep them apart. He never let Jack watch Steve or let Steve go anywhere alone with Jack. At the time, Steve had thought that was just his dad being strict with him. But why had he done that?

It can't be Jack, he thought. There was a rational explanation for all of this. It wasn't Jack. It couldn't be. Someone must have broken into the house. Put the medal in his pocket. It was the only explanation.

And yet, he felt a powerful need to check on Bess and make sure she was safe.

Steve stood up, and the world swam a little. He put a hand on the wall and waited for the dizziness to pass. Idly, he thought about how people said prison was so violent. But he'd been hurt more in the few days since he'd returned home than in his years of being locked up.

He walked over to the window and looked out. Julie's car was gone. She'd probably gone to the cops. Well, at least she'd be safe. But he needed to get out of here. He didn't know why, but something told him he needed to get moving. Things were spiraling out of control. And he needed to know his grandmother was safe.

He'd go stop by Declan's sister's house and just make sure Bess was all right. Before he went—where? It's not like there were a lot of places for him to go. *Declan.* He'd find Declan. Declan would know what to do.

But first things first—Grandma.

He considered walking, but it would take too long, and after his last walk, he didn't want to chance it. He needed a car. He remembered Declan telling him once, a few years ago, that he and his father were restoring a car. Steve prayed they had finished.

He walked through the kitchen in the dark and found the door to the garage. Light coming through the windows illuminated a car under a dusty tarp. Steve pulled off the tarp to reveal a black 1967 Impala. Even in the dim light, the car looked good.

Steve searched the car for keys. Nothing. Next he checked the workbench. Tools were strewn across it, and along the back of the bench were mason jars filled with nails, screws, bolts—and in the last jar, a pair of keys.

Steve grabbed the keys, then, since the power was out, manually pulled up the garage door. He hopped in the Impala and turned the key in the ignition.

The engine roared to life. He would have smiled if a steady ball of fear hadn't been spreading through his body.

It's not Jack. Grandma is fine.

But he was no longer sure if he was saying it because he believed it or because he wanted to believe it.

CHAPTER SEVENTY-NINE

DECLAN AND RUSS rolled up around the corner from Declan's father's house. They'd had to stop by the police station to get more weapons and officers. Declan had debated not telling Keith, but that was his pride talking. Julie's safety had to come before anything.

Keith's smirk had been huge. "How's it feel, Declan, knowing you helped a murderer go free?"

Keith had insisted on running point. Declan didn't argue. He wasn't sure he would be able to bring himself to do what needed to be done, and he had no doubt Keith could.

"All right everybody, let's go," Keith said over the radio.

Russ and Declan stayed where they were. They were not part of this arrest.

Declan stared down at his hands, clenching and unclenching them. How had he been so wrong? He had never seen an inkling of any violence in Steve. Not when he was a kid, not as a teenager. He leaned his head against the window. *What the hell kind of cop does that make me?*

"He fooled us all," Russ said quietly next to him.

"Not all of us," Declan said quietly. Keith had been right this whole time.

"All clear. Suspect's not here," Keith growled through the radio.

Feeling more tired than Declan could ever remember, he pushed open the door and headed for the house.

The front door was wide open as was the garage. He headed through the front door. In the living room, a table was overturned and a lamp broken on the floor. Declan brought his hand to his mouth.

Keith stomped over. "Well, your boy is gone. When this is all over, Reed, I'm having *you* brought up on obstruction charges. You've been helping that murderer ever since he got out. You don't deserve to wear a badge."

Declan opened his mouth to respond, then shut it. What could he say? Keith was right. He just nodded wearily as Keith grunted and stormed away.

Russ came in from the garage holding a tarp. "Is there something usually underneath this?"

Declan nodded. "Yeah—my dad's old car. We've been restoring it."

"It's not there."

The fog in Declan's brain began to clear. "And Julie's car's not here either. That means she could still be alive."

Russ pulled out his radio. "All officers be on the lookout for a —" He glanced at Declan.

"A 67 black Impala, no license plate," Declan said.

Russ repeated the description into the radio.

Keith stormed into the kitchen. "What's with the BOLO?"

"My dad's car is missing, and so is Julie's. Which means Julie was alive when she left here," Declan said.

"You don't know that," Keith said. "Kane could have dumped one car and come back for the other."

"Maybe," Declan conceded, turning for the door, "but until we find a body, I'm going to act like there's still a chance to save her."

CHAPTER EIGHTY

JULIE STUMBLED down the driveway leading to the cabin park. The jogging had helped keep her warm, but she wasn't dressed for this weather. The rain had now shifted over to freezing rain. She gritted her teeth. *I have not missed fall in upstate New York.*

She spied a utility phone attached to the telephone pole at the entrance of the park. She blew on her hands a few times trying to warm them up enough to grasp the locking mechanism. It still took her four tries before she was able to open it.

Finally managing it, she yanked the receiver off. It rang twice and then connected.

"Thank God. I—"

"You've reached the Millners Kill Police Department. All officers are busy right now. Please leave a message and we'll get right back to you."

Julie wanted to scream. But instead, she waited for the beep. Her words came out in a rush. "This is Julie Granger. I'm stranded out at the cabin park. I left Steve Kane unconscious at Fergal Reed's home. He has Mel's St. Christopher medal. There's no doubt—" She swallowed. "Steve killed Mel. He killed all of them. Send help right away."

She hung up the receiver and closed the box. She felt drained, and only partly because of the cold sapping her energy. She had just publicly declared Steve a murderer. It was done. There was no hiding from the truth now.

Not giving herself time to dwell, she pushed away from the pole and jogged slowly down the drive. It was probably going to take them a while to get out here. And with Dee gone...

Julie took a shuddering breath. *Steve killed her too.* She shoved the emotions aside. She needed to focus on making sure she was all right—and right now, that meant getting warm.

Up ahead she could see the log cabins. Each one was pretty basic: two bedrooms, a small kitchen, one bathroom, and a small living room. But in the summer they were always full of people—mostly tourists. Some even had a dock. Not surprisingly, though, no one was out here now.

Julie hurried toward the first cabin, but then remembered that she knew who owned the cabin three down. Jack Kane. She headed for his instead. He certainly wouldn't mind if she broke in, not under these circumstances.

She pictured Jack, sadness creeping over her. He'd defended his brother all these years. It was going to break his heart to learn that Steve was actually the monster everybody thought he was.

Just like it had broken hers.

Jack's cabin was locked, as expected. Julie looked around quickly to see if there was any obvious hidey hole for a key. But honestly, she was too cold for a long search. After only a minute she pulled her gun from her pocket and aimed it at the lock.

Sorry about this, Jack. She pulled the trigger twice.

The lock shattered. She quickly opened the door and then shut it behind her. The inside wasn't much warmer than the outside, but at least it was dry and out of the wind and rain. She made her way to the wood stove and tossed in some logs and kindling. She grabbed the box of matches from the mantel and lit the fire with shaking fingers.

As soon as the kindling caught, Julie placed her hands as close as she could without getting burned. Her hands began to tingle, and then she felt pinpricks of pain as the warmth seeped in.

"Oh, thank you," Julie breathed out.

CHAPTER EIGHTY-ONE

HE HAD FOLLOWED her at a distance and had watched her spin out. He'd held back as she'd slowly made her way to the cabins. It was as if the stars had aligned. *What could be more perfect than for me to find you so easily? This was meant to be.*

From his car, he watched her shoot out the lock on his door. *My, my, aren't you resourceful.* She went inside and shut the door behind her. A few minutes later, a warm glow came from the window.

The rest of the shore remained dark. No one was out here tonight. No one would probably be out here for days. Primary residences would take precedence over these cabins.

His chest felt tight as he watched that glow beckoning him forward. This was right. She was setting the stage for him. This is how it should have been all along. After all, she was the one who knew him best. She should know all parts of him.

He watched the cabin for another few minutes, wanting her to feel safe. He smiled as he imagined the night to come. Finally, after all this time, she was his for the taking.

He stepped out of the car.

CHAPTER EIGHTY-TWO

JULIE WARMED HER HANDS. The tremors had subsided a little. She wasn't warm yet, but she was getting there. She looked around. Jack had decorated a little. There was a plaid blanket thrown over the back of a green futon. Two leather armchairs flanked the wood stove. He'd had new kitchen cabinets put in and had made the space larger by getting rid of one of the bedrooms.

Julie was surprised. It was fancier than she remembered most of the cabins being. *Maybe he spends a lot of time here.*

She glanced over at the bedroom. *If there is a God, there will be some spare clothes in there.*

Pulling the blanket from the couch around her, she walked over to the bedroom and flipped on the switch by the door. Nothing happened.

Of course. She'd forgotten the power was out. She doubled back to the kitchen and scrounged through the cabinets for a flashlight. Finding one under the sink, she turned it on. Light pierced the dim room.

Retracing her steps, she walked back to the bedroom. The

light from the flashlight led the way. There was a queen-sized bed with a log bed frame, one side table, and a lamp.

Her head whipped around as something banged against the side of the house, and her heart thundered. She froze, listening, but there were no further noises.

Just a branch, she told herself, but fear still raced through her. She had to mentally shove away an image of Steve creeping around the outside of the house. *He's not here. He won't find me.*

She ran her light across the bedroom. There was no bedding, which wasn't surprising, seeing as it was the off season. There was a double closet across from the bed. He must have added that; most of these cabins had only one narrow closet.

Feeling a little creeped out by the quiet, she slid open the closet and shined her light inside. An old pair of waders sat on the floor, but no clothes. Disappointment flashed through her.

She moved to the other side and slid the door open. A jacket hung there. She pulled it out and placed it on the bed.

But there was nothing else. *Damn.*

Then she noticed the closet had a high shelf. She reached up and felt around. Nothing. She stretched on her tiptoes and felt the edge of a wooden box.

Stretching as much as she could, she eased the box toward her slowly, only her fingertips at first catching it. As soon as she could reach her whole hand around it, she pulled it down.

The box was about ten inches by eight, with an intricate design carved into the lid. The design looked familiar, but she couldn't remember where she'd seen it before. She could hear stuff sliding around inside. She tucked it under her arm, grabbed the jacket, and headed into the living room.

She knew she was snooping, but curiosity had won her over. Jack kept nothing in this cabin except this little box. And besides, there was nothing else here to distract her except her increasingly horror movie-esque thoughts.

She sat on the floor next to the stove, the plaid blanket over her legs and the jacket resting over her shoulders. She pulled the box into her lap and traced the design. Recognition was at the edge of her consciousness, but it was just out of reach.

She felt a moment of guilt. She was invading Jack's privacy. But something urged her to open the box. Slowly she opened the lid.

Inside was an odd assortment of jewelry, watches, and buttons. *What on earth? Why would Jack keep all this random stuff?*

She pushed through the collection, unable to make any sense of it. Then something familiar caught her eye.

Her hand stilled. *No. It can't be.*

In the box was a small charm—half a heart, with the word "sister" engraved on it.

Julie's world tilted. She had given this charm to Simone two years before her death, and Simone had put it on her charm bracelet. She had been wearing the bracelet when she'd been killed; it had broken, its charms scattered across the room. This half heart was the only charm they had never found.

Why does Jack have it?

She looked over the rest of the knick-knacks in the box. Her jaw fell open as a horrible thought crossed her mind. *No. It's not possible.* Her mind scrambled to come up with another explanation for this box of mementos—mementos that included Simone's charm.

The only reason she'd turned against Steve was because he'd had Mel's medal in his jacket pocket. But Jack would also have had access to Steve's jacket.

What if they *had* gotten the time of death right? Then Steve had been locked up at the time of Mel's attack. He couldn't be responsible.

But Jack?

No one had asked Jack where *he'd* been

But why would Jack kill Mel?

More importantly, why would Jack have killed Simone?

Julie remembered Jack from when they were younger. She tried to remember any interactions he'd had with Simone. But she couldn't remember any time Jack had ever singled out Simone for attention. In fact, he'd never really paid any attention to Simone at all.

If anything, Julie was the one he'd stared at.

CHAPTER EIGHTY-THREE

STEVE PULLED up three houses away from Declan's sister's house. The old car was loud, but it had handled the roads really well. Which was amazing, because the roads were a mess—not just from water, but downed trees and more than one power line. It had taken him more than double the time it should have to get here.

Yet now that he was here, he wasn't sure what he was doing. His grandmother wasn't in trouble; she was with Declan's family. She was fine. Steve felt foolish and guilty for thinking otherwise.

But still, he needed to see her with his own eyes. His world was spinning out of control, but if he knew she was all right... well, then he could handle everything else.

Now that he was here, however, he wasn't sure exactly how to accomplish that. It's not like he could just run up, ring the doorbell, and ask. Julie had no doubt called the cops, and they would be searching for him. He looked around. *In fact, I'm surprised they're not here already.*

Leaning against the steering wheel, he looked at the house. It was a ranch which was good—only one floor to worry about. And no one seemed to be around so that was working in his favor as well. Maybe he could just peek in the window. No one would ever have to know he was here.

He blew out a breath. *Well, here goes nothing.*

He opened the car door and stepped out. No curtains shifted on any of the houses. No one called out to him. Declan's sister lived on the far side of town and houses were pretty spread out. But Steve still paused for another moment to make sure no one was looking.

When he was confident he was alone, he crossed the street. He tried to remember if Declan's sister had a dog. He really hoped she didn't.

He crept along the side of the yard, staying in the shadows of the trees. He'd start at the back. Maybe he could catch a glimpse of his grandmother through the windows. He walked silently next to a row of large evergreens that bordered the property.

"What are you doing?"

Steve whirled around. A boy of no more than eight stepped out from behind a blue spruce.

"Um, I..." Steve had no idea what to say.

The boy peered up at him. "Are you watching my yard?"

Steve tried to come up with a believable lie. He came up with nothing. Apparently, he was not meant to be a burglar. But seeing as how he was already caught, he figured he'd go for honesty. "Actually, I am. I'm looking for my grandma."

"Bess?"

Steve nodded.

"She makes really good cookies."

"Yeah. Did she bring the oatmeal ones?"

The boy nodded.

"Those are my favorites." Steve paused. "Is she still here?"

The boy shook his head. "No, some man came to pick her up."

"Do you know who he was?"

The boy shrugged. "I don't know. Some guy in a suit. He called her Grandma."

Jack. Steve's gut clenched. "How long ago was that?"

"I don't know—a while."

Steve tried to tell himself it was nothing to worry about. Probably Bess had insisted that she'd visited long enough, and she wanted to be back in her own home. She could be very stubborn.

"Well, thanks. Take care."

"Don't you want to talk to my mom?"

"Um, no. That's okay. I need to find my grandmother."

As Steve walked back to the street, he could feel the boy's eyes on him. He turned and waved. The boy waved back and then disappeared into the trees.

Steve ran the rest of the way to the car, just in case the kid was telling anyone inside. *Jack has Grandma.* But that was all right, wasn't it? Jack would never hurt her. He couldn't.

Steve pulled away from the curb, his foot planted a little heavier on the gas pedal than before. Of course Jack wouldn't hurt her. He repeated that thought to himself. But he still drove as fast as the streets would allow.

CHAPTER EIGHTY-FOUR

JULIE CLOSED the box and pushed it off her lap. She stood up, not sure what she should make of this. Was it just because she was alone? Had the frights of the last few days caused her to see threats were there were none? I mean, the killer was Steve, right?

The door flew open and Julie let out a scream.

Jack stepped in and shut the door behind him. There was a look of genuine concern on his face. "Julie? Are you okay? What are you doing here?"

Julie stared at him for a moment, struggling to figure out how to react. She could ask him point blank—but what if he admitted it? Then what? No. She needed to pretend she knew nothing.

"Jack, thank God. Do you have a car? Mine got stranded in a puddle about a mile from here."

"Yeah, I'm parked in the lot." He moved toward her. "You're soaked. Hold on. Let me see if I have any clothes or towels in my bedroom." He took a step, then stopped dead in his tracks, his eyes locked on the box on the floor.

His gaze rose to meet hers, and his whole face seemed to transform. It went hard. If evil was a thing that could be seen, that's what Julie was looking at. When Jack spoke, his voice was cold. "Seems you've already been in my bedroom."

Julie tried to bluff her way out. "Hm? Oh, the jacket, yeah. I found this box, too, but I didn't open it."

Jack laughed, and the sound sent chills down Julie's spine. "Oh, come now, Julie. I think you and I are beyond lying to each other now, aren't we?"

In that moment, Julie knew she was staring into the eyes of the man who'd killed her sister. She knew she shouldn't, but she had to ask.

"Why, Jack? Why did you do it?"

Jack smiled. "I never meant to kill Simone."

Julie felt the breath leave her lungs.

Jack took a step toward her. "You see, it was you I was coming for that night—not her."

CHAPTER EIGHTY-FIVE

JULIE BACKED AWAY, her heart pounding. Jack had killed Simone. He'd admitted it. But he'd meant to kill *her*. "I—I don't understand."

Jack perched on the edge of the futon. "You know, I've always known I was different. I had different... let's call them 'interests.' Ever since I was a kid. Who knows why. Like the song says, I was just born this way."

Julie was terrified and curious all at the same time. But mostly she was stunned. This wasn't happening. "Elise, too? Mel, Dee?"

Jack's smile grew wider. "It's been a fun couple of days. But they're only the tip of the iceberg. There are many others. You've looked in the box."

Julie knew there was no longer any point in denying it. She nodded.

"One memento for each," Jack said. "But they aren't from Millners Kill. Like they say, you don't shit in your own sandbox—until now. With Steve coming back, it was just too delicious to resist. And it's worked out perfectly. In fact, I'm betting you just called the police and told them Steve was the killer, didn't you?"

Julie's mouth dropped open. *How did he know that?*

Jack laughed. "I couldn't have planned it better."

Julie gasped. He was right. The police would shoot Steve on sight—because of her. Her eyes locked with Jack's.

He nodded back at her. "Ah, now you see your predicament. But what you don't realize is that I've been dreaming about this moment for ten long years. Truth be told, I've imagined your blood slipping through my fingers for longer than that. That night, though, it was Simone who let me in. I knew your parents went to bed early. And you said Simone usually did as well."

It was true. But that night Julie had been feeling a little under the weather and had gone to bed early, while Simone had stayed up late studying because she had a big history test the next day.

"When she answered the door, well... I decided to take the opportunity presented to me. It was simply too sweet an opportunity to resist."

Julie felt her stomach turn. He sounded so enthralled with his own acts. He *enjoyed* this. This man standing in front of her right now... this was the real Jack. The polite, concerned Jack that she'd thought she'd always known—he was the fake.

Jack pulled a knife from his pocket. There was already blood on it.

Julie pulled her gun from her pocket. "I don't think so."

He laughed, genuine amusement on his face. "See? This is what I'm talking about. I always knew you'd be special."

"Back up against the wall."

"See, I don't think I'm going to do that." He walked toward her. "And I don't think you're going to shoot me."

"You're wrong."

Julie pulled the trigger.

Jack tried to jump over the coffee table, but the bullet caught him in the calf. He screamed, and Julie dodged around him toward the door. But Jack grabbed her leg as she passed—she fell forward, her arms flailing, and the gun flew from her hand. Julie kicked with her free leg, connecting with Jack's face. He yelled and let go of her.

Julie scrambled to her feet as did Jack. The door was behind her, but the gun was now behind Jack.

Jack raised an eyebrow. "Tough choice, huh? Let me make it easier." He leapt for the gun.

Julie turned and ran for the door. As she shot through it, a bullet slammed into the doorframe right next to her. Heart pounding, she kept running. Too late, she realized she was headed for the beach. She should have turned as soon as she left the cabin. "Shit," she panted.

It was too late to change course now. She looked ahead at the water. She knew it would be cold, and she could see how rough it was. But she was a good swimmer, and there was simply no other choice.

She flew across the beach and pounded down the dock.

Jack yelled from behind her. "Where do you think you're going?"

She lengthened her stride.

She heard the report of the gun three times. Two missed.

One didn't.

It slammed into her lower back. Julie fell forward and tumbled off the end of the dock.

The dark water closed over her head before she even had time to scream. Waves crashed over her, tossing her about, and she began to sink. The pain in her back screamed. She was becoming lightheaded from either the lack of oxygen or the shock of the bullet. Probably both.

She turned and started to swim for the surface, then stopped.

Up above, at the edge of the dock, stood Jack. He was waving goodbye.

CHAPTER EIGHTY-SIX

DECLAN PULLED into his sister's drive. Keith had made it clear that his help was not welcome in the search for Julie or Steve, but Declan planned on helping anyway. He just had to do one thing first.

For a minute he sat and looked at his sister's home. He'd fought with her more than a few times about his support of Steve. She'd always worried what it would do to his career, and she'd never understood how Declan just couldn't let him go.

But Steve had always been like a little brother to him. He'd never had a brother. He wondered for a moment why he'd never felt that way about Jack. Maybe it was because Jack always seemed to know what he was doing, and Steve... well, he always seemed a little lost. A little too innocent.

Declan rubbed his face. *Apparently not as innocent as I thought.*

He looked up at the house and his stomach dropped. He was going to have to go in there and tell Bess about Steve. It was going to break her. All these years, she had defended him. *And now...*

Declan shook his head. *Damn.*

Knowing he couldn't put it off any longer, he opened the car door. Rain pelted him, but he couldn't work up the energy to care. He walked slowly up the front path.

The door swung open before his hand touched the doorknob. Nate, his eight-year-old nephew, stood there. "Um, you forget your umbrella?"

Declan nodded. "Yeah. How's everything going here?"

Nate shrugged. "Okay. I got to play outside for a little, but then it started raining again."

"Yeah. I think it's supposed to stop tomorrow, so maybe we can go for a drive around the island. See the storm damage."

"Cool."

Declan shrugged off his coat. "Where's Bess?"

"She went home."

Declan went still. "What?"

"Some guy in a suit came and picked her up."

Declan felt relief flow through him. *Jack. Good.* He nodded. And glanced back outside. He owed it to them both to tell them himself. Better they hear it from him than from Keith. He pulled his jacket back on. "Well, I need to speak with them. Tell your mom I'll be back." He stepped back outside.

"Okay." Nate started to close the door. "Oh, and your other friend stopped by."

Declan turned slowly. "What friend?"

"The man who was in prison."

Steve was here? Declan's heart began to pound. "Did he come inside?"

"No. He was looking for Bess. I told him she went home, so he left."

He's going after Bess.

"Lock the door and tell your mother not to let anyone in," Declan yelled, and he ran for his car. He threw himself behind the steering wheel and quickly reversed out of the drive.

He slammed the car into drive and tore down the street.

He eyed the radio on the passenger seat, waging an inner war with himself. *Damn it.* He grabbed the radio and keyed it. "Steve Kane is heading for his home. His grandmother and brother are there as well. I repeat, Steve Kane is heading for his home. His grandmother and brother are there as well. All units respond."

He dropped the radio back on the seat, knowing he had probably just signed Steve's death warrant—and feeling really annoyed that he still cared.

CHAPTER EIGHTY-SEVEN

JULIE BROKE through the water near a piling. She'd swum sideways under the dock, stayed under as long as she'd dared, and then surfaced quietly under the wooden planks. She wanted to suck in a lungful of air, but she knew she needed to try to take in only small breaths. She prayed the water hitting against the pilings drowned out the sounds of her ragged breathing. Blood pounded in her ears, and she couldn't seem to stop the tremors in her arms.

The waves were threatening to pull her back out into the open water. She flipped onto her back, letting out a little cry at the pain that radiated through her back. Nausea rolled through her. Gritting her teeth, she kicked her legs, heading for the pilings closer to shore.

She had to battle the waves the whole way there. Each time she got a foot closer, the next wave seemed to push her another two feet back.

Please, Julie begged, exhaustion beginning to weigh her down.

"Don't stop."

At first, Julie thought she'd imagined the voice.

"Julie, don't stop. You're almost there."

Julie opened her eyes. A teenage girl, her dark hair wet from the rain, was treading water next to her. "Simone?"

Simone nodded. "You need to move, Julie. You need to swim."

"I'm too tired."

"No. Stay awake. Look at me. *Look* at me."

Julie cracked open her eyes. "You're dead."

"And you will be too. Now move."

Rationally, Julie knew Simone was just a hallucination. Her body was shutting down. Her brain was shutting down. But she still felt better not being alone.

She kicked with her legs.

"That's it. Keep going," Simone urged.

Julie kicked harder. "I miss you, Simone."

"I miss you too."

Julie kept kicking until her head bumped against a piling. She reached out and grabbed onto a rope wrapped around it. Her grip was weak, but she held on.

She pulled herself around to the other side and wrapped her arms around the pole, resting her head against the rough wood. The waves were now pushing her toward the piling, helping her hold on. Her face was getting scratched up pretty good, but it was making it easier to keep her grip. But even with the water's assist, she knew she didn't have the energy to hold on for long. She wrapped her hands in the rope and closed her eyes.

"Wake up."

Julie struggled to open her eyes.

"Wake up," Simone said again.

Julie cracked her eyes open, not sure if she'd lost consciousness or not.

"Hold on. They're coming," Simone said, still treading water next to her.

"Can't. Too tired," Julie mumbled.

"Just hold on. They're almost here. Look."

Julie could see a flashlight bobbing along the shore. She tried to yell out. "Here. I'm here." Her voice was barely above a whisper.

But the flashlight moved in her direction. For a moment, she worried it might be Jack, but Simone seemed so confident. And at this point, it wouldn't matter if it was Jack. It was going to be over soon, one way or the other.

The light from the flashlight raked underneath the dock. Julie winced when the bright light hit her eyes.

She shut them. Warmth seemed to be calling to her. *I'll just take a little nap.*

"Julie. Open your eyes." A hand touched her face.

Julie struggled to pull herself from the warmth. She blinked a few times and then opened her eyes fully.

Russ was treading water next to her.

"How?" she asked, her voice weak.

He gently pulled her arms from around the pole and put her back against his front. She gasped as his belt came in contact with her wound.

"Sorry, sorry," he whispered in her ear as he swam for shore. He quickly got them to the bank and pulled her out of the water.

Julie felt a sense of unreal. And somehow she felt warmer.

"Stay with me, Julie." Russ rolled her onto her side.

She grunted when his hand brushed her wound. "Shot," she mumbled.

Russ gently picked her up in his arms, his words rushed. "I'm taking you to the cruiser. We need to warm you up and get you to the med center."

Julie felt herself drifting in and out of consciousness. "How'd you find me?"

"I was already in the area, looking for you and Steve, when I heard about your call to the station. I switched directions and came here."

She struggled to focus on his words. That wasn't what she meant. "How did you find me?"

He shook his head. "I don't know. I just... I felt like I should check the dock. And then I heard you call out."

But Julie knew that was impossible. Her voice wasn't loud enough. She closed her eyes. A tear slipped down her cheek. *Thank you, Simone.*

"We'll get you on a medevac to the mainland. Don't worry. And Declan is closing in on Steve. He won't be able to hurt anyone else."

Julie shook her head. She was losing her battle with consciousness, but she knew something about what Russ was saying was wrong. Then she remembered. She tried to speak, but she couldn't.

It's not him. You're after the wrong guy.

CHAPTER EIGHTY-EIGHT

STEVE CROUCHED low against the side of his grandmother's house. Jack's car wasn't in the drive, but there were candles lit in the living room and kitchen, and he could hear Frank Sinatra playing on his grandmother's old battery-operated radio. He peered in through the kitchen window but there was no sign of either his grandmother or Jack.

Steve made his way around the outside of the house to the living room window. He was surprised that the house didn't look damaged. He'd expected broken windows or maybe some more graffiti.

He peered inside and saw his grandmother sitting in a chair. Her knitting basket lay on the ground next to her. He let out a breath. *Thank God.*

He climbed the porch and tried the front door. Locked. He knocked. "Gran? It's me. It's Steve."

Nothing but Frank Sinatra answered him. The hairs on his arm rose. He knocked again, louder and more insistent. "Gran? It's Steve. Open the door."

Still nothing. Steve's heart began to pound.

She just can't hear me over the music. His key only worked
the back door. He ran down the stairs, stopping only long
enough to peer in the window again. His grandmother's hand
twitched, and he let out a breath. *Okay. She's fine. She probably
fell asleep.*

He ran to the back door and tried it. Locked as well. He
unlocked the door and made his way to the living room. "Gran?
Are you all right?"

She stayed in her chair, her head tilted to the side. Her knitting lay in a heap at her feet. He ran to her.

Her eyes shifted to him, but the bottom half of her face
seemed to have frozen, and her lip drooped on one side. Terror
paralyzed him. *A stroke. She's had a stroke.*

He knelt down next to her and ran a shaky hand over her
hair, the same way she had done to him thousands of times. "It's
going to be okay, Grandma."

Heart pounding, he picked her up out of the chair, carried
her to the couch, and laid her down gently. He placed a pillow
under her head, then pulled the afghan from the back of the
couch and tucked it around her.

He knelt down next to her, taking her hand. At first he
thought she was trembling, but then he realized the shake in her
hand came from him. He tucked her arms under the blanket and
wiped her hair from her eyes. "Gran, I'm going to call for help.
You've had a stroke, okay?"

A tear leaked from the corner of her eye. Steve wiped it away.
"It's okay. I'm right here with you. I'm not going anywhere. I'm
going to call for help." He kissed her on the forehead before
standing up. He was almost in the kitchen when he heard a key
in the front door.

He turned around as Jack stepped in.

All his earlier suspicions about Jack were immediately
forgotten as soon as his brother stepped into the room. "Jack,

thank God. I think Grandma's had a stroke. I'm going to call for help. Stay with her."

Steve ran into the kitchen and pulled the receiver off the handset. The cord dangled in the air. It had been cut. Steve stared at it stupidly for a moment, not understanding what he was seeing. How the hell did the phone line get cut?

Steve ran back into the living room, the phone still clutched in his hand. "The phone's been cut."

Jack stood beside the couch, looking down at their grandmother, rolling one of her knitting needles in his hands. "I know."

"You *know*? Why is it cut?"

Jack looked over at him. "Yes. I know, because I cut it. I didn't want her to be able to call for help."

Steve stared at his brother, his thoughts tumbling over top of one another. "What? When? Jack, what the hell are you talking about?"

"She had the stroke about an hour ago. Before I left."

Steve's mind was a jumble. An hour ago? His anger boiled. "She had the stroke *before* you left? You just—*left* her here?"

Jack shrugged and twirled the knitting needle. "I had things to take care of."

Steve stared, dumbfounded. Who the hell was this man?

Jack looked down at his grandmother. "But don't worry, Gran, you have my undivided attention now."

He plunged the knitting needle into her stomach.

CHAPTER EIGHTY-NINE

BESS'S BODY lurched as Jack thrust the needle in almost to the hilt.

"No!" Steve yelled, launching himself across the room.

Jack whipped a gun out of his pocket and pointed it at Steve. "Don't." His voice was flat.

Steve stopped, but his eyes remained fixed on his grand-mother. Her chest still rose, but blood pooled around the needle. She was still here, but he wasn't sure for how much longer.

Steve turned his gaze to Jack. Jack's eyes were hard. His face was that of a stranger. No—not a stranger. Just someone Steve hadn't seen in a long, long time.

"Why are you doing this?" Steve asked quietly.

Jack grinned. "Because it's fun." He gestured toward the kitchen with the gun. "Let's chat in there, shall we?"

Steve glanced at his grandmother, debating what to do.

Jack aimed the gun at her. "I *will* kill her."

Steve wanted to rush Jack right then, but he knew that if he failed, his grandmother would die. Glaring, he walked backward toward the kitchen.

Jack chuckled as he followed, a slight limp in his step. "What? You don't trust me? I'm hurt, little brother. I really am."

Steve clenched his fists, warning himself to stay calm. He needed to figure a way to get the gun from Jack.

Jack waved him toward the kitchen table. "Take a seat."

"I'd rather stand."

Jack's voice was glacial. "I didn't *ask* you to take a seat. I *told* you to take one."

Steve hesitated. Then he walked over and took a seat, his arms crossed over his chest. "Why don't you just kill me and get it over with?"

Surprise flashed across Jack's face. "Kill you? Why would I do that? After all, you're my stooge. You're the one who takes the blame for all my little indiscretions."

"Indiscretions?"

Jack looked at him, his eyebrows raised.

And every doubt about Jack came roaring back. He felt sick. "You killed Simone, didn't you?"

Jack waved his hand, indicating that Steve should keep going.

"And Mel, Elise, and Dee."

Jack smiled. "True. And not a soul suspects me. Not with my brother, the big bad murderer, in town." He cocked his head to the side. "You never suspected me either, did you? Not even when Dad disappeared? I mean, come on, after Dad, that was a pretty radical change of behavior on my part, don't you think?"

Steve stared, confused. "Dad? What does Dad have to do with this?"

Jack laughed and slapped his knee. "God, this is too good. You don't have clue."

Steve gritted his teeth. "Why don't you tell me then?"

Jack wiped tears of laughter from his eyes, a giant grin on his face. "Dad was the only one who ever really *saw* me. Didn't you ever wonder why he never let you be alone with me? He caught me trying to suffocate you with a pillow when you were three. Mom said I was just playing. But Dad knew better."

Cold spread through Steve. He spoke slowly. "Why did Dad leave?"

Jack raised an eyebrow. "*Now* you're beginning to understand. Dad was getting more and more strict. He needed to go away. He was my first. He was the one who showed me who I could be."

"You killed him?"

Jack just smiled.

"But—but why? You were nice to me after that. In fact, you were nice to everyone after Dad disappeared."

"Yes, I was, wasn't I? You, Mom, Gran, my whole 'town boy makes good' persona—you were all my beard."

"Your beard?"

Jack sighed. "Your institutional education apparently has quite a few holes. My *beard*—my disguise, my cover. You guys made me seem like the perfect son, brother, citizen. No one would ever accuse the hardworking Jack Kane of any murderous deeds."

Steve's jaw went slack. His brother was crazy. But as he stared at Jack, he realized that wasn't right. No, Jack was sane—coldly and inhumanly sane. He simply didn't care about anyone or anything besides himself.

"You're a psychopath."

Jack shrugged. "Probably."

Steve shook himself from his shock. "Grandma needs medical attention. What do you want?"

Jack narrowed his eyes and raised the gun. "Don't rush me, Steve. I've been waiting for this moment for nearly twenty years. Twenty years since Dad's death—ten since Simone's. I won't be rushed."

Steve's temper began to boil. *Bastard.* Jack wanted to brag about his accomplishments. The thought brought Steve up short.

"All the letters in prison," Steve said. "They weren't to show me what a good life I could have on the outside. They were an opportunity for you to gloat. To twist the knife I didn't even know was in my back."

Jack nodded. "Oh, it has been fun."

"Why Simone, though?"

Jack waved the gun carelessly. "It was never supposed to be Simone. It was supposed to be Julie."

Steve felt the ground fall out from under him. *Julie?*

"Your best friend," Jack continued. "Your little confidante. But this way worked out even better. You lost her anyway, even while she was still alive—well at least she *was.*"

Steve went cold. "What did you do?"

"I've already taken care of her. Not in as satisfying a way as I would have liked, but fate intervened."

"Julie's dead?"

"Of course. In fact, this is her gun. Nice, isn't it?"

Steve clenched his fist under the table.

Jack tilted his head. "Does that make you mad? Careful, Grandma needs you to be alive to help her. Which brings us to our little game."

"This isn't a game."

"Oh, but it is. And now, for you to win—for you to save Grandma—all you need to do is turn into the killer that everyone thinks you are."

CHAPTER NINETY

JACK LEANED BACK against the counter, his feet crossed at the ankles, looking perfectly at peace—even with Julie's gun trained on Steve. "You've always been so soft. I'm surprised you survived being locked up. If not for Declan, you probably wouldn't have."

Steve said nothing. Jack placed the gun on the counter behind him and then walked over to the back door. Steve looked from Jack to the gun.

Jack smiled. "Go ahead. Take it. I won't stop you. But if you want to save Gran, you're going to have to kill me. I'm not letting you out of here any other way. And if you don't kill me... well, then the first chance I get, *I'm* going to kill *her*. If she survives tonight. Maybe I'll do it tomorrow, or the day after that... or the month or the year. But I'll do it. I'll kill her."

Steve walked over and picked up the gun. He pointed it at Jack. "What makes you think I won't?"

"You don't think I deserve to die."

Steve tightened his grip. "Oh, you deserve to die."

Jack's face changed from confidence to fear in a second. "Declan, help me. He's gone crazy."

Too late, Steve heard footsteps behind him. "Steve, put down the gun."

Declan stood in the doorway of the kitchen, his gun trained on Steve.

Steve moved so he could keep an eye on both Declan and Jack. "Declan, it's not what you think."

"I need you to put down that gun, Steve. Jack, walk over here and get behind me," Declan said.

Steve gripped the gun, following Jack's progress toward Declan. "Declan, you don't understand. It's been Jack all along."

Jack moved behind Declan. His words came out rushed, terrified, but he grinned behind Declan's back as he spoke. "I can't believe it's been Steve this whole time. And now he's killed Grandma. We were so wrong. He needs help. We can get him help." Jack winked at Steve.

Declan adjusted his grip. "Steve, I need you to put the gun down. We can talk about this."

Steve stared at him and then nodded, lowering the gun. Behind Declan, Jack pulled a knife from his pocket with a smile, shaking his head at Steve. He raised it above his head and took a step toward Declan.

"No!" Steve yelled, bringing the gun back up.

"Don't do it!" Declan yelled. "We can get you some help."

Jack shook his head, but he added a plea to his voice. "Listen to him Steve, please. Think about Grandma."

Steve looked between the two of them, his heart pounding.

Jack raised the knife above Declan's back.

"Don't do this," Steve begged.

"I'm not the one doing it," Declan said.

Jack just grinned bigger. And Steve knew that Jack would kill Declan without a second thought.

Steve fired.

"Steve, no!" Declan yelled, firing at the same time.

Blood bloomed across Jack's left shoulder. He fell forward, landing on Declan, who turned to catch him. Jack's knife fell from his hand and clattered across the floor. Declan's eyes grew wide and then flew back to Steve.

Steve dropped to his knees. The gun fell from his hands. Blood poured from the wound in the center of his chest.

Declan's radio rang out with Russ's voice. "Declan, it wasn't Steve. It was Jack. Declan, can you hear me? It wasn't Steve. It was Jack."

Steve fell to the floor. He could feel his life slipping away through the hole in his chest.

Keith stormed in the back door with two deputies behind him. With one quick glance, he took in the scene. He stomped over to Steve. "You murdering bastard." He kicked Steve in the face.

"No!" Declan yelled.

Steve's head whipped to the side, and the world disappeared.

CHAPTER NINETY-ONE

TWO DAYS Later

The insistent beeping was driving him nuts. All Steve wanted to do was drift back into the warm cocoon he'd been in. It had been good there. Comforting. He tried to shut the noise out, but it wouldn't go away.

He became aware of more noises. A voice sounded from somewhere far away, the words indistinguishable. It was followed by movement as someone shifted in a chair—that noise was much closer.

Steve cracked his eyes open. He took in the white walls, white bedding, and medical equipment Then he closed them again against the bright lights. *Hospital.*

"Steve?"

Steve turned his head to the right. Declan leaned forward in his chair and let out a breath. "You're awake. Thank God."

Declan looked awful. A thick, dark stubble had grown across the lower half of his face. His shirt was wrinkled and untucked. Steve couldn't ever remember seeing Declan looking anything but immaculately groomed. "Declan?"

Declan's face was drawn. It looked like he'd aged years since Steve had last seen him. "I'm so sorry. I didn't realize—"

Steve stared at him, confused. What the hell was he talking about?

Then the scene in the kitchen came back to him with startling, painful clarity.

"Grandma?"

Declan hesitated. He grasped Steve's hand. "I'm sorry. She didn't make it."

Steve had thought he couldn't feel any worse. He was wrong. The whole world had just been bleached of its colors. Tears clouded his vision. His grandmother had stood by him through everything, and he hadn't been able to save her.

He looked away and closed his eyes, feeling the tears track down his cheeks. "I should have saved her."

"No. Don't you take that guilt on. It's not yours to carry. All of that belongs to Jack."

Steve's eyes flew open. He turned back to Declan. "You know?"

Declan grimaced. "When Jack fell on me and the knife fell from his hand, I realized what had happened. Then Russ's call came through on the radio, confirming it was Jack. When I spoke with Julie later, she filled in the gaps."

Steve jolted. "Julie's alive?"

"Yeah. She was shot, nearly drowned, but she made it. She's pretty tough."

For a moment, Steve felt a sense of relief, even happiness. Julie was all right. And she knew it wasn't him.

But reality shut the door on the hope that had begun to bloom in his chest. It wasn't Steve who had killed Simone—but it was a Kane. Steve's own brother. Julie might not hate Steve anymore, but he was still the one who'd brought that evil to her family.

"Why did you think it was me?" Steve asked.

Declan looked away. "I matched a print from the crime scene at Mel's to your old fingerprint card at the police station."

Steve frowned. "How's that possible?"

"I checked Jack's prints and rolled yours again while you were out. Jack must have switched the cards years ago. No one ever noticed."

Declan kept speaking but Steve tuned him out. He couldn't believe it. Jack was a killer. He had framed him for murder. And he'd killed their grandmother. He was a monster—and a far worse one than people had even thought *he* was.

Declan was still talking, but it took Steve a few seconds to realize it—he was too caught up in his own thoughts. "Sorry. What did you say?"

"Jack—he killed a lot more people than the ones in town. He had a box of trophies. We're cross-checking missing person cases and unsolved homicides against his known travel. So far we have over a dozen possibilities." Declan stared out the window. "He's been doing this for a decade and we had no clue."

"No," Steve rasped out, feeling dizzy. He then swallowed, trying to get some moisture in his mouth.

Declan stood and poured Steve a glass of water from the tray next to the bed. He held the straw to Steve's lips and let him drink. Steve nodded when he was done, and Declan put the cup back on the tray.

"Thanks." Steve closed his eyes. He was exhausted.

"I'll let you get some rest."

Steve nodded. What had he wanted to say to Declan? His eyes flew open. "No. Not yet. You need to know: Simone wasn't his first. My dad was."

Declan jerked back. "What?"

"My dad disappeared when I was ten. Jack was thirteen."

Declan's face was full of horror. "He started at thirteen?"

"That I know of."

"He's going to have a lot of questions to answer when he goes to trial."

Steve jerked, and pain coursed through him. He sucked air in through his teeth. "He's still alive?"

"It was touch and go for a little while, but he pulled through."

Grandma was dead. Mel was dead. Simone, Dee, Elise, and countless others. Yet his brother, the monster, lived. If Steve had ever believed life was fair that fact would have ended it. But the truth was, Steve had never suffered from that delusion. And his brother was the reason for that as well. Because Steve had come to that understanding when he was ten—the day his dad disappeared.

Steve closed his eyes again, losing the battle against sleep. Declan leaned down to whisper in his ear. "Everyone knows you're innocent, Steve. Take some solace in that. And your brother is going to go away for the rest of his life."

CHAPTER NINETY-TWO

STEVE WASN'T sure how long he slept. He vaguely remembered Declan saying he'd be back. He felt a presence next to his bed and figured Declan had returned. He opened his eyes and stared with shock.

It wasn't Declan. It was Julie. She sat in the chair beside his bed, a hospital gown and robe wrapped around her. She looked paler than usual. She had scratches on her face and a bruise along her cheek.

She looked beautiful.

Steve swallowed. "Julie? You okay?"

She started, then leaned toward him. A small smile crossed her face. "Nothing that won't heal. You were a lot worse off."

"Well, I hate to disappoint everyone, but I think I'm going to live."

"Don't talk that way," Julie said.

Steve tried to smile. He wasn't sure if he succeeded. "Kidding."

"Sorry. I'm a little... I don't know, sensitive? Jumpy?"

"Well, I hear brushes with death will do that." Steve's eyelids tried to close. He jerked them back open.

"I'm sorry about your grandmother."

"Me too." His eyelids closed again, and he knew he wasn't going to be able to stay awake much longer. "Sorry. Sleepy."

Julie took his hand, placed a kiss on his forehead, and whispered in his ear, "Sleep. I'll be right here when you wake up."

Steve gripped her hand, and for the first time in a long time, he had something to look forward to.

An excerpt from
The Belial Stone by R.D. Brady

Two Years Ago
Havre, Montana

Kenny Coleman's dirt drive was doing a number on the Mercedes. It dipped and dived with the bumps. Watching, Kenny's stomach felt like it was doing the same. The last time he'd been this nervous, it was proposing to his Mary.

"It's just a professor. No big deal," he muttered to himself. The butterflies in his stomach, however, ignored him, continuing their maniacal flying.

The Mercedes finally rolled to a stop in a cloud of dust in front of his porch. His old Australian shepherd came to attention and emitted a low growl.

Surprised, Kenny reached down from his rocking chair and patted him on the head. "Hush now, Blue."

The dog quieted. But as the car door opened, he growled again. Kenny could feel the dog's body tense. He grabbed hold of his collar. When the driver stepped into view, Blue emitted a feral snarl and lunged for the steps, nearly yanking Kenny's arm off.

Kenny struggled to hold him back. "No, Blue, no!"

While Kenny might be pushing sixty-five, his life as a cattleman had given him muscle. He wrapped his beefy arms around the dog's torso, carrying him back to the house, ignoring the sting as claws raked his forearms.

Kicking open the front door, he half-shoved, half-threw the dog across the threshold, slamming the door shut behind him.

Kenny stepped back and gaped at the door as Blue slammed his body into it, again and again.

He shook his head, unable to believe what he was seeing. Angry red welts crisscrossed his forearms. This was an animal who'd let his grandkids flop on him while they watched cartoons. In the twelve years he'd had him, he'd barely heard him growl.

With a deep breath, he pushed his concerns for his dog's uncharacteristic behavior to the back of his mind. He felt the professor's eyes on his back and felt the flush creep up his neck. *Damn.* This was not the first impression he wanted to make.

Rolling down his green flannel sleeves, he walked down the stairs and across the expanse in front of his farmhouse.

"I'm sorry, Professor Gideon," Kenny stammered out. "He's never like that. I don't know what got into him."

"No harm done, Mr. Coleman. I appreciate you taking the time to show me your find." A polite smile graced the blonde professor's angular face, but that politeness didn't quite reach his cool blue eyes.

Back in the day, Kenny knew he was considered a handsome man - strong and tall with thick, dark hair. The girls had loved to run their hands through it. And in spite of his full head of now-white hair, he was vain enough to think he still was.

But he knew this professor was what currently stood for handsome. Slim, with pale blue eyes perched above a patrician nose and sharp cheekbones. Dressed in expensive slacks, a brown suede jacket, and shiny loafers, he was one of those "metrosexuals" his daughter talked about.

Can't say he ever really understood the appeal of a man who was pretty, but hell, he never did understand much about what was cool.

Extending his calloused hand, Kenny spoke a little louder than usual, trying to block out Blue's unending barks. "I'd really like to know what I've found. I just can't figure out what something like that is doing on my ranch."

The professor's hand was soft, the shake just shy of limp. "Well, let's take a look. How did you come across it?"

"It was the strangest thing. I was looking for a stray calf one day, and I literally stumbled over the tip of it."

"How much was showing at first?"

Kenny shrugged. "Not much. Maybe four, five inches. It was just such a strange-looking rock, all black with those brown and green veins running through it. I'd never seen one like that anywhere around these parts. So, I marked the spot and went back later to dig it out. I couldn't believe it when I saw it. I took some pictures and posted them online to see if anyone could tell me anything about it. Less than an hour later, I got a call from you."

"Have you spoken with anyone else about it?"

"No. I wasn't sure it was anything important." He avoided the professor's eyes. *And I didn't want to look like some old fool grasping at straws.*

"And no one else has called?" Gideon's gaze was intent.

"No, no. You're the only one. I thought for sure I'd get a couple more people interested. But my pictures disappeared from the site I posted them on and I couldn't re-post them." He shook his head. "I'm not real good with the computer. It really is an amazing sight, though."

"Well, let's have a look, shall we?" Gideon gestured for him to lead the way.

Kenny hesitated, unsure. He glanced back at the house, where Blue's growls had turned to desperate howls. Blue just didn't act like this. Maybe this was a bad idea.

But he knew the medical bills for his grandson were piling up. This strange rock might be his only chance of making some extra money. He sighed. There really was no choice. He nodded and led the professor towards the northwest.

They followed a trail created by wild horses and buffalo generations ago. Kenny tried making conversation. He talked about the Sioux and the Crow that used to summer in the area and pointed out where he had hunted for arrowheads as a kid. The professor only grunted in response.

Small talk about the weather and questions about the professor's research resulted in equally unenthusiastic responses. Soon, Kenny just lapsed into silence.

For the first time Kenny could recall, he felt the isolation of his ranch press down on him. He knew there was no one around for miles. Montana was the size of New England, with only the population of Rhode Island. Generally, the isolation of his ranch was the reason he loved it. But walking next to the professor, he couldn't help but feel uneasy.

It wasn't just Blue's reaction, which, to be honest, scared the hell out of him. It was like the dog had seen the devil himself. It was also that this man looked nothing like a professor. He was too young, too good-looking, and too well dressed.

And there was something about him that just felt off. The man had barely spared a glance at the snow-topped mountains that were a backdrop to Kenny's property. He'd never had anyone come to the ranch that hadn't commented on that incredible view.

Walking next to him, Kenny was reminded of the time when, as a kid, he'd been stalked by a mountain lion. He'd had a vague sense of uneasiness that day. But until the cat screeched as it leapt at him, he hadn't realized the true danger he was in. That day, his dad had cut the lion in half with a shotgun. Kenny gave the professor another surreptitious glance and couldn't help wishing he'd brought his shotgun along today.

"Are we getting close?" Gideon asked.

Startled, Kenny stumbled. Shaking his head at his clumsiness, he pointed to an arrangement of three small boulders twenty yards away that stood out in the flat, almost treeless ground. "Just beyond those boulders is where I started digging. I still haven't been able to get to the bottom of the rock."

Gideon nodded and picked up his pace. As he passed the boulders, he came to an abrupt stop and stared at the small excavation.

The monolith stood five feet tall, although it was obvious there was still more buried beneath the earth. At first glance, the obelisk appeared smooth. Kenny's first thought had been that it looked like one of those fancy granite countertops. On closer inspection, though, the niches carefully carved into the black stone depicting figures and what resembled Egyptian hieroglyphs became clear.

Seconds stretched into minutes as the professor simply stared at the rock in silence. Kenny's nervousness increased. "Uh, Professor Gideon, are you all right?"

Gideon's eyes snapped to Kenny. Kenny took a step back from the man.

But when Gideon spoke, his voice was calm. "It's an amazing sight, isn't it? Would it be all right if I went closer?"

The professor's words reduced Kenny's fears, making him feel foolish. *What the hell is wrong with me today? He's just a professor interested in my find.*

"Sure, sure. After all, you're the expert." Kenny watched the professor gracefully leap into the hole.

Gideon reverently touched the stone, tracing some of the carvings with his index finger. "Finally," he murmured.

After a few moments of internal debate, Kenny's curiosity won out over his uneasiness. He clambered down to stand next to the man. "So, any idea where it came from? It kind of looks like something you'd expect to find in Egypt or down in Central America or some other ancient place."

Gideon looked over at Kenny. "Actually, this site predates those other sites by quite a significant margin."

"Really?" Kenny asked, astonished. "Even older than the pyramids?"

"Yes. Even older than that." He pointed to a spot on the artifact about three quarters of the way up. "Do you see this mark here?"

Kenny squinted at the etching. "That little circle?"

"Yes. That little circle is something I have been trying to find for an incredibly long time."

Kenny's eyes shifted to the professor. The man couldn't be any older than twenty-nine. This younger generation seemed to have a different view of time than his generation.

"Hmm," he murmured. "What is it?"

"Why, it's the end of the world," Gideon said with a slow smile.

"What?" Kenny glanced over at Gideon, thinking he must have misunderstood him.

Gideon turned to face him. His smile looked almost lethal and what Kenny had thought were pale blue eyes seemed to have darkened. "You have been very helpful, Mr. Coleman."

The words were polite, but the tone sent the fears Kenny had been shoving down right back to the surface. The professor pulled a gun from under his suit jacket. Kenny didn't hesitate. He shoved the professor and scrambled out of the hole.

Kenny looked back over his shoulder, expecting to feel a bullet between his shoulder blades at any minute. Instead, he saw Gideon still in the hole, smiling at him. He was even nodding. Kenny didn't understand the man's reaction and he had no interest in figuring it out.

Kenny panted as he sprinted for the house. He didn't hear

the professor behind him. He hoped it stayed that way until he reached one of his guns. He had a shot if he could just get to his truck or the barn. He kept rifles in both of them. That hope kept pushing him forward as his legs turned to jelly, and his breathing to sharp, painful gasps.

His farmhouse came into view and the sound of Blue still barking urged him on.

Footfalls echoed through the empty space behind him and panic charged through him. He knew he should keep running, looking behind would only slow him down, but he couldn't help himself.

Only a hundred yards away, the professor sprinted towards him, his legs moving like train pistons. He didn't even look winded. How had he caught up with him so fast?

Kenny dug down deep for a last reserve of energy, but his body wouldn't comply. He was slowing. Dark spots were beginning to form around the edges of his vision, causing him to stumble and weave.

The professor had no such affliction. Kenny could feel his attention focused on him. The pounding of his feet maintained their steady cadence. He kept coming, like a missile locked on its target, covering the distance to him in seconds. As he caught up with him, he didn't pull him to stop.

To Kenny's astonishment, the professor started to run next to him. He glanced over at the man in terror. Gideon just smiled in response.

Then in a blur of motion, Gideon sprinted a few feet ahead. He came to came to a dead stop and whirled to face Kenny.

Kenny tried to dodge around him, but he was too exhausted and too slow. Gideon's hand snaked out and easily grabbed him by the shoulder. He turned Kenny around and pulled him close.

Kenny struggled and managed to throw a feeble right hook at Gideon's ribs.

Gideon smoothly blocked the punch and trapped both of Kenny's arms with one of his own. He leaned down into Kenny's terrified face and smiled, pressing the gun to his chest.

"Good for you, Mr. Coleman. Everyone should have such a sense of self-preservation. You'd be amazed at how few people actually do. And you've given a good effort, especially for a man of your age. You should be proud of yourself."

Kenny wanted to rail at the man. He wanted to scream at him for doing this to him and plead with him to spare his life, if only for the sake of his daughter and grandchildren. But all he managed to rasp out was a single question.

"Why?"

Gideon's voice was almost a caress when he answered. His eyes looked strangely bright, as if covered in a sheen of tears. "It's the only way for my misery to end. You have brought my search to its conclusion, Mr. Coleman. I will always appreciate that." And with a beatific smile, he pulled the trigger three times.

Pain slashed through Kenny, and then, blessed numbness. He felt himself being lifted as the echoes of the gunshots retreated. He thought of his daughter and his heart already beating unsteadily, felt even heavier. *I'm sorry, sweetheart.*

Blue's frantic barking changed to mournful howls as they approached the farmhouse. *Run, Blue, run,* Kenny shouted in his mind. But the only words that were heard weren't his.

"Don't worry, Blue," Gideon murmured. "I haven't forgotten about you."

The Belial Stone is available on Amazon.com

NOTE FROM THE AUTHOR

This book came about differently than other books I've written. Usually, something strikes my interest—an ancient site, an unusual historical fact—and the story develops from there. But this book was built around an event. The change in approach came after reading Stephen King's *On Writing*.

The first half of *On Writing* is autobiographical. Mr. King describes his childhood and adulthood. And you can't help but wonder if those events helped hone his decidedly spooky imagination, or if he focused on those events because of his spooky bent.

Anyway, the second half of *On Writing* described Mr. King's writing process. One thing that stuck for me was when he said he put people into a situation and then wrote their way out of it. To me, that sounded like fun.

The first thought that came to me when thinking about the storyline for *Runs Deep* was the massive flooding that occurred in upstate New York a few years back. Whole towns were cut off for days due to the massive influx of rain. So I had my situation: a town cut off by floodwaters.

Then all I needed were the people. The first person I thought of was Steve Kane. I pictured this man being released from prison and going back to the town where everyone thought he was a murderer. Then the town gets cut off and the bodies begin to pile up. How would the town react?

So that's how the story was born. And it's been a fun ride. This one was particularly fun to write because I got to incorporate my criminological background into the book with Jack the psychopath. Psychopaths have been a topic of fascination for me since graduate school. As described in this book, psychopaths, like Jack, are often glib, easygoing, and well liked. Contrary to popular opinion, they are not always intelligent, although Jack is. But their most defining characteristic is their lack of conscience.

If you are interested in an introduction to the world of psychopaths, try Robert Hare's *Without Conscience*. It's out of print now, but there are a number of secondhand copies floating around the internet. Dr. Hare does an incredible job of bringing the world of psychopaths to life using real-world examples. An absolutely essential read for those trying to understand the conscience-less among us.

There's one other part of the story that I pulled from the news headlines: Flat Stanley. I read about how this elementary school was sending Flat Stanleys (hand-drawn pictures that could be put in a soldier's wallet) to soldiers for them to carry through their tours. Then the soldier would write back and tell the students about Flat Stanley's adventures. I thought that sounded incredible. I could picture this little friend accompanying a soldier through incredibly difficult times as a reminder that people cared. So when I was figuring out Declan and Steve's relationship, I knew that Flat Stanley needed to be a part of it.

Usually I do a fact-or-fiction section at the end of my books, but that didn't seem appropriate for this book. Still, there are a couple of little tidbits worth chatting about. First off, I mentioned that Steve ate breakfast in prison for a few years at around three in the morning. That is actually taken from true life. Prisons often contract out for their food services, often to restaurants. The restaurants, however, usually will arrange for breakfast to occur before they open their place. And occasionally, that is extremely early in the morning.

The information provided on the BTK killer and serial killers in general is also accurate. As Keith mentioned, there was a serial killer who was an ambulance driver. He would dump bodies before his shift so that he could then be the one who was called to pick it up. Lovely, right?

Dennis Rader, the BTK killer—which by the way stands for Bind, Torture Kill—did actually leave the killing behind in the 1990s. But then in 2004, he contacted the media, writing once again as the BTK killer. And at that time he was married with children, and a pillar of his church community.

Thank you once again for reading. I hope you enjoyed yourself. If you have the time, I would really appreciate you leaving a review. You can go to the Amazon page or connect to it through this link. And if you'd like to hear about upcoming publications, you can check out my website or sign up for my mailing list.

I hope to "see" you again.

Take care,
R.D.

BOOKS BY R.D. BRADY

The Belial Series (in order)
The Belial Stone

The Belial Library

The Belial Ring

Recruit: A Belial Series Novella

The Belial Children

The Belial Origins

The Belial Search

The Belial Guard

The Belial Warrior

The Belial Plan

The Belial Witches

The Belial War

The Belial Fall

The Belial Sacrifice

Stand-Alone Books
Runs Deep

Hominid

The A.L.I.V.E. Series
B.E.G.I.N.

A.L.I.V.E.

D.E.A.D.

The Unwelcome Series

Protect

Seek

Proxy

Published as Riley D. Brady

The Key of Apollo

Be sure to sign up for R.D.'s mailing list to be the first to hear when she has a new release!

ABOUT THE AUTHOR

R.D. Brady is an American writer who grew up on Long Island, NY but has made her home in both the South and Midwest before settling in upstate New York. On her way to becoming a full-time writer, R.D. received a Ph.D. in Criminology and taught for ten years at a small liberal arts college.

R.D. left the glamorous life of grading papers behind in 2013 with the publication of her first novel, the supernatural action adventure, *The Belial Stone*. Over ten novels later and hundreds of thousands of books sold, and she hasn't looked back. Her novels tap into her criminological background, her years spent studying martial arts, and the unexplained aspects of our history. Join her on her next adventure!

To learn about her upcoming publications, sign up for her newsletter here or on her website (rdbradybooks.com).